BLACK AND BLUE WIDOW

RHIANNON ROLLNESS

BLACK AND BLUE WIDOW

Rhiannon Rollness

OLEANDER INK LLC

eBook ISBN: 979-8-9914290-1-6
Paperback ISBN: 979-8-9914290-0-9

Published by Oleander Ink LLC
Cover designed by Miblart

A Note From The Author

This book is not an alternate history. Instead, it was inspired by different elements from across Roman history and mythology, reimagined on an entirely different planet. Considerable creative liberties were taken in the creation of this book and accuracy to a particular era was never the goal. For a more accurate representation of history and mythology, please review non-fiction works.

As a dark fantasy romance about a serial killer, this book contains adult themes and issues. It is intended for adult audiences only.

This book contains:

- self-harm without suicidal intent

- various and pervasive depictions of violence against women

- allusions to sexual assault of a minor (not on page)

- on-page sexual assault

- human trafficking

- on-page physical assault of a minor (a 16-year-old is slapped)

- poisoning

- murder (a lot of it)

- torture (including flogging/whipping)

- other adult content including profanity, obscenity, and con-sensual sexual content

If you have any questions about this list, please do not hesitate to reach out at rhiannonrollness.com.

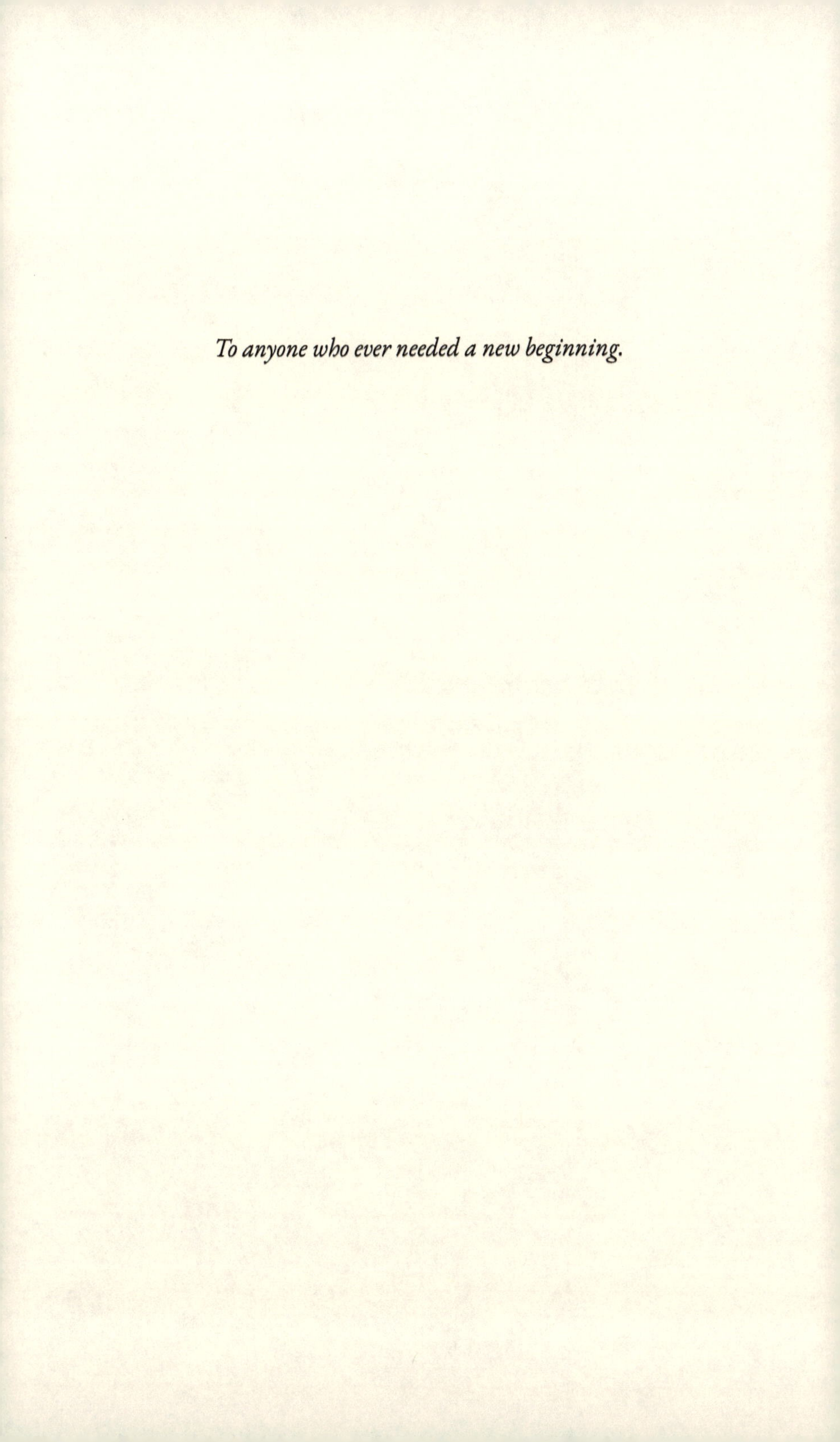

To anyone who ever needed a new beginning.

A Wedding Night

Luella

THIS ISN'T MY WORST wedding night. This one, like the man who accompanies it, falls somewhere in the midst of mediocrity. I might not even remember it, if things go the way I've planned. Of course, that would require Senator Silas to cooperate for once in his miserable life, and the dark hair falling across his reddening face and the veins pulsing in his arms indicate that he's not ready to do that.

Cooperation would look like fear, and he's not afraid.

Not yet.

His eyes are hard instead of wide, and his lips are pressed together in a white line instead of parted or slack-jawed. These are the clues his body gives me, warning me that my new husband is, in fact, livid.

And of course, I can tell because he has me pinned against a wall, fingers tightening around my throat.

"What did you give me, Julia?" Silas snarls, spittle landing on my cheek. Julia is a fine name, but it isn't mine. I'd never allow swine like Silas to put his lips around the vowels and consonants that make up me. Having him around my neck is one thing, but my name is quite another.

Luella.

"*Venefica*," he booms instead, giving my neck a shake. *Witch*. If I cared for his opinion, it might sting, might wound me. I've been called worse things by better people, but I prefer it at a more appropriate volume. There are guards at the bedchamber door, although they shouldn't hear through the thick stone, and if they do, they will think Silas is taking what's his. It is his wedding night, after all.

He wavers on his feet and the motion loosens his hold enough for me to take in a greedy breath. The relief on my face must annoy my dear husband because he leans his weight into me, crushing my windpipe yet again. Stones, he's a large man, and this body feels smaller, more fragile compared to the last.

I'd like to wait it out, but black blurs the edges of my vision. There's not enough time. My fingers grapple at my waist, searching until the palm size blade is in my delicate hand. I bring it up, fumbling around his arms caging me in. Slashing, I meet my target: the soft flesh below his jaw. It's not deep, but it's well-placed. It's enough for him to release me, reaching for his own neck instead of mine.

His eyebrows raise and lips part as his fingers embrace his throat, and I smile. I like when they keep their hands to themselves.

Now he gets it. He finally feels it.

The fear.

He tries and fails to dam the flow of blood spilling from the wound. There's panic mixing with the fear now, and his rapid heartbeat means the blood will flow faster. That makes it messier than I'd like. I prefer potions, poisons, and wits. Women have many weapons, though, and I'm willing to use them all.

Rubbing my neck, I step to the side, air rushing in to fill my eager lungs as I move out of the way of Silas' crumpling body. He collapses on the white marble and I watch his face drain of color for a few moments. *Chamaeleōns* do this. They skitter along the rocks at the edge of the river, and when they sense danger, they change.

Their skin morphs into the stone beneath it, going from green to gray.

In the end, that's all Silas is. A sad little lizard, trying–but failing–to survive.

Was it my knife or my poison that killed him? I suppose it's never one thing, just as I might not have noticed one child missing in a city of thousands. Yet, rumors spread when they're fed with truth, or fear, and Silas' reputation was a corpulent and swollen thing.

His name was easy to scrawl on my list.

His warm blood coats my hands, growing sticky as the night air cools the evidence of what I've done, again. I can't smell it, my nose too damaged from its many breakings, but I remember. Sharp and metallic, until you don't know if it's a taste or a smell, the two senses too tangled with the pain.

The lower half of my wedding dress is smudged with it when I kneel. The dress is objectively beautiful, all white satin with a square neckline and fitted through the bodice. It highlights my petite frame, my large doe eyes, and sweet copper plaits.

I hate it.

No matter, though. Every precise detail served to lure my stupid, predator husband into a place where I could make him what he really was.

Praeda.

I hate the plan I have to use tonight. Too many unknowns, but I'm certain I've profiled him properly. We always do.

"Hmm," I murmur, running my hand along the wall at the back of the bedchamber. No servants' entrance, as I suspected. Too paranoid. They should let me go, though, given the undercurrent of unrest here.

If they don't, I'll have to find out if Janus can grant me gills at the bottom of the Maero. But, even they have limits. No.

It's out the front, dead or alive.

Standing, I peel my dress down, clawing at the back when the laces won't release me. I will not be caged, not tonight.

Not ever.

Liberated, I set to more important matters: smashing my head into the wall. I suck in a breath to steel my nerves, and before I can reconsider, I slam the side of my face into the wall once, twice.

"Jupiter's stones," I mutter. I don't have to put on such a show often anymore, but it's certainly not the first time. Probably not the last, either. This is my best chance.

I bend down in front of my late husband, working the belt to his trousers loose. I wrap the dark cloth around my neck and tie the other end to the washroom door. The cloth is rough against the sensitive and tender skin of my throat, retracing the imprint of Silas' hands from just moments before. My fingers itch to tear it away.

Instead, I step as far from the door as I can, pulling it taut, then kick the door closed. I crash to the floor with a strangled cry and tears prick the corner of my eyes. Gods, I hate the neck. I can only do it once without passing out, so I unwrap the cloth and I throw it across the room. It flutters in an offensive trajectory, landing so close I could kick it.

Naked in the middle of the room, I take stock. The bedchamber is large, as befits one of Silas' station. Its limestone walls are hung with tapestries of Jupiter, Mars, and of course Venus. Useless Gods, all of them.

My white dress and the matching white marriage bed draw my eyes. Perhaps the dress isn't ruined enough. The fabric is soft in my hands once more as I yank at the seams along the back, tear the neckline, and split the bodice the way so many of my dresses have been split before, just not by my hand.

I bite my lip, not in the gentle and seductive way I had in front of Silas, but violently. Angrily. The skin splits and the taste of copper floods my mouth, underwhelming without the scent to assault me. Blood trickles down from my lip, and I let it flow as I walk over to the bed. The white sheets are in a tangled heap, the edges spilling onto the floor.

A vase had fallen off the bedside table earlier and now shards of glass and cool water brush the tips of my toes. My lips curl at the crumpled red roses strewn throughout the scene. Men seem to love roses, adorning their marriage chambers with the disgusting flower. As if to prove they could tame the thorns of beauty.

As if any amount of pretty could justify pain.

I fall to my knees in the glass and pain radiates up my thighs and down my shins. My resolution wavers as I eye the nightstand before cracking my cheek into the corner of it. My eyes water.

I *really* hate this part.

Crawling to the tattered wedding gown, I breathe through the tears and the inescapable sensation of pain. A warning from the body, except the warning I'm creating isn't for me.

Glass scrapes against my lower legs and embeds in my hands as cold water from the overturned vase mingles with my blood. A sharp thorn from a rose gets me, as if it senses my earlier disgust. I glare at it before brushing the useless spike free.

Reaching into the pocket of the wedding gown, I let my fingers trace over the small vials, each a different shape so I can sort them anywhere. Finding the one I want, I tip the purple liquid into my mouth and the familiar bitter tang coats my throat, although I hardly remember the last time I had to drink this particular one. It might as well have been Silas, then, too. They blur together, the men. Each as inconsequential as the discarded rose thorn. A pain for just a moment, and then a fading memory.

Besides, I'm not really here for them. I'm here for the women and children of Divus, and I'll wrap my fist around as many thorns as I must—as many thorns as they need—until there are no more thorns.

I blink, the purple tonic casting a fog over my thoughts. I'm almost out of time. I lay on the floor, tugging Silas' cooling body onto mine. My breath becomes heavy, and the weight is suffocating for a moment. I don't need to pretend as my heart pounds and my vision blurs with tears. A whisper of fear before I remind myself that I'm in control.

He's dead and *I* am in control.

I drag my nails along his neck, his arms, and down the sides of his face until welts appear on his skin and my nails are ready to crack. Pain drags at me, but already it's dulling, ebbing with each heartbeat that circulates the sleeping drought. Satisfied, I relax, focusing on breathing in. Then out. In. Out. Until I convince myself to surrender to oblivion.

THE SMILE

ROSE

THIS ISN'T HOW I imagined my life. My mater would tell me, "You're the sweetest bloom, Rose." She'd seal her final words with a kiss. "Stay sweet." I imagined that I would be pursued, cherished even, by my betrothed.

Instead, I haggle with a man thrice my age, trying to secure his interest before he finds out.

"Gens?" the man in question grunts.

If only I could lie. "Octavius," I answer, standing with my hands behind my back. Daisy says it makes me look demure and highlights my breasts, but it doesn't seem like it's helping. Claude shakes his greying head at my familia's name.

"No dowry, then?" He cuts to the matter and heat floods my cheeks.

"No dowry, but I'm an excellent baker, and–" He's already turning away, and my voice trails off. Venus help me.

From glances and mutterings and unspoken words, I understand that under no circumstances will I be allowed to turn twenty without a husband.

Which means I have only a quad.

Four clipses.

Twenty days to destitution.

"He was hideous," my sister says, coming up beside me. She wraps her arm around mine. Her touch is gentle, but the pressure still makes me flinch as she guides me to the forum steps. The Senate building shades us in the dual shadows cast by the late afternoon suns, Romulus and Remus. I focus my eyes on the central fountain's sparkling water instead of Daisy's knowing look.

"And terribly old," I admit, forcing a smile.

"Terribly old," she agrees, leaning her head on my shoulder. "We still have some time."

I can't look away from the water, the gentle tinkling a contrast to the roaring in my ears. "If I don't..." I clear my throat. "You should be trying to match, too."

"I'm not even seventeen," she objects.

"It's better not to be there alone, Daize."

She doesn't answer, and I don't elaborate. We both know. I tilt my head against hers and scan the square. Most of the men here are older, which is fine since they're the least likely to need a marriage with a dowry. Twenty is old, though, and Octavius is a name that could use more anonymity.

The day is warm for so early in planting season and my cloak mocks me, signaling to anyone with eyes that I have something to hide.

I push the fabric to the side, just to see how noticeable they are in the sunslight. Just to see if I could have a moment of reprieve from the suffocating fabric. No; I'm greeted by the pronounced outlines of hands. The cloak is back up before I let myself feel the cool absence of cloth or whatever emotion accompanies the marks.

I should be used to them by now.

"I'm going to find some water," I tell Daisy, standing.

"Can I visit Ceres?" Daisy asks, pointing to where her friend is in line for bread across the square.

I nod and watch as Daisy's golden blonde hair bounces behind her, the sunslight catching on each strand and casting a glowing aura around her head.

My stomach twists. If only I could see her this happy everyday.

Turning towards the fountain, my face meets a solid wall of flesh.

"Pardon," I say, stepping back. Except my foot finds only air, the angle of my turn putting my back to the lower stairs. My arms flail and I brace myself for the resounding crack my body will make on the stone steps.

Pain does come, but not from the stairs. The wall of flesh reaches out to grab me, hands wrapping around my rings of bruises, and I gasp, part pain and part relief.

The wall is handsome. Red gold hair, bright blue eyes, and a smattering of freckles across his boyish face. He looks to be around my age, if not a year or two younger.

"You caught me," I say, shaken, as he steadies me with warm, sure hands before letting go.

"Of course I did." He smiles. The action lights up his face, and heat stains my cheeks. I should be grateful his hands aren't pressing on my bruises, but something like disappointment moves through me at the space between us. "Your eyes are striking," he says.

"Eyes?" My forehead wrinkles. Did he catch me staring at his jawline, or the dimple on his left side? My entire body is impossibly hot, the cloak suffocating me.

"The objects through which you see?" he says, looking around in an exaggerated fashion.

The only person who's ever spoken to me like this is Daisy. It's unguarded. Non-transactional. "You jest." It doesn't come out as a question, and for that I am grateful.

"I was giving charming a go. No good?"

"I didn't say that." I look to the side, wondering if I've conjured this man out of thin air. Did Venus send him to me?

"May I sit with you? Or were you leaving?" he asks.

I was leaving, until I saw you. "I could stay."

"Perfect," he says. He sits on the step below mine, leaning back on his hands with his legs sprawled in front of him. His dimple flashes when he meets my eyes, and decorum dictates that I have no choice but to sit as well.

"I'm Rose Octavius," I offer, getting it out of the way, refusing to hope, yet. "What should I call you?"

"Octavius?" He raises an eyebrow, and my chest tightens. "I don't think I've met an Octavius before.

Thank the gods. "And you are?"

"I consider myself rather witty, although my pater says I can be dense at times. *Matulo* is his favorite term of endearment."

"Endearment?" I put a hand over my chest. *Blockhead* is certainly better than the words my pater uses, but that doesn't make it kind. "I suppose there are worse things, but I hope you don't expect me to call you that."

"Perhaps, amor?"

Heat and indignation flare in my chest, but he's smiling. My eyes narrow. "You jest." This time it's not a question at all.

"And it seems once again it's not to your liking?"

I glare. Handsome or not, perhaps his pater is right. He is a *matulo*. "I meant your name."

"Ah, well. If I tell you my name, you might think less of me. And I'm not ready for that."

"I have to call you something," I say, perhaps more straightforward than I should be. Does he come from a familia like mine?

"And you refuse *matulo* or amor?"

I cross my arms, trying not to smile. "I most certainly do."

"Augustus, then." The copper of his hair shimmers as he cocks his head at me, the movement simultaneously playful and earnest.

"That's your name?" My body sways towards him as he speaks, like my namesake towards the suns.

"That's what you can call me." He smiles. "Until you get to the others."

Despite his teasing, Augustus is quite easy to talk to. He has three siblings, and while he wants to be a farmer, he suspects he'll be joining the legions in the next two years.

"Pater's orders," he says. He already looks every ounce a soldier. Broad chest, thick arms. My gaze travels lazily down to his hands, remembering how warm they felt, even through my cloak. I snap my head up. He's looking at the fountain, thankfully oblivious to my attention.

My throat is tight, so I nod. I understand duty. Loyalty. Obedience.

"Why do you like farming?"

"I like working with my hands. Growing, painting, building. Creating, you know?" He leans in, like he has a secret. "It's easy to destroy something, to break things. It takes a second." He snaps his fingers in the air between us. "I like things that take time. Clipses and quads of effort, and in the end you can nourish your familia, or shelter them."

"Painting doesn't seem as useful," I point out, trying to remember the last time I saw something beautiful just for the sake of it.

"Not at first." He nods. "Yet, we need it just the same."

I cock my head. "Art?"

His face lights up. "Exactly."

Smiling, I shake my head. He's hopeless, but I like it. I like that he says what he wants in a way I'll never be able to. Passionate about things, even if he can't pursue them. "I wish you could do it." When he looks at me, I add, "be a farmer."

He waves his hand. "It's okay. The things we do for our familia, I suppose."

I don't know why I ask, except I must be desperate and stupid, and I let my mouth be desperate and stupid, too. "Will you marry before you join?" My hand flies to cover my mouth. "That's none of my business."

Augustus raises his eyebrows. "Well, it could be your business." His blue eyes twinkle and I feel myself drawn in. A moth to a delicious flame. This must just be his way, to be vulnerable and blithe and infuriatingly charming, but it doesn't mean anything. It can't.

"You—"

"Brother," a new voice breaks through the noise, cutting me off. A very good thing, since I'm not sure if Augustus is still jesting, and I certainly don't want to know what foolish thing was about to come out of my mouth.

If Augustus is the red at dawn, this man is the light of noon. Yellow hair, tawny brown eyes, and suns-kissed skin.

"Brother," Augustus groans, as if exasperated by his brother's presence. We both stand.

"Excuse my brother's poor manners," the golden man says. "My name is Tristan."

"Rose. It's a pleasure." I tip my head, shooting a glance at Augustus. He didn't tell me much about his siblings. One older, two younger. This must be the elder.

He takes my hand and kisses it, murmuring into my skin. "The pleasure is mine."

Augustus stiffens beside me and I smile politely, withdrawing my hand. Would Augustus have greeted me the same way if we hadn't collided on the stairs?

"Pater needs us," Tristan says, looking from me to Augustus.

"I'm sure he does," Augustus says, voice tight. He turns to me, dropping his voice. "I'd like to see you again."

His blue eyes meet mine and there's that spark again, something tightening in my chest. "I'd like that."

Thank Venus. Finally.

Finally, she's on my side.

Augustus sends me a smile over his shoulder as he leaves, small and secret, just for me. And I can't help but picture it, for just a moment. Him giving me that smile again.

And again.

And again.

A Fickle Thing

Luella

I wake to screams. Rolling to my side, my injuries echo the frantic nature of the room, demanding my attention. My copper hair is matted and stuck to my cheek, dried blood flaking as I shove it out of my face. I start to cry. This part is easy.

Everything hurts after all.

"Good lady, are you alright?" a girl is asking, frantically reaching out to touch my face. Her scream must be what drew in the two guards who roll Silas over, take in the room, and look to me. I hate that I've upset her, but it must be done. I meet the eyes of one of the younger men, Ryle. I won't be speaking first. That's rule number one. I let the tears continue to leak from my eyes as his flicker across my bruised cheek, split lip, and finally down to the red mark around my neck. His fist clenches.

I look away then, allowing my face to be drawn towards the girl tending me. Let Ryle think me shamed. As if I care that they saw this body.

As if it were even my body.

"What happened?" the older guards asks.

"Look at her," Ryle says. I don't look at them, though. Maybe this was the hardest part. The act. Feigning despair when I feel nothing of the sort. Yet I know my role well, and I let out a whimper, flinching away from the servant girl's hands, despite the kindness in them.

"Stones, his own wife?" the older guard mutters, disdain dripping like the blood from my hands just hours ago.

"What?" I choke out, curling my body inward. He's done much worse, but I'm not supposed to know that. Good women don't marry predators.

They would expect that he'd beaten me, violated me, and most importantly, that I was broken by it.

Some of that was true. He did try to beat me when he'd recognized his own sluggish movements, could recognize when someone was being poisoned. Drugged. It's easy to recognize things you are familiar with, to notice the signs you've inflicted on others.

"Who are you?" he'd demanded. Or was that the last one? The details are already fading into the procession of white dresses, red veils, and dead husbands. I've never had an answer to satisfy that question, anyways. They don't care, nor do I know. Who was I, now, with a face not my own? What had I looked like, before?

I shake my head once, twice. It clears my mind and then I'm falling back into the role. "What happened? Is he...?"

"Gods," Ryle mutters. I'd put them in a predicament. On the one hand, they served Silas. I should be arrested for killing him. Wives are meant to obey, and I had not done that. On the other hand, he was dead, and a piece of filth that was worth more on the bottom of their boots than he was as their Senator. Enough of his servants and guards had young girls or boys in their familias. Ones they kept out of his sight, or wished they had. "Gods," he says, louder this time.

I reach for my tattered dress and cover my chest with the rust and red stained fabric. I whimper again and the sound grates on my nerves. I should be laughing. Drinking even, to the demise of such a monster; however, that would not do, yet.

I sob harder when the dried blood touches me, flaking against the matching stiffness coating my fingers. This, obviously, upsets me, so I fall into the servant girl's arms and she instantly begins to smooth my hair, trying to calm me.

"Gods," Ryle shouts and I cry out again, shrinking into her more.

"You're scaring her," the servant girl, Tanya, says. I think that's her name. I can't remember. I need to be more careful about how hard I hit my own head.

But it has to look real.

If it isn't realistic, if it isn't gruesome, there will be too many questions. I won't make that mistake again. I'd lost a good chunk of my hair that time, not from my skirmish with my husband, but from the one with the guard who didn't believe I could have fought off a full-grown man with just a weapon and so few marks on me. He was right, of course, but really it was the principle of questioning a lady that irritated me.

And a *widow* at that.

"Please," I beg. *Beg*. Gods, I hate this part, too. "Please, I... I didn't... He..." I trail off, sucking in a breath.

"Ryle," Tanya pleads. I hate when I have to be here after, when I have to deceive good people. Good women, especially, but I have to live long enough to deceive the monsters, too. Ryle looks to the older guard. I've seen them all around, of course, but Silas had moved fast. His pater had demanded his son produce an heir, so of course, I'd need to get on that, he'd said. As if I'd be getting on anything of his. We'd courted for just a few quads before we wed. I was exactly the type of woman he was interested in. Timid, young looking, with red hair and deep green eyes. Mostly, I was there when he needed to marry, and that was enough.

"Tanya, bring her a shift, and a basin to wash off," Ryle grinds out. I bite back my smile. I guess I didn't hit my head too hard; her name is Tanya.

"It's okay, *pullus*," Tanya murmurs as she stands, stroking my arm once more. "We're going to help you." *Little bird*. The term of endearment thaws something in me, but just for a moment. Empathy is a fickle thing. It comes from a well of kindness, or a chasm of pain. Did Tanya know too well what I supposedly went through?

I say nothing to Ryle or the older guard as Tanya leaves. I cower away from the older one when he moves to throw a sheet over Silas, and after that he stays against the wall near Ryle. His jaw is tight, a twin to Ryle's. Decent men then, although not decent enough to seek new posts. Or perhaps caged by circumstance, as so many are.

When Tanya returns, she places a basin of warm water in front of me, then hisses at the guards to turn around. They turn, properly reprimanded, and Tanya helps me wash the blood from my hands and face. It isn't much, but I don't need that much. Just enough to leave this domus.

My skin breaks out in goose-pebbles and Tanya yanks the shift over my head, then drapes a cloak over my shoulders. She hands me a small satchel that I would guess has a canteen and a few food items in it. Usually there is bread. Something about tears seems to call for flour. Bread, cakes, pastries. I could make my own bread, but what about soup? No one ever sends me off with soup.

"You have to run," Tanya says. "Do you have somewhere you can go?"

I nod, forcing a blankness into my expression, fixing my eyes just above Tanya's head. As if I would use my true domus while luring Silas.

"I have... I have somewhere," I say after a moment of feigned hesitation.

"Good... I'm really sorry this happened, *pullus*," Tanya says. I have my answer now, in the way Tanya wraps her arms around my shoulders. The way her voice cracks over the word 'sorry.'

Tanya's empathy is born of pain.

The List

Luella

No one pays any mind to a running woman around here. They avert their eyes. Even with both suns illuminating my bruises, my disheveled appearance. My pain and my...baggage. They're thinking someone else will help.

That's too generous. They're probably thinking I deserve it. That I must not be obedient, smart, or compliant enough.

Not *something* enough.

That suits me just fine, since I've long since forgotten what enough would feel like and their apathy is its own disguise. What's one broken woman in a city of thousands?

It's not long before I've made it out of the fields and into the forest surrounding my domus, and then even less time before I'm there. I wash the blood and filth from my skin in my rare private bath, scrubbing until I have a clean canvas to work with.

Wrapping myself in a dry robe, I cross my small domus to the kitchen table. The violet tea I'd set to steep before bathing loses curls of steam into the evening air. My mater had loved violet tea.

I groan, falling into the nearest kitchen chair and sliding the mug closer. It's so familiar. I can almost hear my mater's laugh, feel her gentle kisses on my cheeks. My chest aches. It's been years, yet I never stop missing her. She'd be appalled if she could see me now. Perhaps, I'd even be appalled by her, by the complacency that permeated most of her docile life.

My black leather journal lays in the middle of the kitchen table, and I flip it open to the list and profiles we have curated over the past ten years. I have agonized over each mark, and the pages show it. Harsh lines scratch through details and preferences that fell off the list as I learned what mattered and what didn't. Then my fingers rubbed the pages thin when I was ready for each target, etching every ink-stroke into my features, into my soul.

I trace my finger down the page I'd marked earlier, near the back of the book. The others are all done, their bodies rotting stones knows where. There will always be more, but I'm growing sick of skimming the surface. It isn't enough.

I'm almost ready for him, but not quite yet.

The Praetor comes first. He's my way into the Domus Aurea. I review his preferences again, although I know them all by heart.

Preparation precedes perfection.

The Domus Aurea and the Praetors aren't like Silas or my other praeda. Those hallowed halls are devoid of empathy. A few scratches won't protect me from being tried for treason, and they'll gladly place a rope around an already bruised throat.

A loud knock reverberates through the domus and I start, almost dropping my tea. "Gods," I mutter, touching the towel wrapped around my head to make sure it covers each copper strand. I tighten my robe.

The knock comes again, louder this time.

"Hold your stones," I shout, moving to the door.

"This one took forever," Mia complains the moment she sees my face. The tall, dark skinned, raven-haired woman shoves past me, plopping down at the kitchen table, reaching for my mug of tea.

"Help yourself," I say, the corners of my mouth lifting.

"I will. Next time don't make me fret."

"I didn't make you do anything. I told you it would be today," I tell her, shrugging in a way I know will annoy her.

"Yes, and the twins have both set. A few more hours and you would have lied." Mia points to me, emphasizing the 'you.' The edges of the world are still light, fading into indigo as the single moon begins to rejoice in the departure of its dual daytime competitors.

"They couldn't spare a horse or a donkey. I ran here," I chuckle. "Barefoot."

Mia rolls her eyes and sips the tea. My tea. "Mmm, I love this one. Anyway, I'm glad you're alive. You look like the gods cursed you, though. I hate when you do the neck." Mia leans forward, eyeing the offending area.

"I know. It's just so effective." I sigh. My hand moves up instinctively, fingertips brushing the discolored section of skin where countless hands have sought to control me. Or punish me. Or teach me a lesson. They were foolish enough to think they were the first. I was discerning enough to know they wouldn't be the last.

"Something about it, I suppose." We sit in companionable silence for a moment, but then I shift in the chair and wince.

"Jupiter's stones. I guess I could fix that." Mia grimaces, reaching across the table with one hand and withdrawing a stone from her other pocket with the other. Its vibrant blue disappears as Mia's fist closes around it.

I smile, clasping her hand. "Thanks, Mi."

Mia closes her eyes and warmth seeps into my hand, down my arm, like immersing into bath water. The feeling washes through my body, dissolving the pain in my cheek, in my neck. My cracked and broken nails mend along with the rest of me, until I feel whole and healed. As always, Mia's power surprises me. What a gift she is.

"Thank you," I say again, opening my eyes. "Are you faring well?"

"Well? I'm positively blessed." Mia deposits the stone, now shiny black basanite, into her pocket. "Didn't you hear? My apprentice quit."

"And that's... a blessing?"

"It was that stable boy, remember?"

"Oh right." I remember. I really need to be more careful with my head. "He kept dropping your completed potions?"

"After I'd imbued them. Just draining my stores of herbs *and* my magic?" Mia shook her head. "He finally realized he doesn't have the coordination for working around glass."

That was an understatement. He didn't have the coordination to breathe, but somehow managed to maintain the act long enough to find new things to break. "What will you do for an apprentice, though? Surely, you're too busy to do it all on your own."

"Well... I was hoping?" Mia gives me a sad, plaintiff look.

"Absolutely not. We're almost there. The next one lives in the Domus Aurea." I lean forward. "I'm almost there."

Mia shakes her head. "Luella. You're not going to get him. He's impenetrable. I can't pin down a profile. There's no rhyme or reason to the girls, and none of your personas will bear the scrutiny of such a high-ranked betrothal. It's too risky to approach him in a brothel, not to mention I wouldn't even know what would help him pick you and he doesn't have a pattern to where he attends. It would be all chance." She makes these arguments every time. Some, I admit, have truth. Brothels are pointless, because many patrician men have their own prostitutes. Not to mention being a prostitute isn't a great cover to begin with. No one trusts a whore, as one eloquent praeda had informed me. Besides, I'd tried it once and it was a gods damned pain. Wives are easier. Good ladies are docile, obedient. The perfect vessel for someone like me.

And the principle of it always struck me, something poetic in ending the life of a monster on its wedding night, of making myself a widow.

"That's an even greater reason for me to target the Praetor. Maybe I'll learn something. They're friends," I remind Mia. "I just have to wait for an opening."

My blood sparks when I think about going after the Praetor. The challenge. It was the fun part, after all. Being exactly what a man wanted when they didn't always know it themselves, when they were so quick to judge and dismiss the woman they were to marry. Mia helps profile my praeda by working with her network of healers and patients to figure out preferences: hair color, eye color, complexion, age, demeanor. Anything I can use to become the perfect woman and wife, packaged in a body they'll prefer.

The perfect victim, concealing the perfect killer. Because my brand of magic can help with many things, but not that. Once it enables me to get close, I have to rely on a plethora of proven, if unsavory, practices.

"I think you should take a break." Mia leans forward, her dark eyes meeting mine. "You can't do this forever. You're one person, Lue. Yes, what you do is important, but this world is broken, and you're going to die trying to eliminate them all."

If I just kill him, though, that will be enough. Not the Praetor, he was a means to an end, but my final target? That could change everything. For more than a few women.

For all of us.

"I don't need them all. I just need him."

"I wish you'd take a break," Mia repeats, looking away from me.

"After," I say, not sure if I mean it.

Mia lets out a breath. "Well, I had hoped you wouldn't want to know, but I can see that as usual you have more beauty than brains."

"I can't make brains, just beauty." I smile, and reclaim my tea to take a sip. "Wouldn't want to know what?" Mia rolls her eyes.

"The Emperor ended Praetor Ledo's mourning period."

"It's so early." Quads early, in fact. I'd expected some time to plan after Silas. I set the tea down, considering.

"I know, which means he's probably looking." Mia leans in and takes the tea back. "You could still take a break, or I can find you a new praeda. We can wait for someone else in the Domus Aurea."

And let more women die under Ledo's hand? No. That's not something I can stomach.

"You just want an apprentice," I tease, trying to distract us both from what waiting will mean. "And I might have a solution. I hadn't quite figured out what to do with my extra baggage."

"Extra baggage?" Mia arches a brow.

I stand and walk to the back of my domus, down the short hallway. "Boy," I shout. Sitting back at the table with Mia, I wait.

A boy of about twelve comes running out of the back room, nearly tripping over his own feet. His brown hair is poorly cut and his right eye is swollen shut, hiding the brilliant blue match to his left. "Yes, good lady?" he stammers.

Mia looks from the boy to me and back to the boy. "Oh, good lady?" She hates the address. Says it implies something she doesn't quite like. I'd called her 'pain in my arse lady' for a solid quad after she told me, but the boy can't be blamed. He's trying to be respectful.

"Taln, would you like to work in an infirmaria?" I ask, not looking away from Mia.

Taln doesn't hesitate, a trait likely beaten into him. "Yes, good lady."

Mia ignores the boy and glares at me. "How in the gods did you acquire that?"

I laugh. "He has a name, Mi. And remember how I said they didn't have a donkey or a horse? Well, they did, but I couldn't incriminate Taln. He offered to help me but…" I trail off, but Mia doesn't let it drop.

"But what?"

"Well, look at him." I point to him, and Mia lets out a huff, but her shoulders drop and some of the hostility in her gaze falls away. We have an understanding. About what I do, and more importantly, why. To whom.

Only abusers. Only those who deserve it. Those who prey on women and children, like Silas. Taln hadn't told me if anything happened to him, but he'd taken one look at my bruised neck and offered me a horse and clothing. He had no parents and I asked him if he wanted to come with me.

He said yes.

Perhaps I was going soft, but it was too late now. They wouldn't notice him gone for a day or so since we had left the horse.

"Fine," Mia snaps. "Taln, is it? Get in that back room and keep your trap shut until I come for you. You can live above the infirmaria where my last assistant did."

"Y-y-yes, good lady." Taln looks to me and I give him an encouraging nod. He doesn't press his luck and scampers to the back room just as quickly as he had rushed out.

Mia glares at me, but I just smile. "See, problem solved."

"Problem not solved. It was risky to take the boy. And I still don't like this business with the Praetor."

Mia doesn't understand. She sees this every day and watches victims walk right out of her infirmaria and back into arms that sent them there. Sometimes by choice, and sometimes because they have none.

"I couldn't leave him, Mi. He's one of us. And don't worry about the Praetor. His profile is predictable, it'll be easy."

"Don't you dare start thinking like that," Mia warns. "That's how you make a mistake, Luella Amulius. That's how you die."

I shake my head. "I know, I'm sorry. That's not what I meant." I let out a breath, tension and hope and something darker rushing into my lungs in its place. "I just... I have to get him, Mi. I have to."

Mia nods. "I'll work on your batch for the Praetor." The resignation in her voice hurts me, but I can't stop now. I'm so close. Ten years. Ten whole years I've waited for this opportunity, and I'm finally ready. There's finally a way into the Domus Aurea.

"Can I have some extra blue ones? And extra sleeping droughts."

"How many extra?"

"Double the usual. Oh, and can you make the paralytic a little stronger?"

I don't elaborate. Mia helped profile him, she knows his proclivities. Knows that I was being flippant before.

Nothing about my next praeda will be easy.

THE SABINES

ROSE

I DON'T ADMIT IT to anyone, not even Daisy, but I sit near the window every day just in case someone comes to call.

Not someone, actually.

In case Augustus comes to call. He said he would, after all, and he knows my familia's name. I wouldn't look for him, of course, but even if I considered it, I didn't know his gens.

I hadn't considered it, because that wouldn't be proper.

But if I had…

I finish sweeping the disobedient floors, perpetually dusty despite the punishment they see in this domus. They don't have to answer for their failures, instead waiting for me to make them shine.

"Stop looking for that boy," Daisy calls from our shared room. "We need to prepare."

I spare another glance out the window, but the street is empty. When I reach our room, Daisy has our dresses laid out. "What boy?"

"Rose." She rolls her eyes. "I'm younger than you, but I'm not blind. He's very handsome."

I drop into the small desk chair that we share. "Too handsome for me, I suppose."

"No," Daisy says. "Maybe not handsome enough." She taps her chin. "I do think he liked you. He kept looking at you after everything he said, like he wanted to see if you liked it."

Daisy's observant like that. Aware. She cuts to the heart of the matter. "Maybe, but I thought he'd call on me if he did."

"It's only been a few days. And you know how everyone gets around the festival."

Daisy's right. It had only been a few days, not even a full clipse. The Vinalia Prima is close enough to touch and Venus' spell is firmly closing around Divus. Between the fervor of spring blooms and the charged feeling of the air, it's a surprise goods are still sold in the market and the Forum still meets. They won't after today, not for a full clipse after the festivities end.

She grabs my hand and tugs me towards our bedroom. "Let's change and leave before Pater returns. We'll have fun, and maybe Augustus will be there," she says. I don't think she believes it, but the thought is enough to get my legs moving. I need a marriage, and if Augustus isn't there I can't wait for him forever. I only have eighteen days.

My stomach sinks but I hide it with a smile, the way I always do for Daisy. "You're right. We'll have fun."

I keep my hair loose the way I've seen other women do, pinned up on the sides to show my face. Mater had done hers this way, too. I'm dressed in my long-sleeved tunic despite the heat and Daisy eyes my arms for a moment. She doesn't ask why I wear so much cloth, and I'm glad for it.

It's the unspoken agreement between us, that I can bear it as long as I can do so in silence. She used to ask if I was okay, when we lay on our small pallet together at night. I'd cry myself to sleep in her arms until eventually I stopped answering the question; after a time, she stopped asking.

Daisy is perfection. Her white blonde hair makes her eyes appear unnaturally blue beneath her long lashes. She wears white, and it gives her a divine aura, like she belongs in Vesta's temple.

"Beautiful," I say, kissing her cheek.

"*Idem* to you," she says, smiling. *Same.* "Let's leave before it's too late."

But it already is.

His feet announce his arrival before I've opened our door. He's stomping through the threshold, dirtying the floors I labored over all morning. I let out a breath, my hand still on the handle. Daisy freezes behind me.

"Let's wait," I say.

Daisy's already shaking her head. "He won't retire for hours without work tomorrow."

Venus, she's right. "Fine." I take another breath and we quietly file down the hall.

He's in the cabinets already, taking stock. I think we can slip out, both of us moving towards the door.

I'm wrong.

Glass shatters against the door, narrowly missing my head. My body jolts, but we don't cry out, don't scream.

He hates that.

Biting my lip, I turn towards him with Daisy mirroring the movement.

"Where in Jupiter's stones are you going?" Pater asks.

We dip our heads and with my eyes on the floor I say, "The festival, Pater."

"Finally admitting you're a *meretrix*, is that it?" *Prostitute*. He stalks closer, the air chilling around Daisy and me, both of us wilting and shrinking beneath the frost.

"It's the first day, Pater, we always attend the first day." I regret it as soon as I've said it. We always attended with Mater, and she's too dangerous to bring up with him.

"Look at me," he says, hand snaking out to grip my upper arm. I hide my wince, meeting his eyes. So brown they're almost black, they bore into me, judging. "Are you a whore?"

I shake my head. "No, Pater. I would never dishonor you." I never know the right amount to say. Less is usually better, and silence is ideal. Responding to a question is different, though. Too short and he'll take it as insolence, too long and it's an excuse.

After all these years, I still haven't learned the appropriate length, apparently. He yanks me closer, rough. "You already have. I can't even give you away!"

Wincing, I look down again. I should have a dowry, but it's long gone. Maybe Daisy's is, too. A young, respectable man wouldn't be given a wife; he'd be given a wife *and* a dowry. Without a dowry, of course Pater couldn't give me away.

I swallow the frustration, knowing it'll be worse if I say what's on my mind.

Daisy isn't as good at keeping quiet. "Pater, it's hard without a dowry." Her voice is thin and plaintive, as if sounding weak and young will protect her from his wrath. It didn't work when we were children, and it certainly won't now. His face turns red and he looks at her, then back to me.

Pater's free hand wraps into my hair, ripping my head back. "I'm the one who should be given a dowry, for having to raise not just one but two of you." He spits the words, and I know the part he doesn't say. Alone. He's had to raise us alone. Without a mater. He might have been a good pater, if she'd been here. Or perhaps if we'd been boys. Any pity I could feel for him evaporates when he continues. "Yes. Go ahead and make some friends at the festival. The Sabines are paying a pretty denarius for girls like you. And it's about time you bring me something other than grief."

He shoves me away, but Daisy catches me before I hit the floor and guides me through the door. My body isn't my own, it's limp and numb and confused.

He can't mean it.

He wouldn't sell me to the Sabines.

I don't say anything as Daisy leads me through the streets, away from the man who holds my future in his hands.

"He wouldn't sell me." My voice pitches higher than usual, and Daisy doesn't say anything. "He won't," I whisper, lips trembling.

My hands are cold in Daisy's, pinpricks of numbness gathering at the tip of each finger, either from her hold or the way my blood rushes through my ears. Daisy is silent as I struggle to regain control, but when my breathing evens and my heart slows, she finally speaks.

"He's not going to sell you." The lie rolls off her tongue so easily that I almost believe it.

Almost.

Chains

Luella

The meeting is the most important part. It has to feel organic, while also seeming serendipitous. I have to seem like a dream come true, and not just any kind of dream. The kind that will get them thinking with something other than their head. And, I have to do it while hiding the nightmare I am.

Some of that is easy. I'm wearing an everyday face with dark hair and freckled cheeks. There's nothing wrong with my features, but they're a bit asymmetrical, which lowers my desirability enough that I'm forgettable. One face in a river of women, and while it's not a guarantee, it's the closest thing to armor I can wear.

I gather my stones, the opaque yellow and orange charged basanite glimmering in the light from the windows. They're the fire to Mia's water, blessed by a much more fickle god than the healing Asclepius. Nevertheless, the stones are cool as my hand closes around three, each the size of a denarius.

Closing my eyes I feel for it.

The power.

As each drop of blood circulates through my palm, it picks up a parcel of the charge, until my entire body hums with it.

My eyes flutter closed and my mind returns to the preferences I've inked in my little black book. My body stretches and folds and re-arranges, the sensation not entirely unpleasant, until it's done. Each and every word I'd agonized over has been made into something useful or valuable. The very skin on my bones is currency.

I don a light blue dress and turn to the mirror to check my work. Blonde hair and round blue eyes greet me, and the features make me appear younger than my thirty years. No self-respecting man would marry someone as old as me.

But becoming the perfect victim takes more than hair and eye color. Success lies in the details my praeda don't even know they prefer.

My eyebrows are darker than my hair by at least three shades, because he requires all the floras he borrows from the Emperor's harem to darken them with kohl. My lips are fuller than they have any right to be, because he once said that women with full lips remind him of Venus.

He once slapped a flora for having a dimple, so no dimples. He thinks the goddess Diana is too masculine, so my arms are a softer shape.

Every detail from Mia and her sources has been made flesh, until I'm a manifestation of his preferences.

It's make a *meretrix*.

Praetor Ledo doesn't visit the city often, quite content to let his servants and the Domus Aurea provide for him. He only needs to ask for something, and the Emperor grants it. If he didn't ask for such depravity, perhaps he wouldn't be on my list.

If there is one thing the Praetor does appreciate, it's entertainment. And while I would like to rest after Silas, there is no time, unless I want to risk waiting quads more.

Plus, his waived mourning period reeks of his own impatience. He'll be married again, and soon. I missed the last time, and he was married before I knew he was looking.

Not again.

The streets are full as I close the door to my rented room, a place where I can be in the city and have easier access to my *praeda* without compromising my true *domus*. It's the clipse of Venus, or the *Vinalia Prima* to the plebians, a celebration of womanhood and fertility. The beginning of the clipse is for women of higher standing, married women seeking fertility or young women praying for a match. Each day the festivities will become less socially acceptable, ending with *Floralia*, the day of prostitutes.

Divusians are interesting in that way. We celebrate the matron and mater, and then less than a clipse later we celebrate the whore we'd scorn if we met her on the street. I suppose the festival is just an excuse for drinking and rutting in the end. The Senate is willing to suspend their usual moral high ground if it means the populace is too drunk to care what they do. Or, more typically, don't do.

The Praetors will take part in the entire spectacle, but I will need to capture Ledo's attention on day one or two if I'm to tempt a marriage. Last year, the Praetor brought a girl from the village back to the Domus Aurea, but it was the last day. She was never seen again.

I don't want to be noticed on the last day.

Women are performing the maidendance in the main square, twirling their skirts in time to the fast-paced lute music and honoring one another with bows and kisses to the back of hands. It would be a fun pastime if men like Ledo weren't on the sidelines sizing up the dancers like goats for sacrifice. Although, some of the women are blushing, enjoying the attention. Perhaps not everyone views men the way that I do. I even suspect that decent men do exist.

I just haven't met one yet.

That's not fair. I have, but they're dead, too. Divus treats decent men the same way it treats its women.

I wait for a break in the song, then weave my way into the dance. The wooden floor shakes under our stomps and spins as I join in with the other women, smiling broadly and letting my hair fan around me with each spin. I dip low and laugh as a girl, petite with wheat colored hair, brushes her lips across my knuckles. For a moment I enjoy it, the subtle joy of hope. The softness. I let the rhythm take over, carefree, and wink at the girl.

She's the reason I do this, after all. Not her, specifically, but girls like her. Ones who need me to do what I do. While each looks different, they all have one thing in common: they're young. And because they're young, they're one of the worst things you can be.

Naive.

This girl will be given or sold or bartered into marriage after being told all the lies they want us to believe. That it's natural. That women aren't good for much else.

That we need it.

And then, during her engagement or wedding or perhaps not for many years, she begins to learn what marriage usually is.

A chain around her neck, and the cruel master who placed it there.

And when he finally does what his pater did to his mater, and his grandpater to his grandmater, and what any number of men have done to women since gods first walked the realm... That's where I finally come in.

Because *I* am the only master in this republic, and if anyone is going to hold the chains, it's going to be me.

My partner switches to a black haired beauty and my gaze slips past her to a large man rubbing his crotch as he watches and I fight to keep my expression flat, to hide the disgust. The man sees me looking and smiles, raising his eyebrows at me. I avert my eyes in case Ledo is watching. If I went after every man like that, I fear there wouldn't be any left.

Besides, even I know that I can't kill every man that annoys me, even if I want to. This man isn't even worth my vials.

I haven't looked for Ledo yet. It has to be timed perfectly. A parting of bodies, a break in the music. The type of moment that feels preordained. Blessed by Venus herself.

Just then, the girl in front of me sways to the side. Anticipation builds in my chest.

This is it.

I dip my chin, then raise my eyes. He's looking at me, and when our eyes meet I freeze. Only for a moment. Just enough for him to think he affects me. I let my lips part, as if I am letting loose a gasp and it earns the reaction I want. His lips tilt up at the corners and my cheeks flame red.

It's not hard to fake a blush. I think of the men who have dared to put their hands on me, and the rage does the rest. I think of Silas, how he'd wrapped his hands around my throat as if he was in control. I stoke that anger, letting it warm my blood and fuel my purpose.

I continue to dance, stealing glances at Ledo every time I can. His eyes are glued on me each time and I know I've done it.

I've snared him in my web.

And I'm one step closer to holding his chain.

Venus

Rose

Myrtle sprigs decorate every corner of the forum, along with barrels of wine and legumes. Divus is a living flower itself, each person brightly adorned in their most colorful tunics. Goats move around the square, nibbling from eager children's hands, while women twirl in the middle of the forum on a wooden dance floor.

It's just as I remember.

Despite what Pater says, everyone attends today. Men and women. Young and old.

Married and especially the unmarried.

We used to come with our mater, and she'd weave flowers in our braids and remind us of the steps to the maidendance, again. We forgot it each year, our young minds at once sieves and sponges.

We remember now. Daisy and I spin around each other, bowing and kissing the back of one another's hands. Her skin is cool beneath my lips, the way my mater's cheeks always were.

She'd spin us both for hours on the dance floor until Pater would call us back, tugging Mater into his lap. It had always been that way with her, smiles and laughter and love.

Or perhaps this was just one memory I've distorted and layered over years to make our life with her seem better than it is now. Absence makes the heart grow fonder.

Or forgetful.

They wove together, one happening in tandem with the other. It's hard to be fond if you remember too much.

There is a strength to staying soft, of course. A demureness to choosing the good over the bad, to staying sweet. Daisy whirls me into a spin and releases me, following the steps to switch partners. Her hands move to grasp Ceres' and mine fall into a stranger's.

She smiles at me, blonde hair and blue eyes, and she makes me think of who I could be. Her hair is completely loose, and she looks as if she's dancing just for her. Then she smiles, and I think maybe she's dancing for me, too.

I smile back and she winks, spinning me away from her as she switches partners. Daisy falls back in with me, and then the song ends. I spare one last look at the blonde woman as she disappears into the crowd, and hope some of her confidence has rubbed off on me.

Ceres follows us off the dance floor and she and Daisy soon have their heads bowed together, all whispers and smiles. Their faces tilted towards one another, as if they're in their own dance, meeting upturned lips with twinkling eyes.

I head towards the refreshments. Long tables of drink—*sapa*, cut wine, posca, honey water, and goats milk—line the side of the forum in front of the basilica. There's no water, since the fountain near the steps would make that redundant. I trail along the tables, debating the *posca* for a moment before I decide on the honey water. The metal cup is cool and I intend to find some shade to soak up the festival. I even mean to mingle, to talk to the single men who are likely here to find wives.

I *want* to look for Augustus.

Instead my feet carry me away, my mind turning over Pater's words. The honey water turns bitter on my tongue. He will sell me, if the price is right and the barriers are low enough. That's why I want to find my own husband, my own match. If I can choose it, it'll be kinder. Softer.

Maybe it would even be sweet.

"Stay sweet," my mater had bade me. How could I, with Pater's bruises and threats marring every breath I took?

At first I wander aimlessly. Or perhaps I just refuse to admit where I'm going until I'm looking at it.

I bite the inside of my cheek, grounding myself.

It's a small building compared to the temples, but large compared to a domus. The squat, flat roofed building is dark. Bars adorn each curtained window, and it's silent this time of day. The building is at the edge of Divus, pushed to the corner of respectable society.

I shouldn't be here, but I had to see.

The Sabines.

It's not a brothel in the traditional way. The women don't work here for coin. They're *owned* by the domus. No freedom, no money, no familia.

Slaves.

The Sabines are a bedtime horror story. Don't stay out too late, or you'll be kidnapped for a sabine. Don't disobey, or you'll be sent to learn how good you have it.

Don't turn twenty, or you'll be sold for a denarius.

A shiver moves up my spine and I turn to leave, but the door bangs open. A tall man, fully cloaked, flees in my periphery and I hear shouts from the open door behind him.

"You have to pay for it; doesn't matter how cold it is."

Before I can take another step, a ruddy face and dark hair blur my vision as the man from the building grabs my arm. I try to back away, arm throbbing in his grip, and the honey water falls from my hand. The metal cup clatters to the cobblestones and the sound echoes through my bones as the man snarls, "Blessings on Venus. She takes some, she gives some."

Tisiphone and Her Friends

Luella

After the performance, I head to the refreshments. I mustn't appear too eager. Ledo will want to chase. Men like him want to be the predator, so I will play the *praeda*.

For now.

At the refreshment table, two women are leaning in close, talking over the posca. I know they mean to be ignored, because no one drinks the vinegary beverage except those who can't afford uncut wine or the sweetened version, *sapa*, and both carafes are still full. I don't look at them as I fill my cup anyways, always interested in gossip I can share with Mia.

"I heard he was found dead…" a young brunette says. I take a sip of the drink, the sharp tang causing my cheeks to tighten.

"Just like the Senator last quad," the older of the two whispers, her black hair framing her dark eyes.

"It's Tisiphone… seeking vengeance." The younger one's voice trembles, but with fear or excitement, I can't tell. "She sees their crimes. Senator Silas… he took a fancy to my niece a few summers ago." My chest tightens. I hate that I was too late for anyone, that it takes me so long to find them all.

"I thought she was just a girl?"

"She's eleven summers now," the first woman answers. I don't need to hear more. I know Silas' past. That's why he was chosen, but how many were noticing what type of men are dying? I need to be careful. If they're noticing, the men might eventually notice, too.

How will they act if they feel targeted? If they realize it's a woman posing as a wife or sister or mater? I'm not foolish enough to think it can't get worse.

It can always get worse.

I don't want innocent women to pay for my crimes.

"I hope she kills them all," the woman adds, voice guttural. I couldn't agree more.

"Tisiphone should be cutting the head off the snake," the older woman says, invoking the fury of revenge. Tisiphone, the one who metes out retributive justice.

My favorite, obviously.

I should walk away, but instead I say, "Snakes like to live in holes. Sometimes you have to wait for them to emerge."

The older woman gasps. "We were just-" she begins, but something in my face must give her pause.

The younger woman's dark skin grows greenish, as if she's going to vomit. "Tisiphone," she breathes. I'd like to tell her I'm working on it, that beheading the snake is what I've been working towards for a third of my life. Instead, I put my finger to my lips in the sign of silence, and slink away, letting them whisper of the goddesses and revenge.

Weaving past the bards, now strumming a lively song that allows for partners to dance, I head towards a shaded copse of trees at the edge of the festival.

Lowering myself to the ground, I allow the sounds of the music and the birds overhead to fill my ears, seep into my mind. For another moment I pretend that I'm just a woman, enjoying the weather, soaking in warmth from Romulus and Remus as they grow close, shrinking each other's shadows until there is just one, small beneath me in the midday light.

But that's not who I am.

I open my eyes when I realize that Ledo has not pursued me.

Stones. It's never easy, is it? I tip my posca into the dirt, hoping the small amount of vinegar doesn't do to the grasses what it did to my tastebuds, and weave back into the crowd.

It takes me a few moments to spot the Praetor, and I see immediately why he hasn't sought me out. A young woman with dark hair and an inordinate amount of freckles sits in his lap, feeding him grapes.

I hiss a breath out of my teeth, irritation coating my insides. I'm not as good at dealing with women as I am with men. I could come over and compliment her, perhaps give Ledo some ideas that will shift his attention back to me.

That might be too sexual, too 'last day of the festival' behavior.

I could try to slip something in her drink. I do have some nausea inducing potion... but it would be difficult to introduce to her glass. Not to mention the idea of poisoning her doesn't sit well with me.

I'm deep into calculating my options when my eyes snag back on the refreshment table.

The two women are still there.

I don't have time for many friends, but maybe Tisiphone does.

I don't have to wait long for them to follow their end of the bargain. The freckled woman on Ledo's lap lets out a scream as the older woman falls over her, dumping an entire pitcher of uncut red wine onto the woman's yellow dress.

I'd paid for the wine, of course. A handful of the smallest denomination coins, denarii, with the senate building stamped on one silver side and the face of the Emperor on the other. I hope it made him furious that he wasn't on the golden aureus, the larger denomination coin still stamped with his pater's face.

Maybe I'll ask him when he's at my mercy, one day.

"Stones, I'm so sorry," the older woman says. "You'll want some vinegar on that right away, good lady."

"Good luck," the younger woman from the beverage table whispers in my ear as she slips a cloth into my hand.

As the woman from Ledo's lap huffs away, I sweep in with the rag. "Oh, good man, let me help." My tone is direct, no nonsense. Ledo has some wine on his pants, but thankfully it's lower, near his knee.

I keep my eyes on his trousers, dabbing at the wine stain without looking into his face. After a moment I look up between my lashes and my hand stills on his leg. I think he recognizes me, given the way a half smirk plays across his lips. His dark hair brushes his forehead and for a moment he's almost handsome. Tall and dark, with a strong jaw covered in stubble.

I cast my eyes down, then back up. The contents of my stomach threaten to follow the same path as I note how he eyes my face, my form. I start to pull back, like I'm just realizing that I'm touching him, and he grabs my hand.

"I'm so sorry, I shouldn't have..." I trail off.

"You're attentive," he says, the innuendo clear.

Color seeps into my cheeks. "I-"

He cuts me off. "I'm Praetor Ledo." Of course he uses his title.

"Skylar," I say.

"That's a pretty name," Ledo says. "Care to sit?"

I think he means his lap, where the other woman was. Instead, I smile and sit next to him on the bench, close enough that I'm aware of where his hands are placed, the slant of his body towards mine. I can't protect myself here, there's nothing to poison and no scheme would protect me out in the open like this. If I had to defend myself, Divus would see, and I'd be buried or stoned for raising a hand against a man.

The razor thin line of my safety could snap at any moment.

"I didn't mean there," he says, raising his eyebrows.

I lean in, but don't touch him, drowning out the thought of him strangling me in the middle of the forum with a lilting laugh. "Praetor," I scold playfully.

He leans in, smiling as well, but his eyes are mischievous, glinting at the challenge I've given him. His gaze dips to my breasts, and back up. I take a deep breath, letting him look his fill and imagine his own breath stalling in his lungs, his eyes wide when he realizes what's happening.

It's easy to smile back, knowing that one day soon, he'll be dead.

Mistake

Rose

A mistake. I've made such a mistake.

I try to yank my arm away from the man, but his grip is like a mater towing a recalcitrant child. Unrelenting.

"Let go," I screech.

"Come inside, little goat. You'll have fun." His eyes show me otherwise as he drags me towards the door of The Sabines.

Not like this. Not my own stupid curiosity dooming me.

"Help," I scream, my voice unrecognizable in its hysteria. Fear grips my lungs as he drags me forward. The shadow of the building falls over me and its accompanying chill turns me to ice, and my feet lose purchase on the ground.

No, no, no, no.

"I'm betrothed," I shout, the desperate wish breaking free.

His grip tightens, but he freezes. "To who?"

His dark eyes look sunken into his pale face as he leers down at me. I swallow, unable to speak.

He shakes me, snarling. "Who, little goat?"

I say the only name I know. "A-Augustus."

"Augustus who?"

My jaw works, opening and closing, but nothing comes out.

"That's what I—"

"She's betrothed to me."

The familiar voice buckles my knees. Augustus is here. He's saving me.

But when I turn, it's not him. It's his golden counterpart.

His hair is mussed, unkempt almost, and his cheeks are flushed. He wears a dark cape thrown across his shoulders but the clothes beneath are bright, matching the festival.

The man looks between us, laughing as he shoves me towards Tristan, and I fall into the dirt at his feet, looking up at my savior. The man holds out his hand for Tristan.

Tristan sighs and withdraws not a silver denarius, but two golden aurei from his pocket, and without an instant of hesitation places the small fortune in the man's hand.

The man leaves without a word and Tristan reaches for me. I'm still in such shock that I barely register his grip as he raises me from the ground.

The Sabines casts shadows over us to the left and the Maero roars to the right. Sounds the river or the festival or my naivetè had drowned out in front of the building manifest here.

Screams. Crying.

Primal sounds that wash through me, distorted through the buzz in my ears.

The bars on the windows remind me of what almost happened. What still might happen if my pater has his way. We're almost out of the alley when the last window, barred in a grid pattern, is interrupted by something reaching out. It takes me a moment to realize it's a hand, missing all but the three middle fingers, the stumps scarred and red. I flinch, falling back against Tristan but unable to look away.

No sound comes out from these bars, just a sad, tired reaching.

Tristan's grip tightens on my hand. "Let's go before he changes his mind."

My stomach roils. I want to save them, these women, but I don't know if I can save myself.

"You paid him a fortune," I say. No one would change their mind over two aurei.

"Yet, I'm the one with the treasure," he says, not looking back at me.

His words don't register. Instead, I keep looking at our intertwined hands and seeing the scarred hand from behind the bars in place of my own.

Versions

Luella

The magic of Divus is difficult to explain. The gods did not bless this land with the magic of the elements, like the lands to the east where fire and water appear at its inhabitants fingertips. No, the gods of this land were obsessed with themselves and bestowed a magic as multi-faceted and finicky as they were.

I must be blessed by some part of the gods that either hated what they were, or perhaps were just too bored to allow themselves to look the same for the rest of their days.

Ledo had come to call on me at my room in the city after I explained that my parents had died and I'd lost their domus. An easy lie, since I couldn't very well say I had a domus hidden in the woods where I returned every few quads with a different face.

"I brought you these," Ledo says, offering a batch of crushed geraniums. Another pathetic flower, although less deceptive than the rose. "Then a horse nearly trampled me and I accidentally did this to them." He grimaces and shrugs. His explanation reeks of privilege. Horses? I've seen exactly zero horses in the forum. Only the Emperor and the military own horses.

"Oh goodness! Well, it's the thought that counts." I smile at him. This type of lie is so practiced, it nearly escapes my notice. These are the pleasantries expected of a woman, built and tended by every encounter we've ever had. "Although you better make sure to release me if a horse ever tries to trample you!"

He grins. "If I was holding onto you, I don't know that I'd ever let you go."

I smile back. He's charming, because of course he is. I've been balancing the line of spirited banter and meekness to keep him coming back. It's working, although I know I'll need to up the game soon, lest he grow bored of me. Not to mention the clipse is almost at an end. He won't be coming into the city daily after that.

"Ledo?" I ask as we stroll through the cobblestone streets near where we met at the festival. Bawdy music drifts to us from the square over, and I know the festivities will soon become just a tangle of bodies.

"Yes?" he asks, squeezing my arm gently.

"I'm... quite enjoying our time together," I say, hesitating over the words as though I know I'm being too forward, but simply can't help myself. As though I haven't rehearsed these lines for days, years really, since so many men require the same posturing and simpering from the women around them.

"And?" Ledo asks.

"Well," I pause, still unsure, as any good lady would be. "I worry that you're leading me on."

"Leading you on?" he asks, a smirk playing about his lips. Oh, but he is good.

"Yes. Scaring away prospective suitors. With my familia gone, I must be practical."

"Practical." He nods. "And have you had any suitors calling? Ones I have scared away?"

"No, they are too afraid of you." I let the accusation hang in the air, knowing, as we both do, that Praetors do not marry girls from unknown families and not a single other soul has come to call on me.

"Of course. I take it you're interested in whether a particular Praetor has any interest in this situation?" His tone is teasing, and I wonder if he's letting himself enjoy our time together or if he's doing exactly what I am.

Masquerading until I can strike.

I scoff. "Well, don't get a big head."

"Never, Skylar." I like the name. I recycle them, so as not to confuse myself. Skylar, Julia, Luna, Aelia. The same names, just new faces, new bodies, new shapes. A marriage to Ledo would change Skylar's life, but since Skylar doesn't exist Ledo will marry me. And that marriage? That would change *his* life.

"Hmm." I bite my lip in thought, worrying it between my teeth. Ledo drops his gaze to the action, stepping closer.

"Will you come to the ball with me? Tomorrow?"

"Tomorrow? You expect me to have a presentable dress by tomorrow?" I protest.

"If you don't want to come..." Ledo begins, but I shake my head.

"I would be honored to attend." My eyelashes flutter, and it's almost too much, even for me.

"I'll send something for you," he says.

I smile and put a hand on his arm.

He puts his hand over mine, then lifts my hand to his mouth and brushes a kiss across my knuckles. "I'll pick you up tomorrow."

"I can't wait," I say, and I mean it.

Ledo sends a dress. It's light blue, like the dress I'd worn to the festival. The neckline appears nearly modest at first, but when I turn the gown around, I realize that, while it has a high neck, the entire back is open. It will cut so low my back dimples will be visible.

I shouldn't be surprised. Ledo would want to see his prize, but wearing this not accompanied by a man was an open invitation. I stand in my small washroom, curling each strand of my now golden hair around a calamistrum. Each ringlet falls hot against my cheek and neck, but I don't flinch. I try to do them all quickly so I don't have to return the rod to the coals. Thoughts of Ledo slink along me like a second skin. His charming smiles. His teasing. His gifts.

I roll my shoulders back, letting out a low breath.

I set the mostly cooled iron down and apply a dash of color to my cheeks and lips. I run my hands through the curls, breaking them up to make them look softer. Sweeter.

Still, Ledo won't leave my mind. His profile. The women Mia has brought back from death's door. The number of lashes. The hours of sutures. The bruised lips and broken ribs.

I hadn't thought about it before, had put his crimes into a small box, only asking myself if he fit criteria. If he would help me meet my goals. He did, so that was all that mattered. Now... I carefully arrange the dress the way I know Ledo will prefer. The light blue fabric clings to the curves I painstakingly crafted. The perfect proportions.

I take a deep breath, looking into the blue eyes staring back in the mirror. Not my eyes. Nothing about this face is mine, with its small upturned nose, wide eyes, and round cheeks. At least I don't think it's like mine. I haven't worn my own face in over ten years. I tried, once, to let the muscles and bones shift into their natural position, to allow my hair to drift to its own color, my eyes to darken.

I shudder. That girl is dead, and that's how it felt to try to shift back into her.

Like trying to die.

I stand taller, steadying my nerves. Infusing them with stone, with basanite. I refuse to dwell on the question that always lingers in the background these days.

Will this version of me die, too?

TRY

ROSE

I'M SAFE. FOR NOW. Tristan's saying something but I don't hear anything until my eyes find Daisy. She's dancing with Ceres and Ceres' little brother, oblivious to the horror of my almost fate.

"Are you okay?" Tristan asks, and I have the feeling he's said this more than once.

"I think so, just a bit shaken up." I can hear my pulse racing in direct contradiction to that characterization, but it feels like the thing I should say. Hysteria is unbecoming of a lady. I clear my throat.

"Let's dance," he suggests. I start to shake my head, because men can't dance the maiden. Ceres' brother is out there, though, and when I look again I see that indeed, the floor is full of couples. It's later than I thought, and it's the courtship dances now.

"I guess we could." My body is numb, but my tongue knows what to say.

"I'm flattered." Tristan smiles, leading me out onto the floor. The jest makes me think of Augustus and my stomach tightens. What would he think of me dancing with Tristan? What would he think of how I used his name to try and save myself?

As if he hears my thoughts, Tristan draws me flush against him and asks, "You're betrothed?"

My body follows his, the dance giving my limbs something to do with their nervous energy, the memory of the dark alley slipping away in the warmth of the suns. Heat rises in my cheeks at my earlier lie, desperate or not. "No," I admit.

"You said you were betrothed to Augustus?" Tristan cocks his head, leading me into a small twirl, then back into his arms. He's strong, and when he swings me away I'm afraid that he'll let go, and I'll go careening off the dance floor.

"I just thought it might make him let me go, and your brother's was the only name I could think of," I rush. "Please don't tell him I said that. I know he's not..." I trail off, wishing I could sink beneath the dance floor.

Tristan's hand flexes against my low back, making my skin tingle. I've never been so close to a boy before. I've never been held like this. I inhale, slowing my heart against the tangled emotions of earlier and the nearness and newness of this.

"My brother," he says slowly. "Augustus?"

I nod and he laughs. It must be at my presumption, and whether it's from mortification, terror at almost being taken as a Sabine, or relief that I wasn't, I feel the telltale prick of tears. I won't cry. Pater hates it when we cry.

"I'm sorry, I was just so afraid." My voice cracks, but it's better than tears.

"Shh." Tristan presses impossibly closer, our bodies so flush together that I don't know where he ends and I start. "It's alright. You're alright." I don't look at him, but I do nod. I feel like a child, at once comforted and reprimanded for my reckless emotions, for my lack of control. "I was just surprised for a moment. My brother... Augustus? He's not usually serious about girls. Women," he corrects.

"What do you mean?" I tip my head back to look into his beautiful golden face.

Tristan shakes his head. "He likes to flirt. Lead women on." He drops his voice, tilting his head towards my ear. His warm breath makes me shiver as he says, "Then after they've dishonored themselves, he moves on."

I shake my head. That doesn't sound like Augustus. Or does it? I've only met him once. He was charming. So charming, in fact, that I've thought of only him for days. I bite my lip. "So, he wasn't... interested in me?" I manage to ask.

He spins me again, then whirls me back into him, hard. The breath leaves me in a gasp and I look up at him. My savior.

Tristan meets my eyes, the deep amber seeming at once hard and warm, blessed like basanite. "No, but I am."

After our dance, Tristan goes to find me something to drink.

"Don't tell me what you like, I'll surprise you," he says, smiling, and leaves me near a copse of trees.

A new voice interrupts my thoughts. "Daisy looks like she's having fun."

I start, turning to find Augustus. His copper hair glistening beneath the twins, eyes twinkling. My heart leaps, and then falls, remembering what Tristan told me. "Augustus, you scared me."

"I've been looking for you, but when I went to your domus your pater said-"

"You talked to my pater?" I shouldn't have interrupted him, but the idea of Augustus seeing my pater. My domus... What did I think would happen, giving out my name like that? I'm such a stupid girl. A stupid, romantic, hopeless girl.

"I wanted to bring you to the festival, but he said you were already here…"

Venus. I know what that means. It means he said much more than that. "I'm sorry."

"Sorry for what?" Augustus cocks his head.

"If my pater was… unkind."

He smiles. "You're not responsible for how your pater behaves. Besides, you're here." He steps closer to me and I step back. The corners of his mouth dip down ever so slightly. "What's wrong?"

I shake my head. "Nothing, I've just had a bit of a morning."

Hands come around my shoulders, and Augustus clenches his jaw. "Nothing I couldn't take care of, right, Rose?" Tristan says, his demeanor both calm and challenging, like he dares someone to bother me. Like he dares Augustus to bother me. Something foreign flutters in my stomach.

"What happened?" Augustus says, hands fisted at his sides.

I'm saved trying to answer by Tristan. "The Sabines tried to kidnap her."

Augustus narrows his eyes. "Lucky you were there, then."

Tristan's voice takes on a taunting edge. "Very lucky."

Not that it will matter. The only difference is now my pater will receive payment for me. I bite my lip.

"What is it?" Augustus asks, eyes dropping to my mouth.

I can't tell them. My shame, my position? It's mine. It's mine to bear and mine to solve. "Nothing."

"Rose?" Augustus pushes. Does it really matter if they know? Augustus was already just toying with me and Tristan, interested or not, will find out soon enough.

"It might not matter soon." I look down, and Tristan comes around to my side.

"What do you mean?" Tristan says. Augustus steps closer, as if he wants to step between us, but holds himself still.

I shake my head, not looking up. "I'm almost twenty." Their confusion is palpable, their lives on such a distinctly different trajectory simply because they are boys. "And I'm not married."

"That's bad?" Augustus asks.

"Of course it's bad," Tristan speaks for me, the understanding seeming to dawn on him. "She should be married with children by now." He looks to me. "What does that have to do with The Sabines?"

"Nothing," I say again. I can't actually say it. Not out loud. The lie Daisy and I spoke just hours before still clinging to me. Maybe it wasn't a lie, maybe he'll change his mind once he sobers. Maybe I'll have more time. Or maybe...

"Rose," Tristan says, voice stern. "Tell me." It's not a question, it's a demand to be obeyed.

"My pater will sell me." The words are quiet. A confession and a plea. I don't know if I just want someone besides Daisy to hear my pater's plans, to understand my terror, but I can't turn back now. "He's going to sell me to The Sabines."

"Stones," Augustus says, his hand reaches towards me, but then drops. Tristan is silent for a long moment, and I know he must be thinking about what I said to the man who tried to kidnap me.

After impossibly long he says, "Maybe I can fix this."

Augustus snaps his head up to Tristan and they share a look I can't decipher. "No," he growls.

Tristan shrugs at his brother and looks to me. "Let me see what I can do, Rose. I'm not promising anything." Then he takes my hand again, kissing it. He looks over at his brother, his lips lingering. "But it would be my pleasure to try."

Blooms

Luella

Ledo is almost handsome in his black trousers. The barbarian fashion is one I greatly appreciate being adopted here in Divus, compared to the haughty robes that used to dominate. I smile at him as we enter the circular ballroom.

The Domus Aurea is all limestone, circular spires reaching to the dark clouds above them, and the ballroom is no exception. The white tablecloths match the walls, and the colorful roses adorning every table provide contrast.

I am thankful for my lack of smell, but still feel my nose trying to wrinkle at the, probably abhorrent, perfume.

The room is packed full of Senators, Praetors, and consuls. If Silas were still alive, I have no doubt he'd be here as well. I recognize some of the other men that Mia had looked into at some time or other. Lucky for them, her research hadn't warranted a visit from me.

The Emperor appears to be absent, which suits me just fine. I don't need him complicating tonight. It's the end of the clipse of Venus, so there is dancing, riotous music, and more food than the entirety of Divus could eat, much less just this ballroom.

"Care to dance?" Ledo asks, noting my eyes sweeping across the room. The chandeliers above cast flickering light across his face and I can't discern what's in his look. Desire?

"Of course." I smile, taking his arm as he leads me out just as a new song begins to play. The string instruments start out slow, mournful.

"Perfect," Ledo murmurs, drawing me against him. I giggle and Ledo's rough hand finds the open skin of my back while he holds my hand with the other. "This dress is too much."

"Then why did you pick it out?" I say, already knowing the answer. I force myself to lean in instead of away, urge pliancy into my movements. The subtle lies I paint with my body are a dance I've done my whole life.

"I knew you'd be delicious in it," he says.

I make a sound of disapproval low in my throat but wear a smile.

Difficult.

Worthy of chase.

His hand flexes against my skin at the sound, and he tightens his grip as we turn with the music, our chests flush. The musicians reach a crescendo and Ledo leans in close to my ear to be heard. His lips brush across the shell as he whispers, "I'd like to take you to the garden."

I fight a smile. Ledo is as predictable as I'd expected. Now I would see if he'd be pursuing more with Skylar, as was ideal, or if he would try to take me back to his room tonight. I had plans for either, but I want a wedding. Not only would it be easier, but without access to the Domus Aurea, I'd be no closer to my true target.

Ledo's ownership would dispel any suspicion. I might obtain information from him, but also from others in the Domus Aurea. Wives don't try to hurt their husbands and they certainly don't try to poison them, kill them, and flee. Nor would a wife be able to learn anything that might be useful in coming back to kill someone else in the Domus Aurea.

Well, most wives.

As the song finishes, Ledo tugs me through the crowded ballroom, towards the back garden. The suns are setting, the flowers casting deep disfigured shadows across the cobblestone walking path.

He leads me to, of course, the roses.

With the traitorous blooms bursting around us, one of his hands dips beneath the opening in my dress, caressing my backside beneath it, while the other snakes into my hair, tilting my mouth to his. I let out a breathy moan, leaning into him. His grip tightens and he bites my lip, sucking the bottom one into his mouth.

There is no proposal coming tonight. He's too urgent, too needy.

Instead of gagging, I whimper, forcing my stomach to relax, urging the bile to stay down.

"Skylar," Ledo groans, grinding into me.

"Ledo," I breathe back. "Praetor, we have to stop."

"Why?" he asks, trailing kisses down my jaw, finding the junction of my neck and shoulder and sucking the skin into his mouth, trying to tempt me.

Idiot.

"I cannot," I complain, throwing my head back as if in ecstasy. "I cannot dishonor my familia name."

This is the moment. I make sure my eyes are slitted so I can watch every micro-expression on his face. This is the most dangerous part, saying no. It has to go perfectly. His ego must be primed, while still making sure he believes my reasons. He has to believe them, too. He has to agree.

A man like Ledo disagreeing won't end well, but the question is always 'for who?'

"Is this?" Ledo doesn't ask the question, and maybe a lady wouldn't answer anyways, so I just nod.

"I've never..." I let my irritation sweep into my eyes and cheeks, warp it into embarrassment. His lips turn up slightly, his eyes darken.

He's considering. I bite my lip and let my breath come out harsh. Ragged.

Break me.

Own me.

Use me.

I urge him, pleading with my eyes. Pleading with my heaving breasts and my thighs pressed together. Marriage means nothing to him. That means he won't be opposed to the idea itself, but to the ceremony of it. The steps in the way of what he wants.

Yet he must enjoy some aspect of marriage, or he wouldn't keep doing it.

I lick my lips, waiting.

"You're right, Skylar. I'm sorry," Ledo says, kissing me softly, removing his hands. "Let's return to the ball."

I don't relax. The danger hasn't passed yet. "Do you mind if I collect myself?" I say, looking down, smoothing the front of my dress.

"Of course, I'll meet you at our table," he says. I don't need to see his face to know he's smiling like a wolf, thinking I'm a mess of desire.

As he departs, I force my heart to slow its furious pace, allowing each breath to wash through me. Being here, in the Domus Aurea, has me on edge, and I can't afford any distractions.

I reach out to the nearest rosebush. The blooms are bright red, nearly crimson in the fading light. I cup the petals in my palm, careful to keep my fingers high on the stem to avoid any of the thorns.

It's beautiful in some ways. Maybe that's why I hate them. Or perhaps I'm just contrary in every sense of the word.

Maybe I've spent so long pretending to be otherwise that I can't just enjoy a pretty thing anymore.

My palm closes of its own accord, smashing the petals beneath my fist before I give the bloom a sharp tug, ripping it from its stem. I drop the mangled red bud onto the cobblestone path, smiling, then reach for another.

Battlefield

Luella

"By the twins, what did they ever do to you?" a deep voice asks. I spin sharply to an impossibly large man with hair the golden red of the sunrise, his jaw taken over by matching auburn stubble. His piercing blue eyes meet mine and I inhale sharply. He's so familiar, but I don't have time to place it, to sift through my memories to find him.

"Who?" I ask. He gestures to the ground and I realize I've beheaded dozens of roses. The red, pink, and white blooms crushed beneath my fists lay scattered around me, a battlefield of beauty. "Ah... well the gardeners here..." I trail off at his smirk.

"Having fun with Ledo?" he asks. He's been watching me.

I take a step away from him without turning my back. "I should return to him." Jealousy is not an emotion I want to manage in a man like Ledo.

"I'll walk you back," he says.

"I don't know if the Praetor will like that." I keep my tone gentle, sweet.

"What's he going to do about it?" he asks.

Nothing to you. "Who are you?"

He doesn't answer, instead offering an arm. I consider turning away from him, but what if he knows Ledo? I can't be rude. I can't be fierce, and definitely not noticeable. Lightly placing my hand on his arm, I keep the space between us as he leads me back through the garden until we re-enter the ballroom. Neither of us speaks and my shoulders are tight as I search the crowd for Ledo.

He finds us first.

"Dominus," Ledo says, coming up with a tray filled with all manner of sweets. Chocolates, pastries, and fruits piled high as he gestures to a nearby table.

My eyes snap to the man.

"Not the important one." The man grins, as if following my thoughts. "The brother."

The familiarity. The voice. He's the Emperor's brother. Both of them are plastered across Divus, the Imperator and the Dominus.

The Emperor and his Sword.

They're engraved on coins and frescoes, banners and statues. The two men who control the entire empire, and therefore all of us.

I'm surprised I didn't recognize him.

I look to Ledo, but there is no jealousy there. He appears... amused. "You're plenty important, but why are you boring my date?" he says.

"You poor girl," the Dominus says to me. Instead of sounding sarcastic he sounds sincere. Mia's profile didn't cover this relationship. Are they friends?

He's not even supposed to be here.

Ledo laughs, either not catching the note in the Dominus' voice, or more likely, not caring.

"Care to dance?" the Dominus asks, and instead of answering I look to Ledo. He smiles and nods, granting the permission they expect me to seek.

The Dominus draws me onto the dance floor, and I look over my shoulder at Ledo. He's already talking to another Praetor, a portly man in blue.

"What are you doing with him?" the Dominus asks, tilting his head as he leads me into a mid paced dance. His smile doesn't meet his eyes as he regards me, and it puts me even more on edge.

"You ask a lot of questions." I note that the other dancers keep glancing to us. The Dominus must not appear at the Domus Aurea often.

"Call me concerned." He seems determined to unbalance me either mentally or physically, punctuating my silence by leaning me into a dip. His warm hand is on my exposed back, eyes boring into mine.

"How thoughtful, *matulo*," I say, stiff in his arms. I don't hide my irritation. He's going to be a problem.

"*Matulo*? That's the insult you use?" he asks, bemused.

"It is rather block shaped," I say, eyeing his ginger head. I quirk my brow at his fake hurt, forgetting for a moment that I am not myself. I am Skylar. Sweet and with enough bite to be interesting despite my naiveté. Not Luella, not my sharp edges and irritation.

"There she is." He smiles and I quickly soften my features. "Don't hide her." The Dominus reaches forward, his fingertips brushing my eyebrow as it levels with the other.

"Who?" I ask, but the Dominus just smiles.

"I'm sure you know this, but people see what they want to see." My heart thunders in my ears. He can't know who I am. "Ledo? He *makes* what he wants to see." The Dominus leans forward so that only I can hear. "And I'd hate to see you made into anything other than that of your own choosing."

His words are precise. The thoughtful phrasing of someone who, like me, has to tread carefully. I meet his eyes and the flickering candlelight brings out the copper in his hair, the gold flecks in his blue eyes. His jaw is tight, brow just slightly furrowed, as if he's worried.

I smile, my mask firmly in place as I reply sweetly, "I can take care of myself, Dominus."

He nods slowly. My eyes never leave his face, searching for something, anything to tell me if he knows more than he should. About Ledo.

About me.

Then an idea strikes.

"What about..." It's my turn to lean in close. Would he smell of cedar and smoke? Rain? I remember my pater smelling like ash and spirits late at night. Stale body odor in the mornings. Mater smelled like violets and salt. Tears, sweat, and blood: salt saturated our familia in a way I suspect few understand. I don't know what the Dominus smells like. I can't use that sense to determine if he smoked, or bathed, or had rolled with another woman. If he had too much to drink, if I need to be wary. "The Emperor. What does he want to see?"

I tip my head back to watch his eyes, but I don't need to. His whole body tenses, his jaw clenching. His eyes darken, twin storms looking back at me.

"My brother," he says tightly, "is not as blind as Ledo." With that, the Dominus leads me from the dance floor and unceremoniously returns me to the table where Ledo watches me hungrily.

The moment the Dominus turns to go, Ledo grabs my hand.

"Let's go," he says.

And I, still in shock over the Dominus' change in demeanor, allow him to drag me from the crowded ballroom, and out of sight.

My mind spins as Ledo leads me from the ballroom. The candlelit revelry begins to fade as we move down an abandoned corridor and the tall limestone columns chaperon our departure. My blood thrums beneath this skin and sweat beads along my hairline.

The Dominus wasn't supposed to be here.

And Ledo's posture is sending alarm bells ringing through me, the set of his shoulders, the grindingly painful grip on my wrist. Despite his casual air in the ballroom, he was displeased. Was it about me dancing with the Dominus or whatever discussion he'd had with the Praetor in blue? My life depends on being able to manage this shift, the subtle signs on how to steer him. My magic is subterfuge, not force.

I can't engage in altercations I have no hope of surviving, and the likelihood of finding myself in one rises the farther we move from the ballroom.

"Praetor, you're hurting me," I try, suffusing my tone with as much sweetness and naiveté as I can.

Ledo looks down at my wrist as he continues forward, loosening his grip ever so slightly. He doesn't slow his pace, but he doesn't jerk my body anymore, either.

The tapestries around us drip with subtle condescension, each depicting a scene of abundance and privilege. Tables laden with food, women draped in furs beside roaring fireplaces, men surrounded by beautiful servants offering food and drink. Look, they whisper, look at all the things you barely have. I try to take a deep breath, try to calm my center, when Ledo pulls me towards an alcove that leads to a balcony off the main hallway.

The balcony is open to the evening air and the dim light almost makes it seem serene, romantic even, but I know better. He leans into me, using his grip on my wrist to tether me to him.

"I didn't like you dancing with him," he says, trapping me in a bruising kiss.

I gasp at the pain but kiss him back, fiercely, giving myself a moment to calculate. "I didn't like dancing with him, either," I whisper, like it's a secret just for him.

Ledo bites me on the neck, and I don't need to fake the whimper of pain as he digs deeper, the skin tight beneath his teeth.

"I only share when I want to, Skylar," he grates, his teeth scraping against my bruised skin. His rough hands drag at my dress, paw along my exposed back.

The words stick in my throat, but I know I must say them. "I'm sorry," I breathe, hating the way it tastes. "I just want you to be happy. I... I thought you wanted me to."

Ledo groans into my neck, pressing himself against me so I can feel what my timid apology wrought. The tension eases ever so slightly, his shoulders softer. "I just want to make you happy," I say again.

He tilts my chin up to him and kisses me softly, a featherlight brush. It's as close to an apology as he'll come. "You can't make me jealous like that," he admonishes. We both know I'm expected to manage his emotions, to mold myself to his liking.

"I'm sorry," I repeat. I'm not, but Ledo will be.

Very soon, he'll be sorry.

SALE

ROSE

A QUIET KNOCK RINGS through our domus, and my heart stops. Pater should be passed out for hours still and it's early enough that even Daisy snores softly. I throw an extra shawl over my shoulders and slip out the front door.

Tristan's hand finds mine, as if they were never meant to be apart, and he kisses it the way he has every time he's done it. All three times that is. Gentle but insistent. "It's a pleasure to see you, Rose."

I smile, the feeling permeating every inch of my skin, sinking into my bones. "And you, Tristan."

He leads me through the sleepy streets, the twin suns cresting over the Maero. He's leading me into the suns-shine, and I'm quiet until we're descending the narrow stone steps that lead to the walkway along the water. It floods late in planting season, the Maero swallowing the walkways and splashing against the stairways. It's why the city is built on the hill, but this time of year she's mild, rushing by with neither malice nor grief.

Tristan points to troops across the way, swimming. "My brother will be there next year, training."

"He's officially joining, then?" I ask, my heart clenching for Augustus.

"When did you talk to him?" Tristan asks, hand tightening around mine.

I suck in a breath as the bones in my fingers grind together, protesting the loss of the caress they were in. "The day we met in the square."

He loosens his grip, but still holds tightly to me. "Oh, right. Well, he hasn't decided yet, but Pater has."

I nod, trying not to flex my fingers. There's no need to complain when it was clearly an accident.

"I asked you here for a reason," Tristan says. I had hoped so. After the festival, Tristan had been secretive, saying he'd meet me in exactly one clipse.

Today.

"Everything is prepared, you can tell your pater today." Tristan beams, turning to me. The suns behind him blind me and I squint to see his eyes, searching.

"Tell him what?" My heart sinks. I thought he would negotiate with my pater, not ask me to do it. How could I talk my pater out of the Sabines without a proposal? I don't say any of this. The desperation in my belly is too ugly to show Tristan. It's bad enough I told him and Augustus about my problems; I can't complain about his solution, too.

Tristan draws me into his embrace, chest to chest. I gasp as his hand slides into my hair, and he tugs the strands so that I'm forced to look up into his golden face. The world stops when he speaks.

"Tell him that you're to be my wife."

I've always known I was made for love. Softness. I've always known I wasn't made for my pater's version of life.

I just never thought I'd have it.

"Who is he?" Pater asks, his eyebrows furrowing in a look I know as well as the pattern of the freckles on Daisy's cheeks. It usually appears after one too many at the tavern, but I'd approached him early in the day. After his favorite breakfast, but before he'd had more than four drinks.

The sweetest spot for a man like him.

I'd even asked Daisy to help me clean the domus last night. It nearly sparkled in here, and that always put him in a better mood, when he felt proud of where we lived.

"His name is Tristan, Pater," I say, eyes downcast.

"Hmm. What does he do?"

I know what he's actually asking, molding my responses to each expression that flits across his face, reading the pages of his reactions. "He's a son of Tiberius." I wait for the name to sink in, the familia so far above our own that nothing I say will matter after this. "Tristan is set to inherit his pater's domus and position. And he's offered to waive a dowry." I don't use titles, because to Pater that would be boastful, which is unbecoming of a woman. Everyone knows what it means to be the son of Tiberius, anyways. Pater is silent, so I add the real reason he can't refuse, something that has nothing to do with station and everything to do with Paters' situation. "He also offered *coemptio*."

Tristan had been sure that Pater was only interested in The Sabines because he needed denarii, hence his offer of a reverse dowry. *Coemptio* would symbolize that my pater had been caring for me in his absence. I wasn't a burden he needed to be compensated for, but a gift worth purchasing. I extend the small scroll I'd held in the folds of my skirt. "Here is the offer."

At once thoughtful and effective. The butterflies that had been beating their wings in my chest since Tristan and I met yesterday reach a crescendo as I wait. I haven't seen the amount. I just have to hope it's enough.

"*Coemptio*?" he questions. "You didn't offer him the milk, did you girl?" His face starts to darken and I shake my head vehemently.

"The opposite, Pater. I said I wouldn't dishonor myself before marriage..." I trail off, leaving enough for Pater to understand. I'd used myself to earn him more. Used Tristan's desire to line Pater's pockets. He would appreciate that, understand it. And on some level, he'd expect it from me, just as he would from any woman.

It wasn't true, of course. Tristan cared about me, but Pater wouldn't understand *that*.

"Hmm. *Coemptio*?" he says again. Then, finally, he reaches out to take the scroll. He breaks the small purple wax seal.

I fold my hands in front of me and stare at the familiar brick floor, hoping I'll never meet it again. The butterflies continue to swarm, their wings beating in my heart, my lungs, my ears. It's so loud inside me that I almost don't hear the rustle of the paper as his calloused hands unfurl it. I almost miss it when Pater says the words that will set me free.

"I accept."

JUST LIKE ME

LUELLA

"Did you know about the Dominus? I thought he wasn't at court?" I snap at Mia.

Mia raises her hands in defense. "He's been with the legions for the last two years! I didn't know he was back."

"Well he is." I slump into a chair in the waiting room at Mia's infirmaria. The plush blue fabric warms my exposed back and I shiver. It's after hours, so only Mia and I are here, the front door locked and the windows drawn. If Ledo followed me, it's easy enough to fake illness. I have vials just for it and Mia and I have a standing story involving nausea.

"He's not going to be a problem," Mia says. "He's either perfectly normal or celibate, because no one has ever mentioned him." I give her a dubious look. "He won't be a problem," she repeats. "You can handle him."

Mia might warn me, but once I'm in it, she falls in line and offers the support we both know I need. "He *is* going to be a problem. He warned me away from Ledo and when I asked about his brother he said the Imperator isn't as blind as Ledo. Like he suspects something."

"Or maybe he just is a decent man who knows what they are?" Mia shrugs.

"Is he that decent if he doesn't stop them?" I growl. Mia, wisely, doesn't answer. I throw my head back in the chair. "I'm sorry. It was just... a close one tonight. Ledo is more unpredictable than I expected."

"Luella," she says. It's all she needs to say.

"It's fine. Silas was just too easy. I grew too confident." I scrub a hand across my face.

Taln comes into the room, his eyes wide. "Good lady?"

I smile at him, although he hasn't seen me with this face yet, as his guarded look reminds me. He looks to Mia, waiting for permission to speak.

"This is my friend, you can speak."

"We have a patient. She came through the back…" Taln trails off, but we both know what this means.

Someone's been hurt.

I trail Mia and Taln past the rows of healing rooms to the very back of the building. We pass a sign that says 'private' and then the storeroom before we come to the door hidden in the corner.

"Should I wait out here?" I offer. I don't usually accompany Mia. She's the healer; I'm the killer. Nevertheless, something is telling me that what's behind this door concerns me.

I never ignore my intuition, not anymore.

"You can come. If she's uncomfortable we'll send you back out," Mia says, maybe sensing the same thing as me. This isn't a coincidence.

We file into the small room. It has a cot, a washbasin, a few cabinets, and a steel door that leads to the back alley. A small portal towards the top of the door allows Mia to see who is on the other side before admitting them. I don't know exactly how people know to use this entrance, or what the underground network knows about Mia. I just know that when Mia helps those who are afraid or forbidden to seek help, they come here instead of through the front. Mia keeps no records on the patients she sees in this room. The only information that leaves here are the predilections that become profiles for me.

Sitting on the cot is a young girl. I refuse to calculate how young as I take in her state. She's wearing what was once a white shift, although it's hanging in shreds now, covered in dried blood.

The girl has blonde hair and blue eyes. In fact, she bears an uncanny resemblance to me. Well, to Skylar. The girl keeps her face down as Mia approaches.

"My name is Mia. I'm a healer. May I remove this so I can look at your back?" Mia's voice is soft, her words practiced and careful. The girl nods, and Mia starts peeling the gown off the girl's back, using shears to cut it away in some parts. The room is silent except for the girl's harsh breathing, interrupted by small gasps when Mia brushes a particularly tender spot. As the fabric falls away, my skin burns hot. It's one thing to hurt myself in an effort to eliminate a monster. It's another to see what a thwarted monster can do to an innocent.

The whip–probably a flagrum, based on the pattern of the lashes–tore apart the girl's back. My blood heats further, my skin shivering at the contrast between it and the night air.

"Can you tell me what happened?" Mia asks.

"I'm..." The girl hesitates and Mia looks towards the door where Taln and I wait to assist Mia as needed and hear what the girl will say.

"Everything you say here is confidential. This is my apprentice and my partner. I trust them, but if you want them to leave, I will send them out in an instant." It's not a bluff. Mia won't put my curiosity or Taln's learning above a patient. Patients come first. I know that better than anyone.

The girl shakes her head. "It's fine." She takes a breath. "I'm a harem worker. An imperial flora." My stomach drops. A pretty title for a terrible life. "Silly to call us floras isn't it?" The girl scoffs, but there is no venom behind it. It's a scoff of acceptance, an acknowledgement of a ludicrous situation that will never change. "I usually serve the Praetors. Sometimes the Emperor calls for me, but usually just for parties. I'm not..."

Mia takes a washcloth to wet a particularly stubborn piece of nightgown before she tries to pry it off the girls back. "It's okay, take your time," she whispers.

Bolstered by Mia's gentleness, the girl goes on. "I'm not trained for his specific tastes... so I didn't expect..." She takes a deep breath. "A Praetor and the Emperor requested me tonight. They have a routine they like, but I didn't know it." I might vomit. I might actually be sick, no potion needed. Mia listens to this routinely; it's how she creates the profiles. Drawing details from victims, determining if they gave consent, filling in the gaps with her physical assessment. A new appreciation for my friend fills me. She's so gentle, so calm. I breathe, trying to let her calm wash over me, too. I urge it to soothe my racing heart and sweaty palms. My nausea and rage.

Oblivious to my guilt, the girl goes on. "Most of it was... the usual. Then he punished me with the flagrum. I... I didn't take a tonic before because I thought it was another party, and I don't like to be too out of it for those." Mia had told me about this practice. The women would premedicate with a pain tonic to dull their nerves so they could stand the punishments better. Some took mind alterers, too, so they didn't feel like they were in their bodies at all.

"I've removed all this, so I can heal you now. Is it okay if I check you with my power? I'll start with just your back. Then we can do the rest," Mia says. Her power will heal, but if something is lodged under the skin, like the cloth of the nightgown, it could become embedded and cause long term issues.

The girl nods and Mia taps into her power, one hand tucked in her pocket. The girl's shoulders drop, her brow smoothing just a little, as Mia's healing warmth must move through her. I know that sensation—and the relief that accompanies it—well.

"I don't sense anything else in the way, like the nightgown... Can I heal the rest?"

"The rest?" the girl asks, confusion flitting across her face.

Mia bends down to whisper in her ear, but I can still hear. "I can heal your internal injuries."

Internal injuries, from an assault so brutal that she needs healing. I mask my features as the girl stiffens, eyes widening. She looks at me and I refuse to look away, meeting her eyes with understanding but without pity. No one likes to feel pitied, but she doesn't look defiant. She doesn't look like she'd even register my pity if I shouted it into her face.

She looks broken. Empty.

The longer I look, the more undeniable it is. She looks just like me.

Mia puts her hands on the girl, and the girl's face relaxes completely, a soft whimper escaping her lips.

"Excuse me," I mutter.

I leave the room quietly but then I'm running down the hall, towards the front of the building, past the cots and the washbasins and the cabinets of gauze and sutures. Tears blur my vision as the hallway stretches before me, lengthening with each step I take. Finally, I reach the front entryway where I fall to my knees, hugging a trash basin.

I heave, the contents of my stomach burning my throat and nose. My ribs protest each renewed convulsion as Taln joins me, gently patting my back as I sob between bouts of retching. The retching turns to dry heaves, and it doesn't stop until there's nothing left. It doesn't stop until at last my insides are as empty as the young girl's eyes, her body broken in place of mine.

DENY ME

Luella

I sit in front of the small vanity, tucked into the bathing chamber of my rented rooms. My long blonde hair hangs to my waist as I set about untangling the strands, working them into something less wild.

Something less like me.

The comb rips out a small snarl as my eyes snag on the crumpled invitation lying on the edge of the desk. Its thick parchment reeks of privilege, but the words offend me more.

Ledo's invited me to dinner. A very, very late dinner. An unrespectable time for dinner.

He's moving too quickly, growing bolder, and while I'm hardly above sleeping with him to remain close and gather information, the girl's eyes from last night keep looking back at me in the mirror.

I take a breath in, ripping another knot of golden strands loose. My goal is too important to let a body that isn't even mine interfere. I wouldn't be broken by a man like him, not by any man. Playing his mistress could work, even if it means no safe engagement period.

"I can handle it," I say to my reflection, then exhale, meet my own gaze. "I can handle it."

My hand shakes as I lay the comb down. This peculiar, vile feeling worming its way into my gut must be fear. I should never have let myself see what he did. Mia's report would have sufficed, just like in the past.

It's always easier if you don't see.

But that girl deserved to be seen, and now she deserves to be avenged. To know that this will never happen to her again.

I gather my mass of hair to one side and begin to plait it. There's too much hanging in the balance for me to let emotion cloud my judgment. This isn't about me. It isn't even about the Praetor, although he makes an excellent praeda. He's just a means to an end.

This is about the Emperor.

Getting to him might require sacrifice, but I've sacrificed too much already to stop now. It's just pain. Mia can heal me, as she'd healed that girl. Besides, I refuse to let fear over potential outcomes rule me. I will plan for it, and let it go.

I am in control.

I send my response to Ledo and then visit Mia.

Taln answers the door. "Good day, Skylar," he says, eyes widening.

"Good morning," I say as he moves to allow me entry. We don't speak of last night as I head to the staff area. Mia sits at the table while a pot simmers on the small wood-stove in the corner.

"He's invited me for dinner tomorrow." I sink into the chair nearest the door. "A very late dinner. Do you have anything he doesn't have to drink? A powder I can use or something to put on my lips?" She's always experimenting with creative countermeasures for the women of Divus, but she tries to make them perfect and always keeps them secret until they're ready.

Mia's brow wrinkles in disapproval. "Lue..."

"I'm almost there, Mi." I let her see it. The desperation beneath every face I've ever worn. Instead of time tempering me, it's fueled me. Last night was another reminder that for every day I waste, the Emperor and men like him are hurting women, children, and sometimes even men.

They're hurting whomever they want.

Mia takes a breath. "You take your drops?"

"Every day. I'm up to twenty," I say. I'd increased my dose when she gave me the stronger paralytics for Ledo. They counteract the potions Mia crafts for me, so I'm safe from her concoctions.

"I have a small capsule you can crush in your mouth. It's a work in progress, and you have to be kissing him." Mia grimaces. "Or spit in his mouth I guess."

I snort. "I don't need much incentive for the second option."

Mia rolls her eyes but gets up to grab the capsules. She brings a small tin of white beads. I reach out and touch one, rolling the small sphere between my fingers.

"It's soft," I say.

"I thought it would blend in with teeth. Women could roll it between their back teeth, ready to bite down if they needed to use it. I call them pearls." I like this one. Clever, easy. Once she'd created an acid that could be smashed against an attacker's face, burning their skin. I liked that one, too. I was burned by it a few too many times though, and now Mia wouldn't let anyone use it.

"I'm immune with the drops?" I confirm.

Mia nods and then says, "I've been mixing them with the Lace herbs, too. For my other patients."

The herb many women take to prevent pregnancy, it makes sense they want the drops mixed in. A plan for both scenarios. I clear my throat. "I will need some Lace, too."

Mia's eyes snap up to mine but I look away.

"Just in case," I say.

I'm not sure which of us I'm trying to convince.

It's not a secret that the republic is a sham. The Praetors and Senators who make the laws dine with and attempt to influence the Emperor, but in the end only his opinion matters. The same is true of the Gods. No matter which temple you visit, which sacrifices you offer, how many stones you bring to be filled with power, only their judgment matters.

Which is why I make the trek to the temple of Janus every day I'm not pursuing praeda. Black basanite stones weigh down my satchel as I enter the small temple at the edge of the Peridota forest. Jupiter's temples are kilometers high, stone columns and arches reaching to the heavens. Juno's and Venus' are similarly prominent with positions near the Domus Aurea.

Janus doesn't need such fanfare. Or perhaps they wish for it, and that is why they reward my visits so generously.

The square pool at the center of the small temple is overrun with water lilies, the dense green of the pads interspersed with white and pink blooms. Now *that* is a respectable flower, fighting through the weight of the water to burst free at the surface. The archways allow the light from both suns to dance across the placid stillness and allow glimpses of the small fish darting beneath.

I place the basanite at the altar of the two-faced god, and step back. The stone statue above morphs between male and female facial features, the magic shifting continually beneath the surface as the stone attempts to hold the essence of a god. Strong noses, then thin, pouting lips, tight smiles, eyes wide set and then narrow. Janus is a kaleidoscope of features that's both beautiful and dizzying.

Then I make my offering. I have offered much to Janus, but today I bring a meal of goat, grapes, and wine for us to enjoy. I tell Janus of my plans as I eat my portion of the offering. I don't know if they care what I do with their gift from so long ago, but I like to think they do. I like to think they're in on it all, that they blessed me for a reason.

"Then the Emperor," I tell Janus as I pop the last grape into my mouth, bursting it open. "Then I can rest."

I'm not sure if Janus likes this plan, but after the meal my basanite is restored with power. My stones now shimmer, awash in gold, orange, and red.

I don't pray to Janus for strength. If I wanted that I would petition the pater, Jupiter, or the god of war, Mars. No; I pray to Janus for new faces. New opportunities to carry out my plans. New beginnings.

They haven't denied me yet.

LEARN

ROSE

TRISTAN'S LIPS BRUSH ACROSS the top of my hand, sending a shiver through me. He's always doing that, sending shivers through me with his words or his lips or his hands. "We'll have dinner with my parents next clipse, and you'll move in at the end of the quad." We're walking past the forum, but Tristan tugs me down the steps to the sunken walkway. The suns are low, evening creeping up on us.

It feels fast. The moments coursing together and slipping through my fingers like I'm trying to grasp the Maero rushing beside us. "Already?" I ask, breathless as he gathers me closer. A hand slips low behind my waist. The path is empty, most walkers migrating to the forum, a domus, or to the taverns, where Pater headed only moments ago.

"You don't want to marry me, Rose?" Tristan whispers, his breath moving across my neck. He doesn't wait for me to answer before he goes on. "I want to marry you. I want to make you mine in every way there is."

His lips meet the tender spot below my ear, against my hairline, and I gasp. "I love you," he murmurs. "I need you." He kisses again, lower.

My cheeks heat. My skin blazes, bursting into flames beneath his touch. "Already?" I say again, looking around, but I'm not sure if it's because I do or don't want to be interrupted.

"Don't you love me?" He says it like a plea, and I know I'm the one that's broken here. I've never known love from a man. I've known what my pater gave to us, fists and shame, screams and cruel names.

Of course this pebbled skin, and this pulse thrumming through my veins is love.

Right?

"I love you," I say. It doesn't feel wrong, but it feels off. Like the first time I had to bake for Daisy and me, and I didn't know to add salt to the dough. It was still good, still edible, but not quite right.

"You're special, Rose. Different than any girl I've ever known. I know we'll be good for each other." He kisses my cheek, the press firm. "I know you were made for me."

My smile does feel right. It belongs on my face the way the suns both belong in the sky, the way Daisy's hair slips like silk between my fingers, the way it feels to wake up on our pallet warmed by her presence each morning.

"Daisy..." I whisper.

"What?" Tristan asks. Will he think I only said I loved him to get something in return?

"My sister," I say. "I just worry about her."

"Why?"

The question takes me by surprise and I don't answer at first. I can't answer honestly, but I won't lie to my betrothed. "My pater can be... exacting."

He nods. "Is she old enough to be wed?"

"Yes, she'll be seventeen soon." Sixteen was the age it was appropriate to marry. "Although, I'd love for her to have some more time to find a love match."

"Like us," he says, squeezing my hand.

"Like us," I agree. "I wonder if we might have room for her? She can cook." Not well. "And clean." Passably better. "And she's great at mending and sewing, so she could earn some money as a seamstress for the domus?" That part is wholly true.

"I'll have to talk to my familia." Tristan considers a moment, but the pause is familiar to me. It's the intake of breath that comes before bad news, before disappointment. "We certainly have the room, but my pater often has to follow the politics of Divus."

"Of course," I agree.

"And *coemptio* was never in the plan for me. We expected a handsome dowry with my pater's position." I shiver with a different feeling now, the shame coating my skin. I thought the dowry didn't matter to his familia. I'd be in the Sabines if not for Tristan, my hand reaching into an empty alley. Daisy and I have survived our entire lives with Pater, so what's another few years for her? Or even a few quads until Tristan knows us better, understands.

"I'm sorry," I say quickly, throat tightening. "I don't mean to be ungrateful."

He pushes a stray hair behind my ear. "It's okay." I can't tell if he's angry with me, his face impassive and composed. Fear coats my tongue and pricks behind my eyes, but I swallow the bitter taste of it down.

"I'm sorry, Tristan."

"Look at me," he says, and I do. "It's okay, Rosebud." He doesn't smile, but his eyes search mine, like he's trying to read the thoughts even I don't know. Like he wants to see what's written on the walls inside my mind. "Life is just different in the political sphere. We don't always have the choice to do what we want."

"Of course," I say again.

"I already took a chance on you and your familia, and doing more might take time. I won't forget your sister, but you'll have to learn how things work." I'm already nodding, knowing that his familia is worlds away from mine.

And he still wants to marry me. "I'll learn," I agree.

Tristan kisses my cheek again, as if he's dismissing me, and the butterflies that usually reside in my chest have stopped fluttering, the stillness suffocating.

I can't lose him. I can't lose my chance to be free of Pater. My chance for love.

My chance for a better future, for me and for Daisy.

My voice shakes as I say again, "I promise, I'll learn."

GOD'S WILL

LUELLA

I WANTED TO SAY no to dinner, but I don't always get what I want when I'm hunting praeda. I get what I need, and unfortunately that means I'm dressed in another draping and immodest gown, the pockets filled with the tiniest vials available in Divus.

Ledo sends a litter with four servants. Wouldn't want me mauled by miscreants before he has a chance to do it, I suppose.

The city isn't asleep, of course; only the King, Romulus, has set. The Traitor, Remus, casts rare single shadows long and low through the cobblestone streets.

Too quickly the Domus Aurea looms before me, the archways and opulent steps inviting me forward. My sandaled feet seem to know the way as I move up, through, and across to enter the main dining hall.

"Skylar, welcome," Ledo says, sitting alone at the large table set for two. Guards, servants, and floras wait along the walls, ready to ensure Ledo wants for nothing.

"Praetor." I bow my head before sitting beside him. "I was honored by your invitation."

"Wine," he says and one of the servants comes forward to fill both of our glasses. It's a warm night, and the cool wine is more refreshing than it has the right to be. Keeping my limbs loose is a testament only to an iron will and years of dancing with death.

"I hope you had a pleasant day," I say casually. I can't actually ask him about his day, since matters of politics were surely involved and are none of my business.

"I did. In fact, I was feeling quite relaxed."

Yes, abusing women does seem like a rather relaxing pastime for a sadist. I feel the words too close to the tip of my tongue and smile instead.

"I thought it would be a good day to discuss my intentions," he continues.

"Your intentions, Praetor?" I ask. Gods. He certainly has a flair for the dramatic.

"I've enjoyed spending time with you. However, I've just recently come out of mourning for my late wife and I'd like to ensure my next marriage is the right fit."

Stones. He might as well come out and say he killed her. The threat lingers beneath his smile, a hint for what it means to be the right fit for a man like him.

"Praetor, may I serve us?" I ask, noticing that his wine is empty.

"Of course," he sounds surprised. "This is what I mean, precisely." I stand and walk to the servant holding the wine and when I take the carafe from her, I put one hand on the bottom and turn, tipping my other palm over the top quickly as I do, as if protecting it from a draft or debris.

But not from me.

I serve Ledo the wine, chock full of the powder that had been sitting in my palm.

"I'm looking for a wife who can anticipate, Skylar." He puts his free hand on mine while he sips his wine and I send a silent prayer to Janus that the sedative will take effect before the final course of this dinner. "A wife with true Divusian values."

I nod. "My pater would expect nothing less, Praetor." My pater is, for all intents and purposes, dead. And while my mater's fidelity, piety, and chastity would seem to be something to boast, Ledo won't care what I thought of my mater. He'll care what her husband thought of her.

"Which virtue is most important?" Ledo asks. If he were a plebeian, I would say fertility. If he were younger, I might mention modesty, chastity, or marital fidelity. I know exactly what Ledo is looking for, though; what type of woman is a fit for him.

"Obedience, Praetor."

He hums, a low sound of approval. I resist the impulse to urge him to drink his wine, lest I raise suspicion. The drugs won't affect me, but the wine will. Instead, I feign a few small sips, hoping he'll mimic the movement.

He does, sipping and then swallowing deeper when the cool liquid touches his tongue. Mia managed to make it taste nearly addictive, meaning one sip will turn into many, with only a subtle shift in flavor that most don't notice.

"Obedience," he agrees.

"However, defiance is sometimes necessary," I amend. Ledo's eyes snap to mine.

"Explain." He leans back in his chair, arms draped over one another.

"Obedience to one's husband or one's pater, that is the goal. Therefore, I would defy any attempt that would shame my future or current husband, no matter what."

I won't sleep with you tonight, I'm saying. I can't help the breath that stalls in my lungs while I wait. I look down at the table, as though even voicing the thought of defiance is painful.

"What if your husband wishes for something you find shameful?" he asks. Oh it's a tricky question, and I can feel his wheels turning.

"*Vir vult es deus vult*," I say, meeting his eyes. *A husband's will is god's will.*

He smiles, a true smile now, and I know I've hooked him.

"We understand each other," Ledo says. "And I promise, you would enjoy it." It's not a question, but an unsolicited promise. He must sense my doubt, or he wouldn't be trying to put me at ease.

"I would enjoy serving my husband," I agree. It's not entirely a lie. I don't add what I would like to serve him, but a half-truth still rings true.

"I'm an exacting husband, Skylar. I expect unquestioning obedience in all of my tastes." He comes to stand before me and his hand slips up to my throat, almost gentle. Almost. I start to look down but he grabs my chin. "Look at me."

His eyes are hard, dark in the low light. He licks his lips. I'm not sure what he's searching for in my face, what he's hoping to find, so I stare back. I let my desperation for this marriage ooze from my pores and drip from my fluttering lashes.

I need this.

I let him see that part but hide the rest. He doesn't need to know why.

"Do you understand what I expect, Skylar?" His hand slides down the column of my throat, and without warning he tightens his fingers. I gasp in surprise, but don't pull away.

"*Vir vult es deus vult*," I say again, the words rasping against the constriction from his hand. Black spots start to appear in the corners of the room and my eyes water. The experience is all too familiar these days, a foreign name uttered from a man with his hand around my throat.

I keep my hands at my sides, fighting my instincts to resist his hold, and just before I lose the battle with my will he releases me.

"Yes it is," he says, patting the top of my head. "You may go, Skylar."

I stand and bow my head. "Thank you, Praetor."

I don't touch my neck, I don't gasp for breath, and my body doesn't even shake as I turn to leave. I maintain my composure in the litter, and I close the door of my rented rooms before I finally allow myself to relax. I lean back against the door, my legs weak.

The Divusian matrons' mantra had tasted bitter on my tongue, but it was what I needed to say. I won't say it worked until he's proposed, but I know I'm closer than I was before.

My hand finally drifts to my throat, alone in the dark, with only my stones and potions to hear me.

"*My* will is god's will," I correct. "Mine."

BRIGHT AND WICKED

LUELLA

THE LETTER COMES IN the morning. Ledo proposes a marriage contract, where he will waive my dowry due to my orphaned status. His only requirement is an assessment to verify my chastity. A barbaric practice disguising another excuse for men to put their hands where they don't belong.

The men of Divus have obsessed over whom their women sleep with since I was a girl, but the fervor for virginity has risen in tandem with the Vestals' popularity in recent years. The virgin priestesses were always held to their vows, and the public executions after a few were found to have broken them, willingly or not, have cemented virginity as a divine attribute.

Now all of the patricians required it in their marriage contracts. The Vestal priestesses are wed to the god Vestal, so the idea that ordinary men felt they required the same level of chastity and devotion feels presumptuous to me. *Vir vult*, I suppose.

Which is why if Ledo wants the marriage, I'll submit to the vile test. Considering whose blood typically spills on my marriage sheets, I'm happy to indulge his whims.

For now.

I'm in the midst of packing my meager items to take to the Domus Aurea when I receive a second letter.

This one speaks of which tonics may ease my nausea, with an alarming number of words misspelled considering it's from an incredibly talented healer.

Mia's code takes only a moment for me to decipher, and I wonder if her tips for nausea might be needed after all. Ledo sent another flora to Mia's backroom last night, scourged with the flagrum. That explains the proposal today. Whatever he's seeking, he's not finding it with the floras and he thinks he can get it from me.

My jaw aches from clenching and I realize I've crushed his letter in my palm. I uncurl my fingers and select a new piece of parchment to tell Ledo I'll move in today, as requested.

After all, I serve the pleasures of the Praetor.

My rooms are across from Ledo's. Close enough to serve, but not adjoining. That type of arrangement is for couples who love and trust each other, which is an illusion the Praetor has no intention of perpetuating. He most likely plans to have mistresses and floras and me.

I love when men make plans.

Because destroying plans is what Janus and I do best.

The white sheets and the hideous wall tapestries center me as I finish unpacking. I've been in this situation plenty of times before. Ledo isn't different. He isn't special.

I'll survive his grain of cruelty as I have survived every other.

I flinch when a firm knock reverberates through the door. Traitorous nerves.

A young female servant informs me that Ledo would like to take *sapa* with me. I hate it. The name itself is toxic, still named after the leaded sweet wine that once caused confusion, fatigue, and death in those who consumed it.

Oh, how we hold onto the destruction of the past.

I smile at the woman and follow her through the Domus Aurea, towards my new praeda. And one step closer to the final one.

"Will I see the Emperor often?" I ask her, my eyes wide as I look around the halls.

"You may ask the Praetor," she says without looking at me.

With her back to me I can't help the roll of my eyes. Stones, this isn't going to be as easy. Apparently, imperial servants have tight lips.

She leads me to one of the many atriums, and this one opens to the sky, large marble columns supporting archways to the rest of the halls that lead towards the large fountain in the center of the chamber. The fountain features a statue of Bacchus, the god of wine and male fertility who is, of course, nude. He holds a large wine pitcher that pours water onto the several maidens sprawled beneath him. They are, naturally, scantily clad and look horrified by either the wine or the second source of water spurting from his phallus.

It screams of homage to the bacchanalia, but he's always been claimed by the plebeians looking for excuses to practice their deviance and be rewarded for it. The patricians have never needed an excuse, yet here they are, trying to commandeer even the deities of the working class.

Ledo sits in one of the two opulent white chairs near the fountain, and between them is a small table with two glasses of what I assume is *sapa*.

He's in white trousers and a tunic, and receiving a shoulder rub from one of the floras. When he sees me, he motions for me to sit but doesn't say anything. The flora continues to rub his shoulders, wearing the off the shoulder toga often worn by prostitutes and floras. It leaves one breast completely bare while barely covering the second in gauzy material. Even in cooler quads they would wear a similar style, the exposed breast coated in oil to help protect it from the chill. Slits up the sides of the gown reach to her waist, her umber skin contrasting with the white of the fabric.

"Praetor," I say, inclining my head as I sit.

One might wonder why a man would bring a flora to sit with his betrothed, but I know it's a test. A tactic.

A silly attempt to make me jealous so that I feel the need to do whatever he says so he does not seek it elsewhere.

Sadly, I know it works on some. Not me, but some.

"Skylar," he says sweetly.

The fountain splashes in the center of the room, the sound grating on my nerves. If I smashed the stone phallus, would the water come out faster? Less an annoying trickle and more of a soothing rush? I cross my ankles and meet his eyes. "Would you like me to take over?" I nod to the flora but she continues to rub, knowing I'm not addressing her. She's below me, and we are both below Ledo.

"You honor me," Ledo says, snapping at her. She moves to his side, then drops to her knees.

I come to stand behind him and begin kneading the muscles in his shoulders, which are already quite loose. I doubt he's gone a day with any real tension. I work my fingers skillfully into the lower strands of his hair, then back down to his shoulders. Alternating pressure until he groans and tilts his head back to look at me. The flora hasn't moved, her eyes downcast and each line in her body as tight as mine as she waits for his command.

He looks at me, challenge and desire in his gaze.

He doesn't break eye contact as he lifts his hips and slides his trousers down to his upper thighs. His erection breaks free and I let my eyes widen when I see the hard, very average, length of him. Let him think they widen with surprise or lust, instead of disgust.

He's not as unpredictable or shocking as he likes to think. I've seduced and murdered over thirty men. Child molesters. Rapists. Abusers. Not one of them was saved by the existence of their cock, yet they always seem so keen to display it.

But a cock is just a cock.

He snaps again and the flora immediately crawls in front of him. He holds out his palm and she leans forward to rest her head in it, a sign of utmost submission. Her black hair flows over his hand.

"The healer informed me of your chastity." Such a kind phrase for the invasive, and pointless, examination. "So, I know you will need instruction," Ledo says.

My hands are frozen on his shoulders, not because I'm shocked, but because he would expect me to be. "Instruction?" I breathe. I let my eyes linger on his erection, imagining all the ways I would like to remove it. A cock *is* just a cock, but I can think of a few places to shove his.

Luckily, he's an idiot, and he takes my curiosity the way I intend him to, the way I've manipulated him into taking it, and a pleased smile spreads across his face.

"On how to satisfy me. Shoulders, Skylar," he says casually. I return to kneading the muscles, never taking my eyes off the display. Using both hands, he guides the flora's mouth onto his erection. Her brown eyes are locked on his, never glancing my way. She takes him deeper, until I see her throat tighten and her eyes widen slightly. My fingers clench, and for a moment I see myself slitting his throat right here, his blood spilling down his chest and onto his stupid cock.

No. I blink once, twice.

Neither of us would make it out alive. She'd scream, the Praetorian guards would come.

We'd both be slain.

She does this every day, I remind myself. We can both persist until I can dispose of him somewhere alone. Somewhere no one else will be hurt.

She gags, and Ledo doesn't contain himself anymore. He yanks her off his erection and slaps her hard, then slams himself back inside her. She gags again and Ledo wraps his hands around her face, fucking her mouth brutally. I swallow hard, but don't look away.

Her eye kohl smears as her tears fall in earnest and Ledo spits down on her, asking, "Do you want more?"

She answers instantly. It's garbled but sounds something like, "Yes, Praetor." Ledo jerks her off again and slaps her harder, making me flinch.

"Say it," he commands.

"Please, may I have more, Praetor?" she says, but her eyes don't agree. Some women join the floras willingly, but this particular display isn't for her pleasure, nor is it for his. This is a show of power for me. Not all of my husbands were so... direct. They played their games, they groomed, to be sure, but here in the Domus Aurea the atmosphere is different. The subtle viciousness that men use to control us in the city is blatant here. Commonplace and undisguised.

Ledo continues thrusting, and I watch, as his actions demand. I rub his shoulders and as he casually continues this line of training he says, "Your servant will fit you for new garments more to my taste."

"Yes, Praetor." My hands keep moving across his shoulders, not nearly close enough to his neck. "Is there anything I should know about living here, with the Emperor?" I chance. A plebeian might ask out of insecurity.

"I will tell you if there is something you might need to know," he says, voice harsh.

My hands continue their ministrations as he grunts, finishing in the flora's mouth. Then he grabs her unbound hair and pulls her off of him, discarding her roughly.

"Leave," he demands, taking a ragged breath. He adjusts his trousers as she does, then settles back into his chair. I don't watch her go, don't need to. I've already memorized her face.

"Sit," he tells me. I do. "What do you think of my instruction?"

You're a foul creature who couldn't properly bed a woman if your life depended on it. "I have..." I swallow hard, not having to fake my discomfort. "I have much to learn."

He smiles. "Don't be afraid. I will show you."

I just nod, the picture of obedience. Ledo stands and looms over my chair to grab my chin. "You'll learn," he whispers, and I don't know if it's meant to be a threat or promise.

"I want to make you happy, Praetor." It's what I'm expected to feel. Shame and jealousy, and a desire not to lose my place. Fear that I can't please him.

I can see that he believes me. His smile is bright and wicked as he departs, but when his back turns, I smile, too.

Because I can be just as wicked.

WRETCHED

ROSE

"It's wretched," Daisy moans.

"It's expected," I say. It doesn't matter how foul it is, that's beside the point.

"Pater doesn't make us go," she argues.

I take a deep breath, refusing to snap at my favorite person. "Daisy, Tristan invited us for *sapa* afterwards. We can't show up without going to the games first."

"He won't even know if we're there or not." She folds her arms, crashing onto the couch in an equally petulant and dramatic fashion. Pater's away, which is the only reason we're out here and not cleaning, cooking, or washing.

It's not that she's wrong, but it's the principle of it. We were invited.

By my betrothed.

"I'm going," I declare, turning towards our room as if I'm willing to leave her behind. The bluff works, and as I head back to the bedroom, Daisy sulks behind me.

"Will Augustus be at *sapa*?" she asks.

I'm not sure if I want him there. Tristan saved me. I love him, but that first day in the forum is hard to forget. The way Augustus caught me when I almost fell, the way he'd made me spark from the inside...

I shake my head, dislodging thoughts of the brother I should not be thinking of. I'm lucky Tristan chose me before I let Augustus ruin what little reputation I had left.

"I'm not sure." I'd told Daisy about Augustus' reputation for leading women on, for dishonoring them.

Instead of letting the subject of him drop, though, her curiosity has been incessant. "Hmm."

I ignore her, and hand her a tunic. She reaches past me instead, to grab one of a deeper cerulean. I roll my eyes because it's the one she looks best in.

"I don't know what you're doing-"

"I'm not *doing* anything," she says. "I'm dressing so we can go, as is *expected*."

I'm already dressed, so I simply grab a cloak to wrap around my shoulders, despite the warmth. Pater forgets when he drinks that I shouldn't be marked for my husband, that bruises don't befit brides. I dare not remind him.

"Well, let's get this over with," Daisy announces when she's ready.

I'm not sure if she means the games or the *sapa*.

The steps of the Colosseum wind us around and around. Since we don't come often, we have to follow the mass of women and servants to ensure we're going high enough. Up and up we climb until finally we emerge into the highest level.

We can see the entire building from here, albeit seeing down the longer side involves a bit of squinting. All around the oblong structure are seats organized in separate tiers. We're housed at the top, in the attic. If Tristan and his familia are here, they'll be in a place of honor, closest to the pit.

I shudder as the fanfare begins and ten gladiators enter the ring. An announcer screams each of their names and titles, but it's hard to hear over the packed bodies. The gladiators look so small from up here, ants about to trampled beneath the foot of some foul creature.

"Ten against one?" Daisy says as a chimera bursts out of its cage at the edge of the ring. One of its parents appears to have been a Lamassu because wings protrude between its lion's head and snake's tail.

She was right; we don't usually come here. We simply have no desire to see men slaughtered for entertainment.

The formidable beast slithers and flies around the ten men. It's chained so that it can fly just high enough to expose its belly to the gladiators. The men are armored today, each with a unique weapon. A man with a pike tries to stab at the belly of the beast, but its tail whips out, knocking him into another man and they both collapse in the dirt. I bite my lip when the chimera slashes them with its claw, even as it snaps another man in half with its mouth. The crowd gasps, the collective sound echoing across the ring.

Ten to one actually seems unfair to the men. I tug at the ends of my hair, twisting the strands between my thumb and forefinger. How long will this last?

Blood sprays across the sand as the chimera tosses the body against the stone wall surrounding the pit. The crowd screams, pleased with the display of brutality.

A group of three rushes towards the creature's head, roaring their fury. While it's distracted with them, the remaining four rush its belly. One takes a good swipe at the flesh between the creature's chest and leg. It shrieks in either rage or pain.

"Wretched," Daisy mutters. Her teary eyes aren't on the dead men, but instead on the chimera as its dark purple blood spills to the sand.

Perhaps I misjudged why we hate this place. I have no desire to see men slaughtered, but maybe Daisy has no desire to see creatures harmed in a barbaric grab for our attention.

The screaming reaches a crescendo and my ears pop as the chimera's tail wraps around one of the gladiators, choking the life from him while it slashes at another. The man's torso splits from shoulder to groin, his blood joining his battle brothers in the sand as his body crumples.

My stomach turns and I finally allow myself to look away, content to know I've seen enough to prove I was here, if Tristan should want to discuss it.

I've done my duty.

Even if I hated every moment of it.

You'll Learn

Luella

The fountain of Bacchus overflows with crimson. It pours out of his decanter and his phallus. It grows thicker and thicker until it can't be mistaken for anything but blood. The women at his feet recoil in fear. No longer statues, they are the women I've seen brutalized these last days. They scramble back, the blood splattering against their skin, erupting into burns and blisters. One of them looks at me across the room, her wheat hair soaked in blood and her cerulean blue eyes so familiar I feel as if they belong to me. I reach out to help her up but she flinches away from me, too. Caught between the brutal fountain and me, equally afraid of both.

Then she screams.

I jolt upright, the thin blanket slipping down as I survey the room. I usually sleep well. Not deeply, but well, until this clipse. I take a deep breath, then another. I've been to *sapa* with Ledo each day for 'training.' His imagination is, unfortunately, well-developed, and each day is more violent and humiliating than the last. The first few days I could argue that it was consensual, I could argue that perhaps some of the floras enjoyed playing the submissive role, as some prefer. But yesterday...

Some things cannot be argued. Some things are obvious to those with eyes, and I've never wished myself as blind as I did yesterday.

Yet even if I was willing to forsake my plans for the Emperor and end Ledo now, I am never alone with him.

The day passes in a blur of monotony. To take my mind off impending *sapa* and my failure thus far, I read. I wring my hands. I pace. I've asked about the Emperor each day, but have been ignored. I'm not much closer than I was a clipse ago.

And just when the twins touch in the late afternoon sky, overlapping more than the last few days as we grow closer to the end of the clipse shadowing, I'm summoned to *sapa*.

The room is the same. The fountain trickles and gurgles, mocking my dreams. There is a small cart with whatever Ledo plans to use today. And there is the chaise I am expected to sit in. I inhale as I move to it, willing my limbs into a semblance of attentive respect.

There are three floras today, each naked and kneeling before Ledo.

"Skylar, good day," Ledo greets, as if this is an ordinary day. I suppose it is for him.

"Good day, Praetor," I return, dipping my head in respect.

"Today you'll learn about punishment, my betrothed." Ledo draws a whip from the cart. That's all that is atop it today, but it's not just any whip.

It's the flagrum.

Meant to scourge. Meant to flay. Not a riding crop or single line whip that I could believe would be used for those who find pleasure on the border of pain.

It almost looks delicate, just two leather strings jutting from the handle. An immeasurable amount of pain awaits the Praetor's victims, though, due to the shiny bits of metal between knots at each end. I swallow hard and sweat breaks out along my spine.

"Have these floras disobeyed?" I ask, my voice quieter than I wanted. I shouldn't ask, but Ledo doesn't correct me, doesn't remind me of my place.

Instead he ties a leather strap tightly around each of their mouths. As he ties the last one, so tight it cuts across her cheekbones in white harsh lines, he speaks. "Each has spoken out of turn, or without being spoken to, for starters." He looks at me and I know my questions about the Emperor, about the floras, have not gone unmarked.

This is a lesson.

One I brought to them.

He motions for them all to come closer to me, then turn their backs.

Then he begins.

Crack.

I gasp as he strikes the first flora, the skin of her back splitting beneath the flagrum, red bursting beneath the strike like wine from a shattered glass.

Crack.

Another strike, another gasp, but I'm not sure if it's from her or me.

Crack.

My stomach turns and tears prick the corners of my eyes.

Crack.

The back swing of his whip whistles close enough to me that I flinch, realizing I've taken a step forward.

Crack.

This time the flagrum is so soaked that specks of blood accompany the back swing. I close my gaping mouth as copper floods my tongue.

Crack.

A sob finally breaks its way free. The flagrum is too much. The woman from Mia's backroom swims in front of my teary vision.

Crack.

She was my fault.

Crack.

This is my fault.

Crack.

My knees finally buckle, but he doesn't stop. He just keeps swinging. And I do nothing. Like a coward. I should kill him. I should stop this, plan be damned.

Crack.

I flinch back. Memories churning beneath the surface. I tell myself they would have been punished anyways. That this isn't just for me, this is who Ledo is, with or without an audience. The lies are bitter on my tongue, and the guilt and nausea in my gut makes me dizzy.

Ledo kneels before me and I realize the cracks have stopped. Each flora is curled onto themselves on the floor. Will they live? None had scarred backs so he must allow them to be healed. Will they visit Mia?

"Skylar," Ledo says, drawing my gaze. He brushes a thumb across my tear-stained cheek and I feel the blood smear into my salt. "Do you understand how punishments will work?"

"Yes, Praetor," I say, my voice thick.

"I don't tolerate disobedience," he says. We are owned all our lives in some form or another. Our paters force obedience into us, mold our maters into the image of matronly servitude, and pay new men to take over the rod. Some men use their words, some fists, and some like Ledo, the whip.

Regardless of the weapons they choose, the result is always the same.

We obey. And Skylar hasn't broken this pattern. Hasn't seen the wrongness in it, or perhaps has but knows that one woman cannot change it. Skylar needs a marriage because unmarried women have no voice in this republic. They cannot move unmolested in a city that only respects the male claim to women, never a woman's claim to herself.

My chin dips of its own accord. I swallow my terror and my rage. I can do this. I can masquerade as someone who would bow to this man who thinks the pathetic flesh between his legs makes him better than us. Than me.

There is strength in patience.

"You'll learn," Ledo says, accepting my deference. Believing it.

I'm shaking, each tremor wracking my body as I try to master myself. To calm my limbs. To push down the memories.

To gain control.

When he's finally gone I wait until the floras have been removed by the other women of the harem, carried off to be mended. They murmur to each other, soothing nothings to help them contain their cries until they can be healed. They endure.

When I'm completely alone, I whisper into the empty room, with only the disgusting fountain as witness.

"No, Praetor. *You'll* learn."

A Traitor

Luella

WHEN I FINALLY RISE from the chaise, Bacchus pisses on, unperturbed by his lack of audience. It infuriates me.

Everything about today infuriates me, but most of all how Ledo can't just hide his brutality like every other worthless man. Is it better or worse that he puts it on display, where he could be judged? Where I can find him so easily?

I must make some sort of face because the movement causes the dried blood to split across my cheek, itching as if I'm allergic to it.

I should visit the baths in the city, so I can see Mia, but the idea of moving through the city with the blood of three separate women... no. I can't stomach it.

Not that anyone would comment. They'd assume it was mine, and most would think I'd earned it.

The Domus Aurea Baths it is. Leaving the empty courtyard, I make my way down the halls, my eyes flitting down each hallway to ensure I'm on the correct path. I turn down the final hall and barrel headfirst, not into a bath, but into a man. Tall, copper hair, and golden skin.

Venus' tits, it's the last man I want to see. "Dominus," I say, dipping my head at the Emperor's brother. "My apologies."

"I thought I'd seen the last of you," his words are accusatory, although his tone is light.

So insolent. So spoiled. "What gave you that impression, Dominus?" I'm still looking down, refusing to meet his eyes.

"I must have incorrectly judged your intelligence," he says, and now I do look up.

"It happens to the best of us, Dominus," I say, meeting his widening eyes.

"Skylar," he exclaims, "you have blood on your face!"

"Yes. I am heading to the baths."

"No." He shakes his head. "I mean, *why* do you have blood on your face?" He actually sounds concerned. Ledo hasn't been secretive about my 'training.' It's held in a common area of the Domus Aurea and more than once people have come through during the lesson. Yesterday a lower Senator stopped and asked if he could stay and watch. Ledo had simply asked him to join in, "so my future wife knows what to expect."

I tilt my head. "My Praetor has been training me, Dominus," I say, watching for a spark of understanding or knowledge, but I only see confusion.

"Training you for what?" He looks me up and down.

"For marriage, Dominus."

"Stop calling me that," he snaps. "What do you mean for marriage?"

I step forward, glaring even though I feel small next to him. Short and weak, like Skylar. He doesn't know me, though, and I won't allow a man who won't be dead soon to scorn me. "What else should I call you, Dominus?"

"Answer the question, Skylar." He's so close I can feel the heat radiating off of him.

"You first."

"You may call me Cassius." His jaw clenches. "Now, what did Ledo do that resulted in this?" His touch feathers across my jaw and I forget to speak until he narrows his eyes further. "Skylar?"

"I am chaste. Praetor Ledo has much to show me, so that I may learn to be a good wife to him." I keep it simple to hide my rage. I've already been too forward, and I refuse to let my temper undo my plans.

Realization dawns on him, slow and cold. I see the shift in his features, the set of his jaw. "Wait, you've been in the fountain room with him all clipse?" I nod. "Stones! He didn't–?" He grabs my shoulder and turns me around. My jaw clenches as I realize that he's not checking for just any injury. He's checking for lashes.

"You shouldn't touch me," I chastise, stepping away from him. "The Praetor won't like it."

"I don't give a stone what Ledo likes," he spits.

I take another step back when he steps forward. "If you touch me again I'll assume you either have no idea what he is, in which case you're more of a *matulo* than I thought. Or you do know what he is and have no qualms with others bearing the consequences of your actions. Neither option looks good for you, Dominus, or ends well for me."

It sinks in then, what I'm saying. "He wouldn't..." he trails off when I narrow my eyes.

"He almost did, after our dance." I don't say what Ledo almost did, because it doesn't matter what it was. It matters that I didn't want it. It matters that Cassius understands the consequences of his behavior.

And I need to understand whether or not he cares.

"Skylar, why are you here? You obviously see what he is." Traitorous words.

"If you see what he is, then why do you do nothing?" I won't tell him my secrets, but I do want his answers.

"Perhaps the same reason you don't," Cassius says. My mind whirs. What could he know? Nothing. He might suspect, but he can't know. I'm careful. I am new each time.

"What do you mean?" I ask. I don't hold my breath but I want to. I want to freeze this moment for fear of his answer. Is it all about to come crashing down?

"Because I know Tisiphone will mete out judgment, if it's due."

I don't allow my face to change, I keep my spine loose, fighting the widening of eyes and tilt of the lips at this silly rumor that has grown in my wake. "You place all of your faith in the furies?"

"I place my faith in the gods, of course," he says. I can't tell if he's being satirical. His brother is considered blessed by the gods, after all. His blue and gold eyes search mine, and I wonder if he can see beneath the body Janus and I have crafted. Are there cracks in my armor?

"As do I," I murmur, not daring anything further. I've already shown too much Luella, too little Skylar.

Too much me.

"I should go," I say after a moment, turning to leave. But Cassius grabs my wrist, gently leading me into one of the many small alcoves off the main hallway. "Cassius!" I gasp.

"If Tisiphone doesn't come, and you think she should have... I could help you," Cassius says, not releasing my wrist. He's whispering, but the words thunder through me. Treasonous words. Words that burrow into the soft tissue of my resolve.

"Help me what?" I dare.

"Get away from Ledo. Run."

"Why would you do that?" I don't resist anymore. If someone stumbles upon us in this alcove it won't matter what position we're in.

"I already told you," he says. "I'd hate to see you made into something other than that of your own choosing."

"What about the floras? The other wives?" I challenge. I should stop, but I have to know. Is he a good man?

His face darkens, something behind his eyes shuttering. "I have less power than I'd like... but that's all changing, Skylar. Just... find me, if you're in peril."

My hand reaches out of its own accord, betraying me as it brushes his jaw. I shouldn't be doing this.

"Aren't we always?" I whisper. I don't know if I mean me and him, or women, or the people of the republic. I just know that I can feel it, permeating the space between us, breathing down my neck.

Danger.

Sweet Sapa

Rose

I DON'T TAKE *SAPA*. It's too sweet, and certainly too expensive, but perhaps it will grow on me.

The hard back of the chair cuts in my spine as I keep my shoulders straight and my breathing even. The light filters down on the cobblestones and a small circular fountain in the center of the room. It's similar to the one in the forum, a bowl overflowing into the larger circle below. Understated and classic, just as I'd expect of Tristan's domus.

I thought Tristan would return before us, since the attic is the last tier to empty after the games. Somehow, we're still waiting for him. Daisy twists at the table, trying to look around at the small atrium and where it joins with the rest of the domus.

"I thought it'd be bigger," she whispers to me.

"Shh," I hiss, not wanting a servant to overhear.

"Hopefully you're not disappointed by the size of anything else," she says, still in a whisper tone but louder in volume.

"Daisy!"

She laughs, sitting back in her chair. I'm glad she's recovered from the match, but does she have to needle me?

"Laughing before I even enter the room, that's a first," Augustus says, entering from the hallway behind us. Daisy beams as my face heats to scarlet.

He's here.

"Probably not the last," Daisy says, holding out her hand as we both stand.

Augustus takes it, but his eyes find mine. "You must be Daisy," he says. There's something more, something unsaid, but I don't know what it is. "Rose." He takes my hand too, brushing a kiss across the lower halves of my fingers, bottom lip catching on my fingertips.

I can't stop the goose-pebbles that travel up my arm, but if he notices, he doesn't comment. Instead he sits next to Daisy, leaving the space beside me open for Tristan.

"My brother is running late, as is his nature," Augustus says, gesturing for a servant. He looks windblown, as if he's been outside running. Did he *run* from the Colosseum?

Daisy must notice his flushed cheeks and windswept hair as well because she says, "And what has you in such a state?"

Augustus smiles and leans back, shooting me a look before answering. "I may have lost track of the time."

"Doing?" Daisy presses.

I aim a kick at her under the table and she glares at me. Augustus laughs. "I was in the woods when I realized I would be late if I didn't run."

She nods as if this is a perfectly acceptable response to her incredibly rude question. "Ah yes. And in the woods you were…?"

"Daisy," I say. I don't know what's gotten into her today. It's like she cares nothing for expectation. Obedience.

Appropriateness.

Tristan takes that moment to enter, all golden light. "He was wasting his time painting, weren't you brother?" Augustus' jaw tightens at the insult as Tristan's hands snake over my shoulders, fingertips resting on my collarbones. "Rosebud," he says, kissing the top of my head.

"Tristan," I murmur. "This is my sister, Daisy."

"Pleasure," Tristan says, greeting her with a kiss to the hand as well. He snaps for his own *sapa* to be filled and before I can stop him, he asks for Daisy and I to have ours filled as well. Daisy glances at me before taking a sip. "Problem?" he asks.

"No, we just aren't used to taking *sapa*," I say before Daisy can make a comment. Part of her must know that Tristan is not like Augustus because she stays quiet, nodding in agreement.

"I suppose it is rather Praetorian," Tristan muses, sipping his own drink. "So, was I right... Augustus?" His words are barbed, but I'm not sure what about them is supposed to offend Augustus.

Augustus smiles. "Right you are, brother. Perhaps I'll gift it to you when I leave so you don't forget me."

Daisy and I sip our *sapa*, not sure what to say. "Yes, I'd love another dreary naturescape," Tristan quips.

"I could paint a gladiator match for you, if you're so fond of bloodshed."

"You can't paint something you've never seen," Tristan says.

"I'm sure they all look the same," Augustus says, drawing out each word.

"I guess you'll never know."

I have the distinct impression they're not talking about what we think they are. The air is thick with the kind of tension made all the more dangerous because not everyone is aware of its origin.

"When will you leave?" I ask, shattering the stillness between us.

"Three clipses," Augustus says, eyes not leaving Tristan.

"A good time to leave Divus," Daisy remarks. "The storm season is set to be particularly wicked this year."

Daisy's comment does what mine couldn't, and Augustus turns to her, smiling. "I won't envy you."

"I assumed the legions trained here? I've seen men training across the Maero," I ask.

Tristan shakes his head. "Those are experienced recruits. Those just joining are trained further north for a few quads."

"Why?" Daisy asks.

They answer at the same time.

"To experience different terrain," Tristan says.

"To isolate them," Augustus says.

I bite the inside of my cheek and Daisy meets my eyes. I see the set of her brow and know we're thinking the exact same thing. The tension, the crackling in the air. It's like our domus, and the current of unease that surrounds our pater. I'm not sure why, or what is between them, but one thing is certain now.

We need to be careful here, too.

Frigid

Luella

It's not hard to sneak out of the Domus Aurea. I wear a different face, the black stones weighing down my pocket as I slip from the servants' passage. There are enough faceless women here that no one questions me. Isn't that nice?

I meet Mia in the Baths. I don't intend to use them, having just washed the blood from me in the Domus Aurea, instead joining her in her favorite spot, the frigidarium. The large square pool is open to the air, the largest and coolest of the lounge pools here. Outside there are benches and stone lounges, open areas for sunbathing and drying. Beyond that are high arches leading to the other, warmer and therefore better, baths. There are also dressing areas and off to one side a small garden terrace overlooking where the side of the hill gives way to the Maero.

"I hate it in here," I say, wading over to her in the cool water. I could just as well jump in the river if I wanted to freeze my tits off. Her dark purple chest wrap covers her full breasts, the color bringing out the depth of her dark skin. She doesn't stand out specifically for her looks, but instead has the kind of beauty where the longer you look, the more you see.

"You hate everything," she says. She's not completely wrong and I snort my agreement. My wrap is the opposite of hers, a pale lilac shade that looks nearly white against this body's tanned skin.

This is the co-ed area, but there are very few bathers and even fewer men. Mia doesn't like crowds, preferring the Baths at the least busy time of day. I prefer to not attend at all. The things we do for our friends. And accomplices.

"He's the worst," I complain. "Thank the gods it's only a few more clipses." My stomach roils, but I don't elaborate. My guilt is mine to bear.

"And to think you wanted two quads," Mia reminds me. "Has he told you anything about... the reason you are there? Are you learning what you need?"

"No." I can't keep the despair out of my voice.

"So... you'll call it off?"

I shake my head. "No, it still needs to be done. If nothing else, I'm learning about the... layout of my new domus." It's always best to assume someone is listening in spaces like this. They usually are, as Mia and I know too well. It's one way we glean our information after all.

"Well Taln is adapting quite well, for a stray," Mia says.

"You make it sound like you don't like strays." I smile.

"I don't like to make a habit of taking them in."

"Now we both know that's not true," I say, remembering. It's been over ten years, but that room above the infirmaria had once been mine.

"And look at all the trouble that's brought me." Mia splashes water towards me.

"You'd be bored without me." I splash back at her and she just rolls her eyes.

"There's something else." Mia moves closer, swimming up behind me and raking my brunette strands back with her fingers. "Two or one?" she asks, able to speak lower and softer with my ear right next to her.

"One."

She sections my hair into three, pulling the ends taut as she loops them around each other, urging the strands to stay with tension. I let her twist my head this way and that, until she's ready to speak.

"Remember how I hadn't heard about his other friend?" I nod, knowing she means the Dominus. "Apparently he's changed his tastes."

"I just saw him on my way here... he offered to help me," I tell her.

"Help you run away from... your betrothed?"

"Yes, said something about how he's gaining power."

"Power over the girls, maybe." She's whispering now, making sure no one can hear even though there's no one near us. "I had one early this morning, says our new friend punched her and assaulted her. But..." She hesitates.

"But what?"

"Her injuries just weren't what I'd expect based on her story. I think he's just beginning. Like he's working up the courage or something."

"What do you mean?" And why did he offer to help me if he was the same as Ledo? Did he mean to play the savior, and then when I was thankful he'd beat me just a bit less than Ledo and think I'd be thankful?

"She didn't have any internal injuries that supported her assault. That's not necessarily a concern, because that assessment can vary so widely, but she said he punched her. Not hit, punched, with a closed fist."

I can't see her face so after a moment of raised eyebrows I just ask the question. "And?"

"And nothing was broken. She was just a bit bruised." She's whispering in my ear now. "I've seen the Dominus. He trains his men on the banks of the Maero sometimes. If he punched her with even a portion of his strength, something should have shattered." Cassius was not just a general, he was The General. In charge of all of the Emperor's legions.

"So you think she's lying?"

"Or misremembering," Mia says defensively and I regret my words. I didn't mean to make it sound like I would accuse a victim of lying. "Or… that he let her see a healer.. Or he healed her. I don't know, Lue. It just doesn't match."

I let out a long breath. "Can't be too easy, can it?"

Mia gathers my hair back so she's looking down at me. "You can still back out." For the first time I notice dark lines around her eyes. Does this wear on her, too? My oldest friend. It must. She's a widow, but unlike me she loved her husband. He was a good man. He built her the infirmaria, including the back door, because he saw how broken this republic was.

Widows who don't remarry are considered the most matronly. That and her status as a blessed healer means Mia is relatively safe. Unless I bring her danger.

"Are you well?" I ask her, searching my friend. Would she tell me if she wasn't?

She pushes my head forward again, resuming the plait. "I'm fine, Lue. I just don't like you in that place."

I don't like it, either. We don't talk about why, but it lingers between us, unspoken.

The reason for all of this.

A Wedding Day

Luella

I'VE SPENT THE PAST two clipses in the belly of Orcus. Ledo engages in sex acts that begin as consensual–well, as consensual as anything between a harem flora and a Praetor can be–and then dissolve into abuse. Ledo makes them ask for it and thank him for it, and I am to watch without interfering.

This is the hardest part. Harder than it's ever been. Sitting back while women are hurt. I will remember every face I've seen him abuse. Every lash he's bestowed. And I will savor it when he realizes he will never do it again.

"Please, stop," one of the floras whimpers as Ledo uses the flagrum on her. He can't use it too much, or they lose consciousness. They could die, but he doesn't care about that. He cares if they can continue their duties, and he cares if he damages the Emperor's property. They are his flora, after all. And it finally sinks in all the way, why he keeps taking wives. These women act how he wants, but he can't carry things too far. He can't take the ones he wants, whenever he wants. He has to wait for the Emperor to decide who he can have and when, and he has to return them alive. His wives, though... His wives belong to him.

'Til the gods part us in death.

There are five floras today, and Ledo has invited two other *esteemed* Senators to join him. The breath freezes in my lungs and the whole room goes still. She bites her lip as if realizing her mistake.

The man beneath her, another senator, grabs her chin, never stopping his punishing pace below her. "What was that, *meretrix*?" he demands.

She shakes her head, tears streaming down her cheeks. "Nothing. Nothing, Senator."

My nails bite into my palms until I bleed as I force myself to stay still. I don't have enough power to intervene and if I try and fail, Ledo might hurt her worse.

Ledo makes a humming noise. A low, dangerous sound that sets my teeth on edge. He walks to her and drags her off the senator, throwing her to the ground.

"Do you want to stop?" His voice is soft, too soft. Dangerously quiet.

She can't answer, she's sobbing in earnest now. The blood drips down her legs. She was only hit once, but it's the flagrum. It's meant to draw blood, to punish. I bite my lip, holding back a cry as Ledo sends her crashing to the floor with a vicious backhand. She falls flat, her cheek embraced by the marble as if they are as familiar as lovers.

"Do you want to stop?" he says again, yanking her up by her hair.

"No, Praetor," she manages to sob out.

"Silence?" I think he's asking for us to be silent at first, until one of the floras comes forward. She's been kneeling at the edge of the room since I arrived, apparently not needed yet. "Show her what happens to sabines who can't keep their mouth shut."

The flora turns red, but opens her mouth wide. She has no teeth. Not one.

I've never heard of irrumatio being done to a woman, and my stomach turns. The practice itself a vile concoction created during war, but to see it here, next to the pristine marble floors and tapestries of excess wealth and comfort is even more jarring.

I stand on instinct, the sight so unsettling that my legs move of their own accord, trying to flee. Ledo sees, and he removes himself from the floras quickly, coming to stand before me. He's covered in them. Their saliva, their blood. I sway as I meet his eyes, the blood leaving me in a rush.

"May I have some water, Praetor?" The excuse falls from my lips, an attempt to distract him, or me, or the other Senators.

Ledo narrows his eyes. He snaps at one of the nearby attendants who rushes over with a glass. "Thank you," I whisper as I take it. I sit back down, slowly. Ledo stares down at me, his erection now very close.

"Make sure you take care of yourself, Skylar. It's going to be a long night."

Because today is our wedding.

He returns to his demonstration, taking the woman who begged for them to stop and tying her arms behind her back before he and the other two Senators resume using her body simultaneously. Tears prick my eyes. I don't want to see, but at least he's forgotten about the flagrum for now.

I bite my cheek and look at the remaining floras. They were ordered to pleasure each other, which I imagine is a welcome break. One pair of floras is kissing deeply, their hands gentle in stark contrast to the mens', soft and seeking instead of punishing. The women in the other pair are tasting each other, their breaths coming in bursts of ecstasy instead of pain.

The contrast of it all makes my head spin but I don't look away. I can't, because Ledo meets my eyes periodically as he abuses the bound flora, reminding me that nothing is off limits to him. My eyes are open, and perhaps I'm even watching, but it doesn't register. The grunts of pain and pleasure, the warm afternoon air moving through the atrium, the tang of tears, it all surrounds me.

Or rather, surrounds Skyler. Because I can't be here. I can't see this or know this or survive this.

But I must. If she can, I must.

When it's over, Ledo turns and leaves without a word. I don't move. The flora and the Senators follow shortly after him until I am all alone in the fountain room. The sound of dripping water feels garish after what just transpired here. 'Please, stop,' seems to echo around the room, mocking me, reminding me why I'm here.

I can't stumble now, because if everything goes according to plan tonight, these will be the last women Ledo ever harms.

I sign the contract, and then we feast. It's a loud, riotous affair. The Emperor attends and his familiar golden visage is made dimmer somehow by the redder hair, broader chest, and taller build of Cassius at his side. Ledo is to the Emperor's other side, and I am next to Ledo.

This wedding dress is the most daring I've worn yet. The back and front are matching v's, dipping to my low back and my navel. The thin white cloth barely covers my breasts before gathering into a belt at my waist and draping to the floor. I hate it, but that is to be expected when Ledo chooses something.

"Perhaps I shall wed, soon," the Emperor muses to Ledo, who laughs. His voice spikes my heart rate, and I focus on my breathing, refusing to look at him.

"You do need an heir," he agrees. "Perhaps it's best to look after the upcoming rites."

"Perhaps I shall wed, too," Cassius says, but he's not looking at the Emperor, either. He's looking at me. I narrow my eyes.

The golden Emperor turns to him, his smile anything but kind. "That seems a waste, since you are not allowed to have children." I'd forgotten about that. Only the Emperor may bear children. In theory it's to prevent rivalry for the throne, even though imperial siblings have killed one another anyways. But it seems the Emperor and the Dominus play their own kind of game.

Cassius shrugs. "That's not all wives are good for."

Ledo slips his hand under the table, placing it on my upper thigh, exposed from the high slits in the dress. At first, it's almost comforting, like he's trying to protect me. Then he moves his hand in, towards my center. My muscles tighten, pressing my knees together. "I agree," Ledo says. I think he will stop now, but instead he reaches as high as he can with my legs so tight and pinches the sensitive skin of my thighs. Hard.

Tears spring to my eyes at the tender flesh, an area so rarely exposed, being twisted. I exhale slowly, and when Ledo moves his hand up again, I open my legs, ever the obedient wife. He hums a sound of approval that makes my cheeks flame in rage, but I will contain it.

I will not ruin my own plan.

Ledo continues his ministrations beneath the table, conversing with Cassius and the Emperor as if I'm not there. His arm moves across my lap so that it's obvious what he's doing, but no one speaks of it. If anything, the people further down the table smile at me, as if I am so blessed by such an attentive husband. I bite the inside of my lip and look to my plate. I feel Cassius looking at me and a true wave of embarrassment washes through me, quickly replaced again by the rage. If it wasn't me, it would be someone else. Earlier it had been. Now it was my turn.

Of course I am not enjoying myself, but I clench my inner walls and make my breaths come a little faster. I let Ledo think he's affecting anything other than my level of nausea.

He leans over. "Not yet, wife," he whispers and withdraws his hand. I almost choke on his presumption. Careful. I must be so careful now that I am this close. The blood spilled today, the violence, it was all wrong, and my nerves are frayed thin.

The blood coating the floors of the Domus Aurea shouldn't belong to the floras.

It should always be *them*. Ledo. The Emperor. The Senators and Praetors.

I let a small whimper release, as if I am disappointed. Ledo grins. Cassius glares. The Emperor snaps for a flora to attend him as though the show was just what he needed.

And I wait patiently in the center of the web I've woven.

Insects

Rose

She looks at me like I'm a particularly disgusting insect. Like she might try to squash me if I get too close. I try not to squirm under Tristan's mater's scrutiny, but the giant emeralds around her neck glimmer wickedly and the gold bangles at her wrist clang with each sharp and demure movement.

Tristan is to my right, his pater is at the head of the table, and across from Tristan is his mater, Camilla. I assume Augustus would sit across from me if he was here, but I haven't seen him. There is more room, the table so long I can hardly see the other end. I suppose this isn't that sort of dinner.

I continue to meet the discerning eyes of Tristan's mater. She's golden like him, her hair like the aurei Tristan used to barter my life free from the man in front of the Sabines. It's coiled and piled on top of her head, with just a few ringlets bursting free at her neck and temples, like she's made her own crown.

"Mater," Tristan finally says. "Do you have something you'd like to say to me?" He looks angry, his cheeks flushed and his eyes bright.

"It's not my place," she says stiffly. That must be a yes. I look down at the small fist sized roasted hen on my plate. I've never eaten like this. Hens are a luxury. Fish and goat are what Daisy and I grew up on, and half the time we caught the fish ourselves. Well, I caught the fish, but Daisy strung the line with thread and hook.

"Yet, here you are," Tristan's pater says. He asked me to call him Pater, and I suppose he is now. He bought me, after all. "Unable to behave like a Divusian wife should." Unlike Tristan, he doesn't look angry. He looks bored.

She shoots me a look, as if it's my fault that Pater would admonish her so publicly, but I haven't said a word. Besides, she should know better than to be so forward. It's not appropriate to question Tristan and his pater, and a lady of her standing should know that.

Or perhaps, it's because of her standing that she's able to do that? The thought strikes me as odd. I know it's not suitable. What should standing or wealth have to do with appropriateness?

Tristan had said his familia is different than mine. For the first time I wonder what he really meant. What it really looks like, to be part of this familia.

Tristan's pater looks at me when he continues. "A Divusian woman is meant to obey." He doesn't ask, because it's not a question, but I nod anyways. Heat floods my cheeks. Have I done something to upset him? Have I disobeyed without realizing it? "You are weak," he says. "Soft." He stands, coming around to stand behind his wife. "In need of strength and discipline." He clasps his hands over her shoulders, dwarfing her. She doesn't look so threatening now. She looks just as Pater says, weak and soft and so, so small.

His dark brown hair and blue eyes meet mine. "Divusian men must also obey." My eyes widen, confusion unfurling. "We obey the gods by providing for our wives and our children. It's give and take, yes?"

It feels like a test, a trap. I stare at Camilla and she stares back. I can't read her expression though, it's guarded, a virgin Vestal under lock and key.

When no one speaks, Pater goes on. "Marriage is not child-rearing. It's not a domushold matter. It's political. Communal." He kisses Camilla on the top of the head. "It's not a woman's domain."

How strange, to hear that my marriage is not a woman's domain, not mine. I'm half of the equation, and Tristan said he loved me. Is love political?

Am I?

"Rose understands," Tristan says. Lies.

His mater looks to Tristan, as if she senses the deception. She can see right through me, how over my head I am. "If she doesn't, it'll come back on you, Tristan." She spits his name and it hits him in the face like a slap. I feel him flinch beside me, but when I turn to him he looks composed. Confident.

Just then, Augustus walks in. "Sorry I'm late," he calls from the end of the hall. He sounds happy, if a little out of breath, but when he sees me he lets out a soft, "oh."

"*Princeps*," Camilla says. "Come sit." I almost look around to see who has spoken. Camilla's voice is transformed, soft and kind. *Little prince.* A sweet name, usually given to the oldest son as a term of endearment, but Tristan is the elder. Shifting my eyes to Tristan, I see his jaw tighten, his shoulders stiffen.

Camilla has forgotten about the bug of a woman in front of her. She pats the seat beside her and Pater returns to the head of the table, everyone but Tristan seeming calmed by Augustus' presence.

"Yes, come sit," Pater says. "We were just discussing a woman's place."

"Right by your side?" Augustus says, kissing his mater's cheek. She beams.

Tristan stands abruptly. "I think we'll retire. Rose has a long day tomorrow."

Augustus looks worried and I shoot him a small smile. I want him to know things went alright with his familia. Not as bad as it could have been, by far, but I don't have a chance to even say goodbye as Tristan pulls me from the room without another word.

Make it Look Real

Luella

One of the white pearls rolls between my back teeth as I enter Ledo's room. It's a last resort, but I will use it if I have to. Ledo's room is... not empty.

A large four poster bed takes up the majority of the room, covered in white linen sheets and blankets. This country's obsession with maiden blood is obvious, but I know Ledo chooses white for another reason entirely. His intention to paint the bed with his flagrum is not what gives me pause. No. I'm startled by the fact that kneeling beside the bed is a naked flora. She holds a small crop whip between her teeth, and her eyes are downcast.

I fight not to clench my jaw, for fear of crushing the pearl. The customary drink is at the small table off to the side of the room, along with two chairs. The wine will be uncut, the only time of day it's appropriate to have full strength outside of a festival of the gods.

I gesture to the wine. "May I serve us, Praetor?"

"Call me husband," Ledo says, stepping close to me. He grabs my chin, harsh. "And you will serve me."

"Yes, husband," I say. It tastes bittersweet and I wonder how many times I've used that word.

That curse.

I move to the table, my back to him, and quickly dump the white vial from my pocket into the entire bottle of wine. A singular glass isn't wise.

It might look different than mine, we might switch glasses, or he could spill it and demand a fresh one.

These are all mistakes I've made over the years. Mistakes I paid for with whichever body I had at the time. Not mine.

Mia has perfected all of this with me, and I'm never not grateful for her concoctions, or her drops. All of the ways we make this work.

The flora isn't supposed to be here, but I'll deal with her after I deal with the true threat. I pour two glasses, keeping my portion small, as a lady should. I bring the glass to him and he clinks it against mine. "Drink," he commands. So I do, draining my glass. He drains his. "Refill them." I do that, too, returning with two full glasses. I drink again, as does he. The drink begins to make me tingle, but I know he will be even more affected. I'm feeling just the wine, but he'll be feeling much more than that.

"Kneel," he says, lowering his trousers. I do. He snaps for the flora, who comes to kneel beside me. "Show me what you've learned, wife." The condescension in his voice would break me if I was truly his wife. If I thought he loved me. The last two clipses would have broken me. Would have made me afraid, malleable, and eager to do anything to avoid displeasing my new husband.

But I am not truly his wife, and I have never once had any illusions about who he is. These clipses have not broken me. They forged me, as every moment of my life has forged me. Not in fire, but in bruises. Black and blue and broken.

And stronger for it.

He fists my hair, impatient that I haven't begun to pleasure him, but I jerk my head back, not hiding the disgust at his erection, at his presumption that it is anything but ordinary. His eyes narrow and I brace, knowing what's coming.

It still hurts as he backhands me to the floor, then drags me back up by my hair. "Do you want to be punished?" The question almost makes me laugh, because I know he plans to find fault. Why else would the whip already be here? But angry men hit harder, so I don't make a sound.

He puts a thumb in each corner of my mouth, spreading it wide and gripping the side of my face. I try to pull back. Why isn't it working, yet?

Panic courses through me. I can pleasure a man just fine, but that doesn't mean I want to. And once we start, the chance of him drinking more wine drops significantly. He won't have another glass until he's spent.

He thrusts forward but I try to draw back again, and he answers by removing one hand from my face, grabbing his mediocre cock, and slapping me with it.

"I didn't want to have to punish you so early, Sky…" I think he's given me a nickname for a moment, but then his fist slackens on my hair.

"Whaaa?" he slurs. I gaze up at him, giving the paralytic a few more moments to take hold. Something like panic crosses his features as he sways on his feet, until finally, he collapses in an undignified heap.

I feel my reddened cheek and turn to the flora beside me. She's stiff, staring down at Ledo.

"He won't be rising for quite awhile," I tell her.

"What did you do to him?" She sounds more curious than afraid.

"Listen to me," I say, avoiding her question. "You weren't supposed to be here and I don't want to hurt you." I leave the rest unsaid, the part that she probably understands better than me. Want means so little in the face of survival.

Her eyes are hazel and her tight brown curls frame her round umber cheeks. I try to read the expression on her face, searching for a reason to let her go.

"You're her." She brings her hand to her mouth. "Tisiphone."

"What's your name?" I ask.

"Flavia," she says, looking down at Ledo. "What will you do to him?"

"What do you want me to do?"

She looks back to me, her voice softer than the words that escape her. "I want you to make him suffer."

I smile, "I can do that."

"But…"

"What?" I ask. Please don't make me hurt you, I want to beg.

"I can say he dismissed me. That he just wanted you tonight…." She trails off. "But they won't believe it."

"Why not?"

"He'd never leave me unmarked. Even the floras would question me, Skylar. You have to whip me."

The weight of her words settles over me. The truth of them, of Ledo. I swallow hard. Nod once, twice.

She hands me the crop and I do what I would do to myself if I needed to, as I have had to.

I make it look real.

Forsaken

Luella

"Thank you," the flora says, wrapping her arms around me. We're gentle. Each of us too aware of every lash mark I bestowed on her. I shudder knowing the whipping I just gave her is nothing compared to what she's endured. I turn to Ledo. He's lying on the floor, eyes wide.

"Husband," I say, letting the condescension and disgust finally show through. "Have you figured it out yet?" I smile sweetly. "I have no intention of being trained by you, pleasuring you, or suffering even your existence for another night. Do you know why?"

I wait for his answer, but of course it won't come. The paralytic permits him to hear, feel, and see while allowing no actual movement. This might be my favorite part.

The reckoning.

"Because you abuse women. And when you grow tired of that, you kill them. Floras who can't say no, but I know about others, too. Young women like myself with no familia to look out for them." I tap my pointer finger to my chin. "How many wives of yours have you murdered? I found three in the official records, but I know there are more, ones for whom you didn't bother to file the paperwork."

I don't only kill murderers. I kill anyone who abuses women, if they fit the type of profile that allows me to get close enough to poison them, confront them, kill them, and escape. That means I've eliminated plenty of low level abusers. The men like Ledo though? The ones who think they are untouchable? Whose hubris leads them to believe they can do whatever they want to whomever they want, and have the power to not just avoid consequences, but flaunt their conquests? Those are the sweetest kills, even if the planning takes more work.

I drag Ledo's still form to the bed. He's heavy, but I'm stronger than I look. I'm on an errand from a god, after all. That doesn't mean it's easy, though. I'm panting as I arrange him into a star, stretching and tying each limb to a separate bedpost. Once there, I test each knot, making sure they are secure. Then I pour powder from another vial into Ledo's mouth. The powder is a combination of things, a reversal for the overall paralytic, but also a very special kind of replacement that Mia has been perfecting over the years.

"I'll kill you," Ledo seethes. He can speak now, because I need him to admit what he's done, but the new paralytic still immobilizes his limbs.

"Try," I shrug and watch as he realizes he can't move his arms or legs. "Do you know the part you haven't heard about Tisiphone?" I ask as his face pales. "That I don't tolerate liars. You can have a quick death if you tell me how many women you've killed. If you don't, I'll make you suffer."

"You don't know what you're talking about," he spits.

I lean down, just above his face. "I know everything about you, Praetor Ledo Ballona. I know about the eleven-year-old girl you whipped last mortua, and I know about the flora you used the flagrum on the night we met." His eyes widen. "I. Know. Everything," I growl. I don't, but I know enough. I know enough to know he deserves to die and enough to make him afraid when he does.

He tries to shake his head, but the paralytic results in it looking more like a tremor. "No, you can't."

"I can. I'm here to make you pay, Praetor. You decide if you pay with your life now, or your blood for the next six hours." It's mostly a boast. I don't actually like to torture men; I like them to admit what they've done. I've done some unsavory things to gain their confessions, but the difference is that I didn't enjoy it.

Much.

"Fuck off," Ledo spits at me. The warm liquid lands on my cheek and I make a noise of reprimand.

"That's not how good boys behave. Don't worry, husband." I smile. "You'll learn."

After Ledo's confession, I dump the red vial of poison into his throat and watch as he dies. My first kill in the Domus Aurea, after all this time, and hopefully not the last.

Poison, potions, and wits.

I'm in the process of untying the ropes along his leg when I hear the door handle jiggle. I locked the door behind the flora when she left, and on our wedding night no one should be bothering Ledo and myself unless he rings the large bell off to the side of the bed that calls a servant.

I freeze, looking down at Ledo's dead body.

I could shift my face, and pretend I found him like this. Or climb on top of him and pretend we're having sex and tell them to leave. Bile rises in my throat at that idea, but I do plenty of things I loathe, all so that I can do this one thing I relish.

The noise stops. I remain frozen for several minutes. When I hear nothing further, I finish untying him and return the ropes to their places in the closet. I drape a sheet across his waist. If anyone were to look in, they might for a moment think him sleeping, recovering after his nightly activities.

A last glance around tells me the room is tidy. Now to return to my room as if nothing unusual had happened. Men like Ledo don't sleep with their wives, and I intend to use that to my advantage.

I don my robe over the wedding gown that he never removed, and quietly unlock the door. The hallway appears empty and I step over the threshold.

A hand slides across my mouth and I'm pinned back against a warm wall. No, not a wall; a chest. I bite down hard on the hand and try to bring my elbow back into the attacker's stomach, but they're holding me too tightly.

"I knew it was you." A deep, satisfied voice rumbles through my chest. Janus appears to have forsaken me tonight, because the voice is none other than Cassius Evander, the Dominus.

And he's caught me.

This Face

Luella

Cassius tugs me back into the room. I haven't given up, but I have stopped fighting. I need to be careful. Clever. My priorities just became avoiding a cell and keeping my stones. A new face won't do me any good if it's locked up, and I still have work to do.

He shoves me towards the bed and moves to lock the door with a small key. How did he get that?

I can't read what's on his face. Fear? Anger, perhaps? He's impassive. And he's pulling a trick from my book by refusing to speak first.

Circling me, he goes to the bed and folds back the sheet I'd thrown over Ledo. He casually slides a hand to Ledo's neck, checking his pulse. Cassius raises his brow at me after a moment. His movements are un-hurried, worryingly apathetic.

The usual rules are out, and I speak first. "You were not invited to our marriage bed, Dominus."

"A blessing, don't you think?" He doesn't smirk, as I expected. There's no gloating, just understanding in his steel blue eyes.

"Why are you here?" I ask. The possibilities filter through my mind of where this night will end for me. The dungeon. In Cassius' room, where he's likely grown more brazen with his abuse. Here, murdered next to my last victim. Public execution. All end up with me, dead or close to it.

"I was wondering why you brought up other floras being abused, but were so willing to marry Ledo anyways," Cassius says.

"I'm sure it's not a secret, Dominus, the way you and your brother and the Praetors treat women." I spit the words now. If I am to die, I want him to know exactly what I think of him.

"Is that all?" he says, stepping closer.

"What else does there need to be?"

"Are. You. Her?" He growls, still advancing. I take a step back, but now I'm against the wall.

"Her?"

"Tisiphone." He's caged me in, an arm on each side. I crane my neck to look at him, forcing confusion into my face.

"I'm Skylar," I say.

"Why did you kill him?"

He doesn't know. Not really. He guesses, and I can work with a guess. "I didn't mean to. I meant to give him some sleeping drought... to lessen his..." I let myself take a breath, as if steadying myself. "To lessen his appetites. For the first night."

"You knew what he was, I saw it in the garden. You're not what you pretend to be," he accuses.

"So? Who is what they pretend to be? I had no prospects, no dinarii, no familia!" I raise my voice. "I thought I could handle it. I would have. I just got..." I trail off. He would believe this. He has to. My life depends on it. "I got scared. When it was my turn." I gesture to the cabinet on the side of the room. Atop it, Ledo's whip glints with flecks of Flavia's blood.

Cassius' face softens, then just as quickly darkens when he sees the whip. "You've never done this before?"

"Done what? Accidentally overdosed my husband on sleeping drought?! Of course not."

"What will you do if I let you go?"

What will I do? I'll come back and kill you.

"You'll never see my face again." It's not a lie. Not this face.

I'll never wear this face again.

BETROTHED

ROSE

"YOU SHOULDN'T WEAR YOUR hair like that," Tristan snaps. I flinch back at the venom on his tongue. My hair is down in ringlets, except for the sides which are pinned up the way I wore it at the festival. The way my mater wore hers. I wasn't quite daring enough to wear it the way the beautiful blonde woman had at the festival, down and free.

"You don't like it?" My gut sinks. I should have asked him how to wear it. I should have known how much it meant to meet his familia. I'd agonized for hours over my dress and hair.

And I'd chosen wrong.

"It's common. Plebeian," he spits.

I don't know what to say. I *am* a plebeian. I look down at the flagstones in his familia's garden. The citrus and grapes around us fill the air with a heady fragrance. The twins have both departed, casting us in the indigo of twilight.

I'm already making mistakes.

"Did you hear me, Rose?" Tristan grabs my upper arm, squeezing tightly. I bite my lip to keep from crying out, more with surprise than pain, at first.

"Yes, Tristan," I say.

"And?" He demands. He draws me closer, and I conceal a wince as his grip neatly overlaps the last bruise my pater had left. "Are you a common *meretrix* or are you my betrothed?"

They sink in slowly, the words I've heard many times before.

Whore.

Meretrix.

Sabine.

I'm not sure which hurts worse. His words or his hands.

"Your betrothed," I answer softly, refusing to let my voice crack.

His grip tightens and a gasp escapes my lips without my permission. Tristan leans closer and drops his voice to a whisper. "Then act like it."

"I'm sorry." My voice finally betrays me, cracking over the words. It shatters something in Tristan's expression. He drops my arm, then grabs my wrist, gentle.

"Stones, Rosebud. I'm sorry." He folds me into a hug and I stiffen, unsure. "Did I hurt you?

"No," I lie. "It's okay."

Tristan straightens his arms so he can peer down at me. "She ruins everything. I just... I thought she wouldn't ruin this." His mater *had* upset him. Was it her words, her view of me, or the way she had called Augustus *princeps*? Perhaps it was all of those things.

"You're not close with your mater?" It feels dangerous to ask, but I think that maybe, just maybe, it's more dangerous not to know.

Something conflicted and ugly passes through Tristan's eyes. It breaks my heart when he says, "I wouldn't say that."

"What would you say?" I lift my hand to his cheek, urging him to come back to me. Begging him to be who I know he is. The man who saved me from the Sabines. From my father. From my future. The man who loves me.

And maybe, the man I was made for.

At first he's frozen, and I fear I've stepped into the minotaur's maze, only for the entrance to be swallowed in hedges behind me. Then he leans into my touch, closing his eyes. "She's... she favors my brother. Her precious *princeps*." I sense the bitterness in the way his eyes narrow and his shoulders tighten. "And she never lets me forget it. That I'm not him. That I'm my pater's son."

"She doesn't care for your pater?"

He laughs, turning in to bite my palm. "I spent my childhood learning all the ways she didn't care for him." He's so beautiful like this, his face open, eyes hooded. Like he's being himself for the first time ever, and he's amazed at it.

"I think I understand," I say. "My pater feels the same about me. That I can be the target for him, now that my mater is gone." I've never said it out loud before, but I know it's true.

Tristan steps forward, resting his forehead against mine. "Did he punish you, for what she'd done?"

My eyes flutter closed against the memories; against the pain I've hidden from Daisy. From myself. "Yes."

"I'm sorry," he says, but when I nod he interrupts me. "For that, but more for me." He tips my chin up, gold eyes searching mine. "I don't want to be my mater, or my pater. I don't want us to punish each other. I want to break it." His eyes flare, as if small candles are consuming the oxygen behind the iris with each word.

"Break what?" I whisper.

"Break the cycle. The chains. This," he gestures to his golden, privileged domus. It's a beacon of Divus, but I understand. We could fix the broken things we inherited. "Whatever it takes to be free of them. So, we can give our children what they deserve. You and me."

I let out a soft breath, and the butterflies that have been lying dormant since the day Tristan offered to marry me seem to wake. They stretch their wings, tentative.

I rise to my tip-toes, lips finding his. "You and me," I promise.

We could break the cycle. We will.

Because I was made for love.

Replacement

Luella

It's the most welcome sight, my domus. I pass it, though, and head along the forest path. I need to thank Janus. I'd like to kiss both their faces for the simple fact that I am alive.

I kneel in front of the shifting statue. The twin suns have not yet risen, and I wonder, not for the first time, if gods sleep.

I place my used basanite on the altar, along with a loaf of bread I took from the kitchens on my way out of the Domus Aurea. It's an especially delicious looking loaf, but I know mine are better. I'll bring one of my own next time.

Cassius is suspicious. I don't know how to infiltrate the Domus Aurea this time, how to get close. I don't have years of information to help me understand him, the way we did for the others.

I place my head on the altar and tell Janus about Ledo. "Seven wives and countless women from Divus. He didn't even know the number." I pause, then, "I'm adding the Dominus to my final praeda. I want to eliminate them both." I tell Janus the rest of it, and when I lift my eyes, my stones sparkle once more with fiery hues.

Tisiphone. Black Widow. *Vidua. Venefica.* The names I hear for me are multiplying, but I like *vidua.* Widow. I have lost many husbands, and while I do not mourn them, I am in constant mourning for humanity. That this is what women endure, still. But I am not divine like Tisiphone or Janus. Cassius reminded me of that tonight, and I will not rush these last two. I will not make a mistake, not now.

Freckles adorn my new features, and my black hair remains long, a preference I've never been able to abandon. I make my way to my domus and slowly, so slowly, my shoulders move away from my ears. My breathing slows. My heart rate returns to normal.

It was too close, but I will be more careful.

I retrieve the bag of flour from my storage cellar, bringing it to my kitchen workstation. Bread. What I need is bread. And soup. It's definitely a good time to start soup.

I'm sliding the last of my carrots into the pot as the suns begin to rise when Mia lets herself in. I grunt at her as she drops a parcel onto the kitchen table. It clinks.

"What's that?" I tilt my head towards the parcel, stirring the soup one last time before coming to sit beside her.

"The Dominus has been busy."

"Busy? He was bothering me all night!" I fume. Why did he let me leave if he was going to hurt someone else?

"What?" Mia asks. I tell her everything. The flora, Flavia, who saw me. Cassius sneaking into the room. Cassius letting me go.

"It doesn't make sense," I finish.

Mia shakes her head. "I don't know, but the reason I came right away? The flora injured last night? She looks exactly like you." I stare at her and gesture to my new face, brow furrowed. "The you that met Cassius. Blonde hair, blue eyes, petite features..."

I don't know what game he's playing. "How old was she?"

"Same as you looked, around twenty summers."

"So what's all that?" I gesture back to the parcel.

"Refills for your stash," Mia says. She opens the bundle and the rainbow of familiar vials greets me, including one filled with little white pearls.

"I thought you wanted me to quit?" I ask, sliding the vials towards me.

"I don't know what he's doing to them," Mia says. "But, they're... off." She shakes her head. "The injuries don't match the intensity they describe. They're so terrified..."

"What do you mean they don't match?"

"I think he's...blessed? A healer..." Mia trails off, confused. That can't be right. Men aren't blessed, at least not often. Perhaps with strength or speed: blessings for war. A healer, though?

"A healer?" I shake my head. "Mia, how?"

She throws her hands up in frustration. "How could they be mostly healed? What if he...?"

I already know where she's going. What if he heals them so he can hurt them again? Her eyes are searching mine and I know what she wants. Her worry for me isn't enough to let this go, not when her patients are scared, terrified to tell her what's going on. If he's bad enough to worry Mia, I can't wait. "Okay, Mi. We'll get him." I nod. Once, twice.

"We'll get him."

THE BEST BAKER

LUELLA

"YOU SHOULD BE A baker," Mia says, grabbing the piece of crusty sourdough from my hand and taking a bite. It's been a clipse since I left the Domus Aurea. A clipse of planning and plotting and wondering why Cassius let me go.

"I was eating that," I say, rising to grab a new piece from the table. Mia sits in her favorite rocking chair in the common area of my domus. I return to the bench below the window so I can see the small pond behind my domus. "Besides, I have a job."

"A job," Mia laughs around the bread. "I guess you could call it that. You do something dangerous that you hate." I don't know that I hate all of it. There are parts I rather relish. And, does it matter if you're called to it? Janus didn't bless me so I could play *chamaeleōn* for myself.

"I could say the same about you," I say, stuffing a piece of bread into my mouth.

"I don't hate my job," is Mia's curt reply.

"Well, the dangerous part," I amend.

"The difference is, I love it." Mia takes another bite. "Oh, and I receive compensation."

"I love parts of this, even if it's not a job. And you know I don't need the money." My pater hadn't been rich, quite the opposite, but I'd gotten enough from him. Between that and small amounts I've stolen from my praeda, I have plenty. Enough not to work and to pay Mia for all of my potions and poisons.

Mia raises her eyebrows. "Which part?"

"The part where your backroom is empty, for longer." I watch a goldfinch hop along the edge of the pond, probably looking for bugs. Just like me.

Mia sighs. "I like that part, too." I can feel the tension in her as she wrestles with something. She wants to say more.

"What is it?" I ask, turning to her when the goldfinch flies away.

"The Dominus is hosting a ball," she says quietly. "To find a wife."

"What about the Praetor?" I ask.

"What about him?" Mia's brow furrows.

"Have they replaced him? Is there an uproar about it?" Maybe this is all a ruse because Cassius regrets letting me go. Does he think I'd come to the ball and he could arrest me?

Mia crosses her ankles. "They already replaced him with a Senator, and the Senator had a cousin who took his role. They're saying he died of exertion."

"No mention of his wife?"

"No." Mia shakes her head. "They don't like the Tisiphone rumor. It makes it seem like their behavior isn't okay. No one from the republic will mention you and I bet your wedding papers were never filed."

I look out the window. "So, a ball?"

"Taln and I have had a girl each night. All blonde. All terrified. A few even said he called them by your name."

"Stones," I say.

"Stones is right. He's obsessed with Skylar. This ball? I think it's him trying to find you or the perfect replacement."

How do I maneuver him into picking me without looking exactly like Skylar? I don't want him to be too suspicious. "All blue eyes?" I ask.

"No, after the first one eye color has been mixed. All floras, though."

"I have to go."

We're more aligned than ever, and Mia doesn't argue.

I reach for the colored stones in my pocket and close my eyes when I feel the cool surface. I concentrate hard on my brow bones, cheekbones, and nose. Shift the set of my eyes, my skin tone until I feel the familiarity of something I know to stay away from. My real face. I pull back, just a bit, and then open my eyes.

My blonde is more wheat than Skylar's had been, and my eyes are a greenish blue instead of Skylar's sapphire. I raise the cheekbones, but keep the pert nose. My freckles are gone, replaced by barely tanned skin. "How's this?" I ask Mia.

Her eyes widen just a bit. "You look... beautiful. Like someone I used to know," she says, voice soft, sad. I nod and finish transforming my body. It's not painful, exactly, just uncomfortable. Like stretching sore muscles. I've done it more times than I can remember, drained my stones hundreds of times.

I wonder for the first time what will come after this, when I've finally reached the last name on my list. Him. Will I hunt monsters for the rest of my life, or will I really feel satisfied? Will I rest? Could I, knowing about Mia's back room?

"I think I'd be a good baker," I say, finally replying to Mia's first thought.

Mia smiles, coming to sit beside me on the bench. She leans her head against my shoulder, and I rest mine against hers. We're quiet, both lost in our own thoughts. Is she thinking about her husband, Agrippa? I'm thinking about mine. The vows and contracts and bodies.

The way I've been broken and formed, new each time, so that I'm never really me, except when I'm with her. My bread, my irritation, my sharp edges. I can only show them to Mia, and maybe to Janus.

When Mia breaks the silence, I try not to wince at her words, at the pleading in them.

"You'd be the best baker."

There You Are

Luella

I'm nervous, like it's my first time all over again. As if I haven't killed before, haven't hunted monsters for ten years. Cassius confuses me, and I don't like being confused. I don't like surprises.

Yet, the best way to understand something is to study it.

I'm studying everything as I enter the Domus Aurea ballroom. It's in a larger atrium than the last ball I attended with Ledo. A large fountain in the center of the room makes me pause for a moment. It can't be.

And yet it is. It's the fountain from the room Ledo trained me in. It was moved here, and the women still shrink away from Bacchus' pouring wine and pissing phallus. Everything about this room is an homage to my courtship with Ledo. White tablecloths, colorful bouquets with more roses than are ever necessary. The fountain. Even the floras around the room are all familiar... the ones he trained me with.

The room is full of women. A bachelor ball is not an uncommon occurrence for men seeking a marriage, but the Dominus? I'd bet all my stones that nearly every eligible female in the city and surrounding farms and vineyards is here. And, of course, men are allowed to attend. Partially as chaperons for their chaste familia members and partially in their own attempt to find wives. The floras are here to keep the marriageable women chaste when the heathen men can't control their urges and need something to take the edge off.

Gods forbid anyone expect them to control their urges on their own.

I make my way to the wine, which is unfortunately quite close to the fountain. The trickling water freezes me for a moment and I take a deep breath to steady myself. One. Two.

Cassius is sitting directly in front of the fountain, a flora kneading his shoulders and another kneeling beside him. Both are blonde. It does nothing to discourage women from approaching him, as a young woman and her male chaperon are doing when his makeshift throne comes into view. They incline their heads and Cassius looks her up and down before waving a hand.

He's changed. More arrogant, more open about his proclivities, and I wonder again if this is a trap.

Does it matter if it is? If I isolate him, I can set off my own trap. It won't matter what he suspects if I have him paralyzed and restrained.

I wish he wasn't handsome. I wish I hadn't thought him... something different. Because I had thought he was different for a moment. Maybe for two.

I thought perhaps I'd finally met a man who wasn't obsessed with destroying. A man who wished to build. Instead, I'd just found one who hadn't begun breaking yet. And now that he has...I shake my head. There is too much work to do for such trivial thoughts. I wait until he dismisses the next woman that approaches, then I cross to stand before him. I incline my head in respect, but maintain eye contact.

"Dominus," I say.

He leans forward, intrigued by my lack of manners. I should be complimenting him, the ball, or introducing myself. "What's your name?" I've debated all day how to respond to this question, should he ask, but now I decide to take a risk.

"This is a beautiful ball, Dominus. The fountain especially," I say. His eyes darken and I know Mia's insight is correct. He's looking for Skylar.

For me.

"What's your name?" he asks again.

"I'll tell you if you ask me to dance," I say.

"And if I don't?" he asks as he rises.

"Then I'll find another victim." I smile my most charming smile as he leads me to the dance floor. There are couples all around us and floras dancing alone. The one closest to us is swaying her hips to the slow string melody, her hands caressing each of her own curves in a sheer dress that leaves nothing to the imagination. She looks well compared to how she looked when I saw her under Ledo's hand. I swallow.

Cassius follows my gaze. "She's fully recovered." His voice is flat as he draws me close, one strong arm wrapping around my waist and the other lifting my hand as he leads me.

He's sturdy. Commanding. The warmth from his hands seeps into my hip, my hand.

"Tell me your name." It's not a question this time. His eyes are intent, rapt on me. His scrutiny is so heavy my knees nearly buckle under it.

"What do you think it is?"

"Skylar." It's not a question and now I spin another thread for him.

"It's a pretty name," I admit.

"But it's not your name?" He leans in. His attention is unwavering. I use that to begin a new web, even if it's different from the others.

"It is if you want it to be."

"Is it Tisiphone?" he demands. His grip tightens, not painfully but possessively. Like he wants to hold Tisiphone, not harm her.

"If you want it to be," I say again.

"I'd hate you to be made into anything other than that of your own choosing." He'd said those words to me that first night. And like a fool, I'd believed him. And if I want to replicate whatever it is he is trying to find in Skylar, if I am to step into his trap in order to set off mine, I must pretend to believe it again.

"I can take care of myself, Dominus."

He stops dancing. Just, stops. I have no choice but to stop with him, lest I spin out of his arms. Heads turn our way, but he only has eyes for me.

"What if you let me take care of you, instead?" For the first time in a decade, the words of a man make me consider, perhaps even make me want. Not to be taken care of exactly, but to be cared for. What a silly time to be inconvenienced by such a human thing as feelings.

I cock my head in confusion and Cassius searches my eyes, catching on the right one. His eyes widen a fraction, and his lips part. The breath in my lungs stalls, frozen beneath his gaze. What does he see?

Cassius claps his hands three times, the sharp sound stopping the instruments and the chatter and the dancing. His voice is strong and confident as he says, "The ball is over. I've found my bride."

The guests look at each other, at Cassius, at me. They murmur. Someone even laughs, an insecure and shrill sound.

"Now," his voice booms and the confusion turns to surprised obedience. He is a general, after all. Servants shoo guests towards the arched doorways and the floras who have disrobed don their sheer shifts and garments once more.

Minutes later, only the Dominus and I remain.

"I never said yes," I say, keeping my voice light. I look around the room, not daring to meet his eyes again.

"Can you say no?" He smirks.

"I can always say no," I snarl before I can stop myself.

He grins—truly grins—and steps closer so I have to look up at him, his chest nearly touching mine. "There you are."

The Crown

Rose

"Ouch!" Daisy yanks her head forward, her silken strands slipping free from my hands like spun gold.

"Sorry." I shake my head. "I was distracted." We sit in our shared room for what feels like the last time, the small space taken up by the sleeping pallet we've always known. Daisy had hung her drawings on the wall since she only reached my knees. There are wax rubbed renditions of roses and daisies and violets. Sunflowers and fields of green. As she grew, she used ink, shrouding the beautiful flowers in grays and blacks, same as us.

"Why? What could possibly be on your mind?" Daisy teases, an easy smile on her full lips.

I smile back, not wanting her to see my hesitation, my shame. "I'm going to get you out, too."

Daisy's smile drops, just a little. "I don't want to be a burden, Rose. Don't push too hard. I'll be okay."

I nod in agreement. Of course she'll be okay; she'll survive as we always have. But she shouldn't merely survive.

She should bloom.

I gently coax Daisy's tresses into a crown, the braid wrapping across her brow. If anyone deserves to wear one, it's Daisy. She's not common like me.

I look down at my outstretched arms. Fresh bruises in the shape of Tristan's hands add a purple hue atop Pater's yellowing ones. I'll get better at reading him, at knowing him, at navigating his mater.

No one said it would be easy to wed, to break cycles. To change.

"What will you wear?" she asks.

"For the wedding?" When Daisy nods, I continue, "You'll help me choose, of course. I think that's part of why Tristan wants me in the domus by the end of this clipse. So, we can start planning the wedding."

My heart flutters. The wedding. *My* wedding.

My *freedom*.

"I think you look best in statement pieces." She nods, agreeing with her own assessment.

"Statement pieces?" I raise an eyebrow.

"Yes! Think sharp lines, unconventional colors. Like a rose colored gown!"

"Rose for Rose? Doesn't that seem a little on the nose?" I laugh. "Besides, I doubt a pink gown would compliment the wedding veil." It would be red for luck, of course.

"Oh! Red. Everything red. It's cheeky, like you." Daisy winks and I roll my eyes. I secure the braid with a pin and admire her perfectly polished hair. She is the cheekier of the two of us.

A door slams at the front of the small domus and I feel my smile drop. Daisy's shoulders tense and we both fall silent. I don't stop though, strategically pulling just a few golden strands loose at her temples and around her jawline. It frames her rounded cheeks. She's a vision.

"Get out here," Pater shouts from the kitchen. Venus. I'd hoped he'd fall into sleep, that he'd be in his cups for days with that *coemptio* gold lining his pockets.

Daisy worries at her lip as we hurry into the front room. It's spotless, as usual. The pillows on the worn green couch are perfect, the scratched wooden floor shines with its most recent coat of diluted orange oil.

Dropping our heads, we say in unison, "Yes, Pater?"

I know it's coming–it's why I always stand on his left side–but the backhand still makes me whimper. My shoulder knocks into Daisy, but we immediately right ourselves. His boots will find us if we fall.

"They're talking about you in the forum, girl." I can hear the expression on his face, the twisted sneer. "You're embarrassing this familia with that boy."

Of all the things he could have said, this was one I wasn't expecting. Tristan, embarrassing to them? He should be ashamed of us. Pater is a woodworker, when he can stay sober enough to keep his jobs. He has one right now, but it likely won't last any longer than the others.

Before I can determine whether a response or silence is safer, Pater shoves me. This time I do fall, but he doesn't kick me. Instead, a sharp slap reverberates through my bones, despite the fact it never lands on me. Daisy flinches, but keeps silent. Obedient.

"You're whoring around now that your sister is getting married?" he whispers, the volume so dangerous that the hair at the nape of my neck stands on end. No. Not her. He can't do this to Daisy.

"No, Pater, I would never," she pleads. I know her fear must be choking her, the constant tightness we live with squeezing her chest intolerably.

"Someone saw you," he screams. He goes to hit her again, but I can't stand it. I'm the one who can handle this, not Daisy. Not her.

"No, Pater" I cry. "I bet it was me and Tristan. People can't always tell us apart." That isn't completely true. We're both blonde, but my hair is a touch more dishwater than Daisy's sunshine. We both inherited Mater's curves, but my figure is more pear than Daisy's hourglass. Nevertheless, perhaps it will be enough to cast doubt. If nothing else, perhaps he'll be so upset at me talking back that he will spare Daisy.

He looks down at me as I dare a glance up. *Please*, I want to say. *Please, hurt me instead*. His dark eyes focus on me, his intoxication and rage evident in his flushed cheeks and ruddy neck. His calloused hand reaches down and grips my chin, rough. Always so rough.

"You're both whores. Just like her." He shoves my face away, the anger leaving him at his own mention of our mater. He pushes Daisy to the ground as he walks by and she makes a pained sound as she falls, but for once Pater doesn't revel in it. He keeps walking towards the back of the domus, enters his room, and slams the door.

I look to Daisy, my sister's braided crown half out from the force with which he struck her, her cheek red, her eyes watery.

I have to get her out. I have to make sure Pater can't keep ruining her crown.

The Same, but Not

Luella

"WILL YOU MARRY ME?" he asks. His warmth seeps into me and for once I don't have to fake the breathlessness that comes with his nearness. Did he drug the wine? I feel hot. Hyperventilating. Sweaty.

I can't answer, so I nod instead.

Cassius puts a palm against the side of my cheek, gentler than I expect. "And what shall I call my future wife?"

I should lie, but I don't. Instead, my traitorous lips form the word I've never let my praeda say.

"Luella."

"Luella," Cassius says, nodding as if it fits. His hand moves to brush a strand of wheat hair away from my face. "I'd like a longer engagement than your last."

"My last? I've never been engaged, Dominus." Not as Luella. If this is to work he can't know for certain. He can suspect, but he can't know. Doubt is its own web.

"My mistake." I can't tell if he's humoring me or questioning himself. "Where shall I send for your things?" He asks.

"My things?"

"You're to move in tonight." He snaps, which draws my awareness to the space, or lack thereof, between us. I step back.

A flora appears beside us, and I realize with a start that it's her. The flora from the night I killed Ledo, the one I let go.

"Flavia, show the future Domina to her rooms." Men can be Dominus. Senator. Praetor. Emporer. And since women are of value only in their relation to men, Cassius Evander has the right to call me Evandia. Or rather, future Evandia. But Domina? His master and respected mistress?

I furrow my brows as the flora bows and doesn't lead me out. Instead, she questions him. "Yes, Dominus. Do you still want the rose rooms?"

Cassius shifts his attention to me. His eyes travel from my eyes, down to my deep violet gown, across my hips, and down to my cloth clad toes. "For tonight. Your things?"

I tell him there's nothing I need tonight, and he doesn't argue. Instead, his eyes rove over me, sharp and assessing.

He steps close to me and I have to fight the urge to step back, to keep him away. He brushes the back of his knuckles against my cheek, just below my right eye, and I shiver. "Goodnight, Luella."

The rose room is, of course, hideous. Filled to the brim with colorful blooms, I can hardly see the rose themed tapestries, furniture, or bedding. It's larger than the rooms I was in while courting Ledo.

I bet it stinks in here. I wrinkle my nose and Flavia opens the door to the room and begins setting vases out in the hall.

"What are you doing?" I cry. I can't make a true scene over roses or anything else. Skylar never made a scene.

"It's clear you don't like the roses, future Domina." Her words carry no judgment, but her agency is startling in comparison to her submission around Ledo. Ledo ordered. Demanded. Ledo spoke for everyone in the room.

And now he's dead.

"I can't actually smell them," I admit, "but no, I don't particularly care for them. Don't trouble yourself moving them. Perhaps they will grow on me." They won't, but it appeases Flavia. She doesn't bring the vases from the hall back in but she does stop worrying over the ones in sight.

"Is there anything I can bring you?" she asks after she's turned down the linens, drawn the drapes, and ensured I have a lamp and nightgown at my bedside.

"Flavia," I begin. "Is the Dominus as he seems?" I feel foolish. I am foolish. "Is he kind?"

Flavia looks at me. Really looks at me, as if she hasn't had the chance to do so all night. Finally she says, "Are we ever exactly what we seem?"

He's invited me to *sapa,* which in and of itself is not worrisome. Yet given his homage to Ledo and Skylar last night, with the fountain... I pace the room. How long will I have to endure this time?

Perhaps I'll try something new and simply slit his throat in his sleep. I smile. Alas, I am a creature of habit and my hand drifts into my pockets, reassuringly full of the necessary potions. The smooth white pearl in the back of my mouth carries a similar comfort. I started altering my teeth when Mia first gave them to me, and now I have a small gap that allows it to sit perfectly hidden.

A knock sounds at the door and I stop my pacing. One breath in and out. Two, in and out.

Upon opening the door I instinctively step back. It's not Flavia, as I expected, nor is it any flora.

It's Cassius.

Stones. "Good afternoon, Dominus."

"Good afternoon, Luella." He's in a white shirt and dark trousers and boots, as if he's just come from the stables. I note the short sword at his hip and surmise he must have been training. His ginger hair is tousled, and his afternoon stubble does nothing to detract from his attractiveness. How irritating. If only our outward appearance matched what hid inside. Then perhaps he'd appear monstrous and rotting from the inside out.

Instead he's tall, ginger, and handsome.

He holds out an arm for me and guides me down the hall. Of course, our destination is the atrium in which Ledo conducted most of our training.

The fountain gurgles, mocking me, as Cassius brings me to a small lounging chair that wasn't here before. I work to keep my shoulders down, to appear hesitant and confused instead of revolted.

Cassius sits in a high backed chair next to me and I take a breath, readying myself for whatever type of 'training' Cassius intends in his efforts to replay my—well, Skylar's—courtship with Ledo. But there's no sign of the depravity that is sure to come. The room is bare except for some additional chaise lounges.

And that's all: No whips, or ropes. No Senators or Praetors.

There aren't even any floras. Of course, I can't ask if this is what I think it is. I can't compare this to my time here before.

"I'm pleased about our engagement, Luella," he finally offers.

"As am I, Dominus. It is an honor." I've said worse, simpered more.

"I tried to replicate the room," he says, watching.

"Replicate it to what?" I ask, furrowing my brows and leaning forward in my seat.

"Ah, of course you've never been here before," he says the words mockingly, teasingly. "This room was used recently as a bridal training ground for an esteemed Praetor."

"Blessings to the happy couple," I say.

"A blessing I'd rather not repeat," Cassius says.

"Oh?"

"I'm sure you'll hear all about it. Servants talk." He gives me a mean-ingful look. "As do floras." Flavia. Flavia told him about me that night.

Traitor.

But it doesn't matter. That face is gone.

I hum. "You mentioned a long engagement, Dominus?" I steer us towards useful information.

"Yes, I think that's appropriate. I hardly know you, after all." I don't know if I should laugh, but I'd like to. There is no point in knowing this face, this mask. It dies when you do, I want to tell him.

"I see," I say instead, even though I don't. Since when has something as trivial as knowing stopped a Divusian man from, well, anything? "How long?"

"As long as it takes," he says.

"To... get to know me?" I repeat.

"To get to know you," he confirms.

I nod. Perhaps Cassius is one of them. A self-proclaimed *good man*. One who tallies his charitable deeds to throw them in your face at a later time. The type who says, "I got to know her before I gave her a black eye; she really should have been grateful." I had very little experience with good men, but if you have to tell someone you are good, it probably isn't true.

"Flavia," he calls. The flora comes in, followed by a number of other floras. Perhaps it's all of the imperial floras, because I lose count after twenty-two. I stretch my legs out on the chaise, ignoring the lambs being led to slaughter. What cruelty will Cassius force me to watch? And why does he need so many?

The last flora enters, pushing forward a cart. On it there are the usual *sapa* refreshments. The *sapa*, of course, but also bread, cheese, and grapes. The women begin to serve themselves and after confirming that I don't want any, Cassius serves himself. He brings the plate to his chair, then goes back to the cart and helps serve the remaining floras.

Then he comes to sit next to me again. The floras find chaises, spots on the fountain, and on the floor. And they just... eat. And drink. And talk to one another.

It shouldn't startle me, but it does. It feels normal. Like if Mia and I were out with twenty other Mias and Luellas, chatting about our day and our plans.

Floras don't do that. They exist *for*. For pleasure. For pain. For those in power to do with as they wish.

But right now they don't exist for anything.

They just exist. And it's beautiful.

"Different from *sapa* with Ledo, I hope?"

"Dominus... are you sure you mean to marry me?" I ask. I let my voice wobble just a bit, allow my nerves to escape into each word.

His eyes narrow. "Why do you ask?"

"Last night you called me Skylar. Now you speak as if I know a man named Ledo? You mention this room as though I've been here before..." A patrician would know the name, or someone involved in politics, but not a plebeian. Not someone like I am pretending to be. "Perhaps you wish to marry Skylar?"

He shakes his head. "I know exactly who I wish to marry, Luella."

I cross my ankles. Uncross them. "As you say, Dominus." A deferment, a polite and politically correct response. Ladylike.

I wait. I wait for a retort, for the catch or the cruelty that he must be hiding in this charade.

It doesn't come.

Flames

Rose

The forum is still recovering from the festival, half the stalls closed and the other half wishing they were. The smell of wine and goats and sweat still hangs heavy in the air, and I hope a breeze builds off the Maero today.

"This is pointless," Daisy whines. She only does it to annoy me.

"Well, I still think Ceres' little brother would do it," I say to annoy her back.

"Rose," she groans.

"Well, at least you know he's kind." I'm being serious now. He is kind. A bit young, and likely to join the legions in a few years, but that could work in her favor anyways. "Ceres' familia is a good one, and you know they don't need the dowry." They weren't like Tristan's familia, could never pay *coemptio*, but they wouldn't starve with another mouth to feed, either. That's more than half the city could say.

"He's like my brother." She rolls her eyes. "And just because they don't need it doesn't mean they don't want it."

Wasn't that the truth of everything. "You'd get to live with Ceres," I add. Daisy looks away, her cheeks pinking.

"Not for long," Daisy says. "She'll marry soon, too."

"I'm sorry," I say. I mean it. Not for one thing, but for all of them. For Ceres, for Pater, for the way I'm leaving her. My guilt nearly swallows me for a moment, but there's no time for sentimental breakdowns. "There's still a chance I can convince Tristan to help with money, or perhaps if Tristan gives me some jewels I could give you one to sell. That might be enough." His mater was draped in them, after all.

Daisy looks down at the ground, her slippered foot tracing a cobblestone. "Let's just wait awhile. As a last resort, after your wedding... if there's still nothing. Then we can ask." I know she doesn't want to look at me, can feel the fear and embarrassment rolling off of her.

"I'm sorry, Daize."

"I just... wish it wasn't like this."

"Like what?"

"I want to choose. I want to decide if I will join the legions, or obtain an apprenticeship, or work the fields..."

I'm already shaking my head. "Daisy..."

"I know, we can't. Because we're not men. That's my point, Rose. Why do they get to choose?"

"I think that maybe they are beholden to their circumstances in a similar way, soror. Augustus wants to be a farmer, but his pater is making him join the legions. Tristan wants to join the legions and instead he's destined for the forum."

"At least they have more than one option," she sighs, sitting on the bottom step of the forum. "What if I don't want to marry?"

I stare down at my sister, wondering how long she's thought about this. "You know that's not an option."

"What are our options? A virgin until we marry, or a whore if we don't," she says, the words sharp and bitter.

"Daisy Octavius!" I should scold her for her language, for her views, for something. But I can't see past the truth of her words, so I settle for the weight of her name. It lands on her like a yoke, her shoulders slumping.

"I'm sorry, Rose," she says. "I'm just really going to miss you."

A clearing throat has us both turning.

My mouth falls open in surprise. "Augustus."

He smiles. "Good day, good ladies." The man in front of the Sabines flashes before my eyes. What if Augustus had saved me? What if he knew what I said?

"What brings you to the forum?" I ask, shaking those thoughts away.

"Ah, I just left the Sabines." He meets my eyes brazenly.

"So that is to your... tastes then?" I don't know why I ask, except I have a habit of saying stupid, unladylike, inappropriate things in front of him. Daisy and I are both feeling defiant today, it seems.

His mouth falls open in silent horror. "What? No," he splutters. "No," he says again, more firmly. "I was serving them a notice of inspection."

"A notice of inspection?"

"To check for citizens of Divus. They're not allowed to hold citizens against their will. And when Tristan told me what happened..."

"What about the others?" Daisy jumps in, catching on to the conversation.

"The others?"

Daisy stands taller, almost looking down her nose at him, if that's possible from a girl half his height. "The non-citizens. Do you think they chose to be there? It's against their will, too." She's right. If they're from a conquered nation, they're not any more deserving of such a fate.

Augustus, Venus bless him, looks aghast. Like he never considered this. "Oh," he says.

Daisy tilts her head as a sort of triumphant look spreads across her face. "So, maybe your pater can work on that next?"

He just nods, a glazed look in his cerulean eyes. "I'll speak to him."

"Good," Daisy says. "Now, I'm going to talk to Ceres." She points a finger at me menacingly. "And you're going to stop trying to sell me like a goat for at least a few minutes."

She's gone in a flash and Augustus looks to me. "She's... spirited."

I sigh. "She is becoming more and more. She certainly doesn't get it from me."

He smiles. "I don't know about that. Besides, what's this talk of you selling her like a goat?"

A small laugh escapes me, and Augustus' eyes drop to my mouth, my lips. Heat rises in my chest and I look away before answering, the laugh dying in my throat. "I'm not trying to sell her, I just worry about her now that I'm marrying. I don't want her alone in our domus. I'm trying to find her a suitable husband."

"Your pater?" He asks, somehow knowing.

"Did Tristan tell you?" I don't know why I'm surprised. They're brothers, after all.

Augustus shakes his head, holding out his arm for me to take. My brow furrows. If not Tristan, then who?

I let my hand rest on him, the heat of his skin seeping into me. We start to walk around the forum, the way many couples do, enjoying the weather together. "No. A pater who threatens to sell his daughter to the Sabines isn't too hard to figure out," he says.

My throat clogs up, so I don't say anything, and after a few rounds around the forum, Augustus speaks again. "I'll see if I can find her any matches. I have friends who won't need a dowry. I'm sure I can find one for her, if you'd like. Someone not like your pater."

I stop in my tracks. "You'd do that?"

"Of course." He puts a hand over mine on his arm. "Anything you need, Rose. You say the word, and I'll make it happen."

The heat from our joined hands, from the way his words sink into me, from the look in his eyes all threaten to set me aflame. My mouth opens, then closes. I can't find the right words to express my gratitude, or my fear.

Because I can't feel this, not for him.

Vidua

Luella

I am invited to *sapa* again, and again Cassius arrives to take me to the same room. Instead of the floras from the day before, a table sits near the fountain.

Ledo's table.

My stomach clenches, then plummets when I see what sits atop it.

The flagrum glitters in the afternoon suns, the black gleaming with a recent oiling. This moment is a jarring reminder that no matter how shiny Cassius tries to be, I know exactly what he is and why I am here.

I have a role to play: Appear unthreatening. Get him alone.

Kill him.

Cassius follows my gaze and nods. "Yes, that's his." But I've done this longer than him.

"It's whose, Dominus?"

"Ledo's." His eyes are drinking in my face, reading my expressions. The same expressions I've spent years mastering.

He spent yesterday attempting to lower my guard and since that didn't work, he's trying a new tactic.

Fear.

But fear is a friend I've known my whole life. Instead of my lower eyelids tensing or my eyebrows raising, I channel surprise. A slight widening of my eyes, a tilt in my head.

Cassius brings me to the chaise so I have a perfect view of the table, the fountain, and the entire room. I'm close enough to make out the details on Bacchus' statue, the masks and bulls etched on his wine carafe reminding me of the deception and rutting he symbolizes.

I meet Cassius' eyes but refuse to speak. My skin pebbles in the cool air. Tomorrow is clipse, so Remus is covering much of Romulus, making midafternoon feel more like dusk.

"Luella," Cassius says once I'm seated. "I'd like us to trust each other."

I look from him to the flagrum and back again.

I have been whipped before. Struck. Chained. Everything Ledo did to his floras has been done to me.

Every.

Single.

Thing.

"I'd like that, too, Dominus," I say, swallowing.

"I don't think you trust me," Cassius says.

And you think whipping me will help? "Why do you say that?"

"Because you think I'm like him." He holds up a hand when I open my mouth to ask who. "And that's my fault. I didn't know how else to find you."

I'm trying to decide how to respond when he begins removing his white tunic. The planes of his stomach remind me that he's a general. A fighter. His muscles ripple as he tosses the tunic to the floor and picks up the whip, letting it dangle between his fingers. My eyes cling to it, trying to decipher its path and its pain before it ever touches my skin.

"Flavia?" Cassius calls out. Flavia enters not in her flora wrap, but in a shift of dark cotton, as if she were lounging in her room. Dressed for comfort instead of pleasure. "Bring them in."

She steps out into the hall and returns with about ten floras. The majority are varying shades of blonde, but there is one with black hair and dark skin and another who is brunette with hazel eyes and freckled skin. They line up near the fountain and Cassius approaches. Flavia is in front.

"You've all helped me these past clipses. Sometimes that involved injuries I wished you did not have to endure." He turns to look at me. "You volunteered and for that I thank you. I think it worked."

It's a trap. My mind screams at me to run. My friend, fear, says, run.

Run, Luella!

I won't, though. I let the blood pound in my ears and I listen to the voice telling me to run, and then I refuse to do as I'm told.

I do many things I hate. And I do many things that are dangerous. I furrow my brows as though confused and cock my head at Cassius. I let my eyes travel down the line of floras and realize these must be the women that Mia treated. The ones who said Cassius beat them. "They look like you," she had said.

Most of them do.

The ones he just admitted to beating. As volunteers?

"I know I can't undo what I did, but I do offer myself as compensation." It feels ceremonial. As if he's practiced. Does he think they'll ask to pleasure him after he beat them? I suppose they will if he's forced them too. I would be surprised at the audacity if anything surprised me anymore.

Cassius hands the flagrum to Flavia and drops to his knees in front of her, facing me. His bare back is towards her and she holds the whip in her fist.

Before my mind can process what he intends, Flavia speaks. "I forgive you, Dominus." She hands the flagrum to the next woman in line and leaves the room.

The next woman, the one with black hair, nods down at him. "It was an honor, Dominus."

The next woman was clearly chosen to model Skylar, with blonde hair that's almost white and striking blue eyes. "I hope it works," she says.

The whip passes down the line, each flora saying something to Cassius that is equally cryptic.

"I forgive you."

"It was an honor."

"It will be worth it."

Finally, the last woman holds it. Her hair is golden, her skin umber. She looks freshly beaten. A large black eye and swollen lip look from me to Cassius and back to me. I know the life cycle of a black eye all too well and hers happened after I came to the ball.

"I'd give my life for Tisiphone. I'll volunteer until I have nothing left to give." She drops the whip beside him. "Thank you, Dominus." She looks at me as she leaves. "Thank you, *vidua*."

Thank you, Widow.

Cassius is watching me, his back bare but unmarred. Not a single flora whipped him. Did he plan this? Were they told what to say?

I swallow, hard. Who am I to be in this moment? I wrack my mind for the move that will put Cassius on guard, instead of me.

"And will you prostrate yourself before me, as well, Dominus?" I move towards him until he's looking up at me from the floor and the bottom of my skirts whisper against his knees.

I remember that first night, when I felt his words were measured. I measure myself now, calculating each syllable before I speak.

"Perhaps," he says. He doesn't move, but he doesn't hand me the flagrum either. "Perhaps I would do whatever you asked of me. Perhaps I want the same things you want."

Impossible. "Perhaps," I say. "Or perhaps you don't know what I want."

"You could tell me," Cassius leans forward and for a moment I think he might wrap his arms around my waist, around my knees. A man drowning in the Maero, reaching for something solid to save him.

Of course, he does not. And he sways back again. "Are you drunk?" So much for measured words.

"I thought they were going to whip me," he protests. "Of course I'm a bit drunk."

"Then why did you hand them the whip?" I ask.

"Because I don't know how else to show you... Because I don't think you know what I want, either."

"You could tell me," I repeat to him.

For once, I do want to know. Never before have I struggled to understand what my mark wanted from me. It is not difficult to guess the desires of mortals. We want pleasure, comfort, safety, power, or any combination of those. I always fit in one of those spaces, molding into the cracks of desire. Always. But right now I don't see where I fit, and not knowing that is very, very dangerous.

"You don't like roses," he says. Says, not asks.

"I don't care for them particularly," I say.

"I don't like that gods-forsaken fountain," Cassius says.

I almost laugh. "I hate the fountain." His eyes widen, like I've con-firmed it, but this is measured, too. Surely a woman who hates roses could also hate a fountain. A woman who watched women brutalized next to one, though? She would loathe it.

Another doubt, another seed. Yet I recognize another master, because his act has planted some in me, as well.

Drunk

Luella

Cassius tugs his white shirt down over his muscled chest and I'm only disappointed because for once I was not the object of lust in the room. That's the only reason. Besides, all good things must come to an end.

The whip still sits beside him. The fountain bubbles in the center of the room. The Dominus doesn't rise, and I don't step away.

I wonder how long we can stay this way, each taking the other's measure.

Then Cassius sways again and a very undignified hiccup escapes him.

"Stones," he murmurs.

"Dominus, you are very drunk."

He lets out a sigh and scrubs his hand across his facial stubble as he rocks back on his heels. He teeters, then ends up on his bottom, legs sprawled out in front of him and his powerfully built arms reflexively reaching back to catch him.

"Domina, I am very drunk," he says.

No one else is here. I could easily tip a vial of poison into his mouth and be done with everything right now. If I take advantage of my knowledge of the Domus Aurea, I can escape as easily as I had before, posing as a servant. The thought makes me angry. If he suspects me as Skylar, why does he have so little self-preservation? He can't even keep his wits around a known murderer.

I should kill him.

"Come," I say. I put out my hand and he quirks a brow. After a moment he acquiesces, grabbing my wrist and using me as leverage to stand.

"You're thinking about how to kill me." He sounds resigned.

Yes. "Why would I be thinking about that?"

"Because you still don't understand." His face is so open that I want to bite. I want to ask what I don't understand. I want to ask about the women and why I am here and why he would risk not being in control with anyone, especially women he hurt.

Especially with me.

"I certainly don't," I confess.

"I had to hurt them, for you," he says. I flinch. "No, no. No. I mean. Just..." he searches my eyes and lets loose another sigh. "Can you just wait to kill me? Just a little longer. You'll see." He nods. "You'll see."

I don't answer as he wraps his arm over my shoulder and uses me as a crutch towards what I assume are his rooms.

"Right around this corner, almost there and you can tie me to the bed if you want." He giggles as if this is an inside joke between us. It is. Of course, I pretend not to know it.

When we turn the corner, I stop in my tracks. Cassius falls against me, looking up.

"Stones," he says. Stones, indeed.

"Brother!" The Emperor says. He's resplendent in his white robes with golden trim. His blonde hair is highlighted with a small golden leaf crown. The Emperor of Divus is known for two things. One, his rakish good looks, which the Dominus shares. Two, his absolute and unyielding cruelty. On his first war campaign, the Emperor was nearly beaten multiple times. At one point the enemy said they would surrender when the boy king bent over for them. When the Emperor final-ly won, he personally reinstated the ancient practice of *irrumatio*, breaking out the teeth of every soldier and messenger who had called him the boy king so as to... assault the orifice, which he purportedly did with gusto for days, fine with blood and open wounds.

My stomach turns at the sight of him and his Praetorians, all six of them lining the hall on either side. The sweet *sapa* burns the back of my throat, threatening to coat the floor in front of us.

"Imperatus," I murmur, shoving Cassius off of me so that I may bow at the waist. It would not do well to draw attention to myself here, in this form.

"Ah. The *venefica*," he says. The witch. "You've cast a spell on my brother. The man who never had interest in man nor woman in all the years I've known him. Suddenly betrothed."

He looks me up and down as if he wonders what could be so special about me. I see it when the wondering shifts to something else, a decision.

"The floras bore me," Cassius says. Any trace of drunkenness has vanished, and he's standing tall. Controlled. "I decided to try something new." He shrugs, as if it's no matter at all.

"When you grow bored of her, let me know," the Emperor says. I keep my eyes down as is expected of me.

Cassius nods, the idea of sharing his wife as benign as sharing a meal. Both things to be devoured, nothing left but bones. "Perhaps after the wedding night you can try her out." I should have killed him next to that gods-forsaken fountain, but he definitely won't be making it past the wedding night. "Come," Cassius says, hand on my arm. "Good day, Imperatus."

As we move to pass the Emperor, he grabs my wrist, stopping Cassius and me with the movement. I look up shyly, not hiding my intimidation. His interest in Luella, in me, will ruin everything. "Yes, you'd make a fine addition," he hums his approval, his hand tightening painfully around my wrist until I feel bones crack. I whimper and on the other side Cassius tightens his hand, too.

It's only pain. But the Emperor must like my reaction because he squeezes harder, the small squares in my wrist grating against each other, fracturing my breath until I'm crying out, trying to pull away. He reaches his other hand forward to grab my forearm and I know he's going to break my arm. I know it before he does.

Then Cassius yanks me back hard, and a surprised grunt leaves me. "Brother, leave me something for the wedding night," Cassius says and a forced chuckle leaves him.

The Emperor smiles. "Of course, little brother. She just screams so pretty." The blood drains from my face. I can't fake the trembling that overtakes me then. Those words.

She just screams so pretty.

I will do it. I will vomit all over the floor in front of them and then I will smash this pearl between my teeth and spit on them both and watch as their bodies decay.

Cassius yanks on me again, harder this time, his grip nearly making me cry out again except I refuse to let the Emperor hear anything but silence from me, now. "So pretty," Cassius agrees, the words a growl as he tugs me down the hall. I spare a glance back at the Emperor as he watches us leave, and my wrist throbs when I meet his eyes. I know what will happen even if they don't, yet.

These brothers will rip me apart.

Kiss or Kill

Luella

It hurts. Stones, it hurts. Sweat beads between my shoulder blades and my breath comes in staccato as Cassius continues to tug me down the hall, and into his rooms.

It's... green. The jewel green chamber reminds me of the temple of Ceres, where the jade hewn floors of polished chrysoprase reflect the sky above through the numerous arches and skylights.

The floor is the same here, as are the skylights. The walls are limestone but each tapestry is a scene from nature. An ancient temple covered in ivy. Baths filled with lily pads instead of people. The coliseum seats cracked and broken, and the pit filled with wildflowers.

His room is the opposite of the republic. It's nature and nurture. It's freedom and joy.

It's treasonous, and I might love it if I wasn't ready to cut my own wrist off for the pain. That probably wouldn't help, though.

I lean against the nearest wall. I have a vial for this, a vial that is half opium and half stimulant. It masks the pain and gives a burst of energy, but I won't take it yet.

"Stones, Luella." Cassius guides me to a plush bench at the foot of his large canopy bed. Gauzy white curtains hang around the dark green linens. I sit, cradling my left wrist with my right. It's swelling already, the tiny bones inside screaming in protest as the fluid inside begins to press on the injury.

He's on his knees in front of me for the second time today as he cradles my wrist gently in his hands. "Shh," he murmurs when I try to remove it from his grasp. "Just let me look." The confrontation with his brother has sobered him and he moves smoothly, earlier signs of swaying gone.

I try not to hold my breath, blowing out softly as he twists my whole arm to look, not letting my wrist shift. Hot and sharp, the pain explodes when he underestimates where his elbow is and bumps it into my shoulder, jostling my wrist in his hand. I bite down on my lip to stifle the cry that begs to be released.

She just screams so pretty.

Maybe I will rethink my stance on torture. Maybe I'd like to see the Emperor scream so pretty.

"I'm so sorry," Cassius says. "It's definitely broken. I'll summon a healer."

I shake my head, pain clouding my ability to mask myself. "I want to see my own healer." I trust no one but Mia. Healers, the ones blessed by Aesculapius, feel inside of you. Mia says I feel different. She's never said if that's because of Janus or because I make my own bodies, or because of something else.

I don't want to find out.

"Luella, you're in pain," Cassius argues.

"This is the least of my pains," I say, eyeing him.

He tosses his hands up. "Then I'm coming with you."

Stones. That's not what I want. "Please, Dominus. I am fine. You have more important things to do."

"What could be more important than this?"

Beating floras. Fighting with your brother. Drinking *sapa* and fucking and playing mind games.

"I see a plebeian," I say instead.

"So?"

"Is that really a place for the Dominus?"

"Is it where you're going?"

I pause. "Well, yes."

"Then it's a place for me," Cassius says and shrugs as if the second most powerful man in the republic often follows women around. I narrow my eyes.

"Why?" If he thinks he will catch me as Skylar or that Mia will implicate me, he couldn't be more wrong. Any lady would think it strange for her betrothed to attend her personally. Send for someone, yes. Send her to someone, yes. Scoop her into his arms to carry him herself? No.

"Cassius, careful!" I screech as he does just that, wrapping arms around me to lift me off the bench. I brace my wrist against my chest, shielding it from him.

"It'll be faster this way. You look like you'll faint any moment." He's not wrong. I feel pallid and ill and weak. It's just a bit of pain but it's pain I hadn't prepared for.

She just screams so pretty.

I shake my head once, twice. I'm so close and the pressure is getting to me. Cassius has succeeded in confusing me, yes, but he won't ruin my plan. He won't.

I won't let him.

"Hurry, boy," Cassius says impatiently when Taln asks why we are here. I glare at him.

"Please," I stress the word. "Tell healer Mia that Luella and the Dominus are here to see her."

Taln pauses, just for a moment, at the name. Cassius is watching him, of course, and notices it. Stones, gods, and offerings, this man is too observant for his own good.

Thank Janus Taln doesn't know this face nor does he know my abilities, and he leaves to bring Mia.

When she enters she knows her role well.

"Good day, Luella," she greets. "I hear you have injured your wrist. Did you fall?" The nice way women tell each other what's been done to us. How many falls has Mia treated over the years, without a single woman having slipped?

I nod but Cassius interrupts, not understanding the language of women. "She didn't fall." I shake my head at him and he looks between us. "You didn't fall, Luella. It's okay to tell her."

If I was a younger woman, a more naive one, I might find this charming. If I wasn't so broken, I might find his honesty refreshing.

I am none of those things, so instead I find him stupid. "Women *fall* all the time, Dominus," I say each word slowly. Urging him to understand. "Floras. Wives. We can be quite clumsy."

Cassius narrows his eyes and understanding must dawn on the entitled fool because he doesn't argue and instead asks, "Can you heal her?"

"Of course, I've healed much worse," Mia says.

Cassius' gaze darkens further and he asks, "On her?"

I'd like to roll my eyes. I'd also like to kiss him. What? That can't be right. The pain is making me delirious and rational thought is slipping between the sieves of my mind. I need Mia to heal me and then I need to sleep. I need to stop thinking about Cassius and it would be much easier if he'd stop being kind.

It would be much easier if I'd killed him already.

Mia doesn't answer, instead she lays my wrist in her lap, arranging my arm so that all is in proper alignment. She makes a noncommittal noise in the back of her throat.

Nice or not, Cassius isn't used to being ignored. "Have you healed much worse on her, healer?"

"I cannot disclose information about the patients I treat, Dominus. You know that," she says instead. He does. It's not an explicit rule, but it is an oath the healers swear to Apollo or his son, Aesculapius.

If he's put out, I don't know or care. Mia clasps one of her hands gently around my forearm and asks, "May I heal you, Luella?" She's asking if she can look for everything, everywhere, and I dip my chin. I wouldn't hide anything from her.

The familiar feeling of sinking into a warm bath envelops me and the tightness in my shoulders loosens just a bit as the pain begins to ebb away. She's incredible.

"Thank you," I murmur.

Mia pats my hand. "Always."

Cassius doesn't speak, watching the way Mia holds my hands, the familiarity with which our skin brushes. His face is unreadable, still as stone, and my stomach sinks.

He sees too much.

Neither of us speaks on the walk back. The fog of pain has receded and my mind feels sharp again. I'm irritated at Cassius and whatever game he's playing, but I'm more irritated at myself for starting to consider that maybe he was right. Maybe I don't know what he wants.

He doesn't return me to my rooms. Instead he steers me towards his own. I keep my steps sure, but I check the pearl between my teeth, rolling my tongue over the smooth sphere. I reach into my pocket and feel the unique shape of each vial, counting and recounting the small thumbnail sized life savers. Well, subjectively speaking.

Silas and Ledo and dozens of others might call them something else.

I twist my wrist, testing its movement, making sure it feels functional. I listen for the sounds of anyone else in the hall, and I look at Cassius out of the corner of my eye. He's slumped, shoulders rounded. His copper hair is disheveled, and he runs his hands through it for what is clearly not the first time.

He stops at the door just before his. "I'll have your things moved in the morning, but you'll stay here now."

I clasp my hands behind my back and debate for only a moment before I decide that if I have said I am Luella, and Luella is who Cassius says he wants to marry, then I will show him her. Well, pieces of her. The pieces he saw when I was Skylar and the pieces he seems to be gravitating to. The jagged ones.

"Why?" I don't hide the challenge in my voice.

"Why? Because my brother just broke your wrist," Cassius says. He reaches forward and tugs my arms, easing the once broken one forward to look at it again, scrutinizing it. It's nearly dark now and the sconces of the hall cast flickering light over us, the firelight dancing across his mussed hair and his golden face. "I should have known," he whispers.

"Known what?" I ask.

He looks up from my wrist, the gold in his eyes brighter in the firelight. "That he would notice you. That I couldn't keep you safe." He shakes his head and nothing in his expression matches the confidence I've seen so far, or the coldness in front of the Emperor. "This was a mistake."

"You... you want to call off our engagement?" My wrist falls from his hands as I take a step back.

"No, I just..." he trails off, because he doesn't know what he wants. I can see it, the struggle playing across his face. "I want us to work together. To trust each other."

I laugh. A cold, broken sound. A sound the real me would make. "Trust would kill me," I say, shaking the laugh away. It's not an admission. It's a universal truth. A plebeian and a Dominus. A man and a woman. A killer and praeda.

"I'm trusting you," he says. "And I keep wondering if it will kill me."

He steps forward, until my back is against the wall, my chin tilted up to him as he looks down at me with something I can't believe. It's want and desire, but it's care and curiosity, too. It's lust but it's reverence.

The warmth of his body seeps into me and our breath mingles, so close I could touch him.

I just can't decide what I would do with that touch, what I want.

Kiss or kill?

THE LOSER

LUELLA

I slip into my new room before I can do something I might regret. My skin is too tight, my bones not right. Everything about this body feels poorly designed, ill-fitting. Reaching into my pocket I grab a red stone and begin to shift, trying to find something that doesn't fit so wrong. Higher cheekbones, no rounder. A prominent nose, a sharp one, a hooked one, a dainty one. Narrow eyes. Wide. Full lips. Thin. Flared hips and straight, curves and bones, and rags and jagged edges.

Until I hold the last stone, more golden than yellow. Tears soak my cheeks and I kneel on the floor, folding over my chance to be honest with myself.

I know the shape my body is yearning for now, but I can't be her.

I won't.

I sob over my last stone, and when it drains and reverts to black basanite I stay there, in a liar's face, until morning comes.

Morning dawns to illuminate my quarters, which are awash in light greens and sunshine yellows: the sunslit version of Cassius'. Potted ferns nestle in the corners and skylights illuminate tapestries similar to his naturescapes, a well overflowing with vines, a temple flooded to the deities' eyes. A second door surely connects to his neighboring room.

And I'm lying in the middle of it all, surrounded by black basanite. All of my stones drained, leaving me powerless and one step from my enemy's door.

I ache from sleeping on the floor, from shifting my body relentlessly. From sobbing and feeling and dying.

From living.

There is an adjoined bath and the cold water jolts me awake. I avoid the gaze in my mirror, this version of Luella that I had created for Cassius. With wheat blonde hair and greenish blue eyes, it's almost there. Almost her.

I'm almost me.

I planned to visit Mia today, and I will, but now I will have to visit Janus as well.

I don the only thing in the wardrobe, a pale pink dress that flows to the floor. It reminds me of something, although I can't say what it is exactly. Perhaps one of my praeda had given me a similar gown in what Mia calls the hits and gifts cycle. Healers have a morbid sense of humor.

I don't intend to truly sneak out, but I also don't want to draw attention to myself. I press my ear against the door that leads to the hall. It's quiet.

I try the handle and pause, then try again.

It's locked.

Some moments feel as though they balance on a precipice. The decision you make could either slide you into victory or topple you into an abyss. I walk to the door that leads to Cassius' room and slowly try the handle. It turns.

I take a deep breath, then another. I knock softly but there's no response. Perhaps I will be lucky and find Cassius is already out.

I am, of course, not lucky. He is sitting at a small table to the side of the bed, a soft beam from the skylight casting him in profile. His strong jaw and nose are regal, proud. A game board sits in front of him full of dark green and white Latrones pieces.

"Do you have company, Dominus?" I ask quietly, nodding towards the two person game obviously in progress.

"Luella." Cassius smiles, the pensive expression on his face shattering with the flash of his teeth. "No, but I'd be happy to start a new game with you." I must look confused, as he offers an explanation. "Flavia and some of the other maidservants for this wing, will move a piece when they are here. Of course I play with friends a faster game, but this one I like to leave going at all times. Long strategy," he explains. Flavia must be his favored flora. A man often keeps one after marriage; it's not unusual. It's also not unusual for men to introduce me to them, to the new normal, in casual terms like this. It's less brutal than Ledo's method, and for that I am grateful. Besides, I'm not jealous.

Cassius will be dead soon. Well, not imminently considering his wish for a long engagement. But too soon for me to consider whether or not I care about Flavia being his favored. Because I don't.

"I haven't played Latrones," I lie.

"Sit, I'm sure you have a mind for strategy," Cassius says. Ah, so the game is back on.

"Yes, Dominus," I say as I sit. He resets the board game. "Will Flavia be upset that I've ended her game?" I should not ask.

Cassius smiles. "Why would she?"

I shrug. "Perhaps she will feel replaced."

"Ah," he says, lining up the pawns in two rows on each side of the board. "You believe there is more than a game between us?" His pieces are white carved birds, except for the dux, which is a white tree. Mine are dark green lily pads and the dux is a large lotus bloom. It's the most beautiful set I've seen. Many plebeians play with circle stones, and the dux a colored one or a small wood carving.

"I wouldn't question you, Dominus." If he wants to play strategy then let us play strategy.

"I think you would. In fact, I'd like you to. I meant what I said yesterday."

"If you want to gain my trust, perhaps you could start by not locking me in my room." I look up from the board, moving my first piece forward.

"If I hadn't you wouldn't be in mine right now," Cassius says, smirking. I don't hide my glare and he laughs. "I was worried about my brother. There's a key in your nightstand, Luella."

His eyes are steady, no flicker to the left or right, no crease in his brows. Open. My shoulders tighten and I stand, turn, and march into the other room. I move to the nightstand and as I rip it open, something clangs inside.

There, in the middle of the almost empty drawer, is a small iron key. I glare towards Cassius' room, even though he can't see me. Tearing the key from its place I stomp towards my door.

It works.

I return to the table with the key in my pocket but I don't meet Cassius' eyes. He's moved one of his pawns so I move mine. He touches a pawn but doesn't make his next play, and I finally look up. Once he's sure he has my attention he says, "And I didn't lock the door between our rooms, even though..." He must think better of that sentiment because he clears his throat. "Even though you haven't given me any reason to trust you."

"I haven't given you any reason not to trust me," I retort.

"That is still up for debate," Cassius says, finally moving the pawn he's been holding. It captures one of mine and I frown at the move. It's allowed, but it's not common.

"Fine. If you trust me, I'd like to go into the city today." I narrow my eyes at him. "Alone."

"I have concerns about that," Cassius says, "but of course, I won't stop you."

"What concerns?"

"That my brother will..." he doesn't finish this thought, either. I clear my throat when he doesn't add anything after a moment.

"I know his type." I leave the *and yours* unspoken. "I'll be careful."

"Am I allowed to ask where you are going?" Cassius says.

"I need to visit temple." I move a new pawn forward, making the same move he did previously, and it allows me to take one of his.

"A pious woman, then?" He contemplates the board. He's a worthy opponent, which doesn't surprise me. "Do you have much to atone for?" His tone is teasing, joking. He's trying to catch me with honey, and for a moment it almost works. My lips quirk, but I refuse to smile.

"Simply asking the gods to bless our union," I say.

Cassius finally makes a move, opening a path for me to take his dux without realizing it. "Perhaps you should visit Fides," he says. The goddess of trust and good faith.

I roll my eyes and take his dux. "That's not necessarily who I had in mind," I smile at the victory and he huffs. I've shown I'm not a novice at Latrones after all, but Agrippa hadn't taught me for nothing.

"Just stay away from Mars, please?" He shakes his head as he clears the board. "I don't want to go to war with you."

"Because you'll lose?" I tease.

But Cassius just nods. "Because I'll lose."

Yours

Rose

Tristan arrives, unannounced, to take me to dinner. He's quiet as we walk to his familia's domus, the suns reflecting off the surface of the Maero and the scent of orange blossoms and myrtle masking the wet smell of the river.

"Did you have a pleasant day?" he asks, guiding me away from the yellowish, rushing water of the Maero.

"I did." I lean into him. Romulus is starting to dip in the sky and our dual shadows overlap at the ends. "How was yours?"

"Fine," he says. "It was fine."

I try to glean a few more words from him, but he answers me in only a handful of staccato sentences.

He doesn't take me inside, instead leading me behind the domus to the gardens. The orange trees and grape vines sway in the light breeze, and I can't help a small shiver that moves through me. There is a small table set for two, with large clear glasses and an assortment of bread, cheese, and grapes. Servants line the walkway, holding lanterns and pitchers and trays.

"Tristan, this is beautiful." I turn to him, but he doesn't smile, his face as still as the marble of Mars.

"Sit," he says, pulling out my chair.

I take my seat, the hair at the back of my neck prickling. The silent servants glide in as soon as Tristan sits and pour us both a generous glass of *sapa*. Tristan waves them away, dismissal etched in each muscle.

He drains his *sapa*, then sits back, crossing his arms.

Still, he doesn't speak. "Tristan, is something the matter?" I ask. Tension rises in me, intensifying with each breath.

"Where were you today?" he asks, leaning forward. I finally see what I didn't before. He's not quiet; he's angry. His jaw is set, eyes wide.

"I went to the forum with my sister," I say. I don't know what I've done wrong, what's upset him.

"That's interesting, because it looked like you went to the forum with my brother," he says. His voice is level, calm, but I know better.

"We ran into him there, that's all."

"It looked like more than a run in."

He followed me. Something hot and irritated tries to rise, but I shove it back down. Stay sweet, I remind myself. "I was talking to him about Daisy," I say, thinking if he knows Augustus wasn't interested in knowing me, it would help.

I'm wrong. Tristan stands, and he quivers with it, his rage. He takes his empty glass, and smashes it against the cobblestones, glass scattering in tiny silver shards. "I told you I was taking care of it," he screams, then tosses mine less vigorously. The shards glint with red *sapa* I hadn't had an opportunity to drink, a dark puddle sinking into the cobblestones. He looms over me, tense and angry.

I don't bother correcting him, although he'd said nothing of the sort. I don't move my feet away from the glass and I certainly don't cry. Instead, I do what I know works best.

"I'm sorry, Tristan. He overheard us talking." Tristan heaves a breath, looking down at the glass. I reach my hand out to his. "I would never ask him for help rather than you." I wrap my fingers around his, tugging him closer. The movement masks my trembling.

"I'm yours," I remind him. His head snaps up at that, eyes searching mine. I pull him even closer.

"I need to know where you are. Who you're with. I need to keep you safe."

I nod. "You're right. I thought I'd be safe with him since he's your brother."

He shakes his head. "No, you're not. I told you, he's not a good man."

He is though. Between trying to close the Sabines and looking out for Daisy, he is. But Tristan is a good man, too. He saved me. And if he wants me to stay away from Augustus, then I will. It's probably better anyways, considering the traitorous heat that rose in me this afternoon.

"I'll stay away from him," I promise us both.

Tristan comes closer, resting a hand on either side of my chair. He leans down, capturing me with his lips. "Say it again," he pleads.

"I'm yours." I don't need to ask what he meant.

"Again," he says into my mouth, hands tangling into my hair. He tips my head back, deepening his kiss.

"I'm yours."

He swallows the words, again and again, bruising my lips with his kisses. I'm back in my domus, in the dark on my pallet with Daisy, before I realize he never once said it back.

Confirm

Luella

I GASP AS THE ice cold water hits my stomach, refusing to lower any further. "You're supposed to keep a low profile," Mia hisses as she looks me over. I already visited Janus and used a stone when I entered the Baths so that I came out of the changing room dark haired and freckled. I don't want Mia to be seen with Cassius' Luella again.

"I didn't exactly seek him out and say 'please break my wrist, oh powerful Imperator! Look how your brother has me and you don't. Doesn't that annoy you?'" I snap, lowering myself another inch. "Stones, can't we talk in the tepidarium or the sauna next time?"

Mia huffs, ignoring my request. "Might as well have. Don't think I didn't notice the face you chose." I ignore the jab and she goes on. "Well, he's livid, Lue."

"What do you mean?"

"He did it again," Mia says.

My heart pounds in my ears and the words lodge in my throat. I don't want to ask. "Cassius? What did he do?"

"No, the Emperor," she says softly. "They were young. Sisters."

I'm shaking my head. "Mia, please." I can't hear the details. I know them. I know them like the back of my hand. Like my true face. Like my soul.

"I know, Lue. Please be careful, but be quick, too."

I swallow the lump in my throat. "What if Cassius is telling the truth? What if he didn't hurt those women?"

"Then why hasn't he arrested you?" The question I keep asking myself.

"He says he wants me to trust him," I say. Mia's up to her neck in the cold water, her hair piled on top of her head.

"Do you?" she asks.

I don't answer, because I don't know.

"I did think it was odd that their injuries didn't match. They weren't as bad as what they said he did." Mia shrugs. "It's entirely possible. And I haven't seen any new girls since you went to the ball." She leaves the 'not from him' unsaid. "There's something else, too."

"Gods. Do you have any good news?" I feel bad as soon as I say it. "Sorry, Mi. I'm sorry."

She smiles. "I know soror, but this is important. The pearls? They don't work. Well, they do... but the drops won't be enough to counteract it."

"Stones, gods, and offerings, Mia! I almost used them."

"Well, don't." She grimaces. "I'm working on it, and once might not kill you... but if you survived it would knock you out, too. It would still kill them, but you wouldn't be able to escape. Defeats the purpose."

I blow out a breath. "Okay. Thank you for telling me. And let me know if you work the kinks out. I can up my drops a bit, too." I assume that's the issue. The antidote isn't strong enough.

"Just start with five more. I don't want you moving faster than that," Mia says, confirming my thoughts.

"Yes, Mater." I give her an exaggerated bow and she splashes at me. "Stones," I hiss, jumping back and slipping on tiles beneath us. The frigid water rushes into my ears and eyes, shocking my lungs. I stand, gasping.

Mia's smirking, but leads me to the more shallow steps so I can be mostly in the suns, their dual shadows short at midday.

Mia looks around to ensure we're still alone. "What are you going to do about your betrothed?"

"I think I've run out of options." I know I haven't. I could stop, I could leave. I could just go to his room and slit his throat. I could go to the Emperor's room and slit his. I'd probably die trying, but I'd have met my goal before the Praetorians killed me. But if I want to live to see Mia again, there's only one option. "I think... I might have to trust him."

My things were moved from the rose room into the green room while I was out yesterday. It's called the nerium room, Flavia informed me as she brought over the last of my dresses this morning. How fitting that he'd put me in the toxic flower's namesake.

Janus filled more basanite than I'd ever brought to them before and I hide the ruby and golden stones throughout the room, in each gown's pocket, under the mattress, in the washroom. I even sew a few into my undergarments for emergencies.

Flavia returns with a note and waits for my answer. I consider it for long moments before I say anything.

"Would you trust him, Flavia?" I don't know if she will answer but I have to ask. I have to know.

"I trust him with my life."

"Did he beat you? Those floras?" It comes out more accusatory than I mean and I bite my tongue.

"Do you know how floras are chosen?" she asks instead.

I shake my head. I know some of it, but not the details. I assume it's done the way all things are in Divus, chosen by men with more power deciding fates for those with less.

She comes to stand beside the bed, gesturing to the small bench. I nod, and she sits softly. "We are chosen by our pater. When a familia of high respect wishes to earn a favor from the republic, they can offer a child to it. Boys for the ring, girls for the harem. When a child turns six, they may be gifted. My pater had seven girls, and now the republic owes him seven small favors."

My stomach roils and heaves and I can't make words come. I want to say I am sorry. I want to cry. Pity will not change her childhood, though, so I sit silently and wait for what she really wants to tell me.

"Seven girls, and I am the last," she says. "Would you like to guess why?"

I don't need to guess, because I know this republic and I know its Emperor. "No."

"He took volunteers." It takes me a moment to realize she means Cassius. "We are scared, not of him, but of what will happen if we are caught. Every one of us volunteered. We want you to help."

"How do you know I'm the person you think I am?"

She shrugs. "I don't, but it's worth it for the chance that you are." I circle my answer on the note from Cassius and hand it back to her. She looks down at it and back at me. "It's worth it for hope."

Cassius' note wasn't special, simply a list of activities and the request for me to circle one. I was tempted to write something rude and circle my own answer; however, my meeting with Mia and her information about the Emperor sobers me. Every second I waste is another opportunity for someone to be hurt.

I curl my hair, apply some berry stain to my cheeks and lips, and don a green dress that dips low in the front and accents my hips. It flares to the floor and I can't help admiring that I look every bit the betrothed to the Dominus.

A gentle knock comes from the adjoining door and I call for him to enter.

"Oh," Cassius says, eyes widening.

"Oh?" I feel the line appear between my brows.

"You look beautiful," he says and I'm surprised he hasn't tried that kind of honey before. He doesn't look too bad, either, but he doesn't need to know that his white sleeves pushed above his forearms highlight the strength in his arms or that his dark mahogany stubble makes me want to drag my nails across his chin.

"Hmm. Shall we go?"

The early morning light slants through the archways, creating bars of shadow on the floor. Cassius could still betray me. This path could so easily lead me to the dungeon.

He has a sword strapped across his back and when I place my hand on the crook of his arm to move through the halls I feel the heat emanating from him, even more than usual.

Cassius wipes his brow with his arm, the one I'm not holding, and answers my look of inquiry. "Ah, I didn't have time for the Baths. I was training."

On the streets people call him Dominus the Dominator, the violent general who secures glory and land for his Imperator brother. There is respect in it, certainly less fear than they have of the Emperor, but he's still a killer.

Just like me.

The silence is at once comfortable and awkward. His presence isn't demanding, but the weight of my secrets and my decision tightens my shoulders and jaw. I roll my shoulders back and breathe steadily in time with our steps as we leave the Domus Aurea. The city streets are nearly deserted this early and they will be until the suns have both cleared the horizon.

"I was surprised you wanted to come here," Cassius says as we approach the temple. It's one of the most grand in Divus, the tall columns dwarfing the temples of Janus and Mars. The only larger is that of Jupiter himself, and while you might think his wife, Juno the mater, had the second largest temple, you'd be mistaken. This is the temple of Venus.

"We are to be married, are we not?" I say. "Venus is who we should visit."

"Is Venus who you prayed to yesterday?" he asks, leading me up the steps. The temple is surrounded by flowers, but its most notable feature is the brilliant myrtle trees that grow in the center of the temple courtyard. Their white and pink blossoms occasionally float down from their branches to rest on the surrounding grounds.

I shake my head. "No, I have never paid much attention to Venus."

"Have you ever been here?" He leads me to a small bench between the myrtle trees and the silence of the temple is interrupted only by us and a soft breeze.

I take a deep breath. "Once before."

He notices the change in my tone or the way I've stilled, or perhaps he just knows things he shouldn't, because he turns to me and takes my hands in his.

"Luella, tell me what to do to earn your trust? I don't have the luxury of time—"

I cut him off. "I thought you wanted a long engagement?"

He lets out a breath. "I did. I do. But there are things outside my control and..." He searches my face. "You asked me about my brother once. About what he liked to see..."

He's remembering his dance with Skylar. Once I do this I can't go back, but I do it anyways. I confirm all his suspicions with a single nod.

My Type

Luella

CASSIUS SQUEEZES MY HANDS tight. I know I should pull away, but instead I lean in as he whispers, "It's you."

"If it was… I'd be very curious about why it mattered now. About why you hurt those women. And why you'd want to marry me."

"My brother…" He shakes his head and starts again. "I need help."

I shake my head. "If you want my trust, I need yours. Tell me everything."

"There is a lifetime to tell." He swallows. "My brother… is a *belua*." *Monster.*

"I know about your brother," I say.

"Luella, you don't. It's more than you could possibly know." I don't correct him; there is too much I cannot tell him. "But it's only become worse. The floras know much of his… worship."

"Worship?" What a word.

"Of Bacchus. That's why he does what he does." The Emperor belongs to the mysteries. I didn't know, but of course I wouldn't. Bacchus followers are a legend, a nighttime story to keep children and virgins inside when the suns set, just like The Sabines. Some even believe The Sabines exist solely for the followers of Bacchus.

"So he's a *belua*. A deviant. So was Ledo, so are 90% of the Praetors and Senators," I say. Which now makes more sense. Many of the men I've killed were likely followers, appointed by the Emperor himself. "Why do you suddenly care? And what do you want from me?"

"I've always cared."

"You've never stopped him."

Cassius flinches at the accusation. "I couldn't."

"Because men are allowed to do what they want? Because he's the Imperator? Why couldn't you do anything, mighty Dominus?" I sneer. I can't help myself. Over ten years. Ten years of women being beaten, raped, and murdered. Perhaps he called it worship now, but I know he hadn't always. He was a twisted man who found a way to justify his deviance, and convinced others to join him in it.

"Because he had my siblings," Cassius says, his voice cracking over each word. "Because he had the twins, kept safe in his wing to protect them from assassination." The lie he's had to swallow sounds cold, distant.

"Had?"

He looks up at me with eyes so haunted that it's my turn to flinch. "They're gone now... last year after we lost the battle at Nocia. He said they were kidnapped but..." The confident man I've seen has been replaced with a broken-hearted brother and I wonder for the first time if he might cry. "I found their bodies."

He doesn't elaborate, and I don't want him to. I don't want to know anything more about them because I can feel my heart breaking and I can see the thread forming between us, the one woven by loss.

He takes a deep breath and I see the steel in him once more as his shoulders straighten, his chest inflates. "He's kept me at bay for years, using our siblings as leverage. I mourn their loss every day, but I won't let their deaths go unavenged. My brother made a mistake, because without their lives on the line, I can do what needs to be done.

"What's that?"

"Whatever it takes," he says. "Whatever it takes for things to change."

Everything falls into place. Warning me away from Ledo and his brother, then letting me go, then baiting me back with the floras once he realized who I was. And if he's wrong about me, I could destroy him.

Because he wants to kill the Emperor.

"You want…" I look away. Venus is known for her deception, her affairs, her promiscuity. She blesses brides but curses married women. She is love and passion and jealousy. It's fitting to discuss this here. "You want me to do your dirty work, take your revenge?"

"I want to help you do what I think you were planning to do anyways. Isn't that why you asked me about him back then? Why you chose Ledo?"

He's right, of course. "Why can't you do it yourself?" I waive my hand over his form. "The Dominator? I'm sure you could best him."

Does he blush? "Him, maybe. Him and his six handpicked Praetorians? No. I'm still just a man, and many of those men trained me. He's only alone in his chambers with the floras, and even then not always. The Praetorians are always stationed outside. I'd never get close enough, but you could. The floras come and go, they don't have an escort in or out."

"Why would they," I say, not as a question, just a reminder of the hubris of men like the Emperor. Men who think our pretty heads are too occupied with how to please them than with anything else.

"We can work together. Whatever you need, whatever I can do, whatever the floras can do. We can stop him, together."

It is what I want. On some level maybe that's why I decided to trust him, to admit who and what I am.

Because I'm driven by want as much as the Emperor, as much as Ledo or Silas or any other praeda I've killed. I want to end the Emperor more than I've ever wanted anything and the ache of it sets my blood on fire.

"Perhaps," I say again.

"So, you're not going to kill me?" He smiles in that charming way of his, sadness forgotten at the thought of taking his own revenge.

"*Matulo*," I say, rolling my eyes. "I didn't say that."

"Fine, you're not going to kill me, yet?" he clarifies, still smirking.

"Yet," I agree. "Turns out, you're not really my type, anyways."

He throws his head back and laughs. The sound spreads through the temple, through my chest, through my core and I find that I'm smiling too when he says, "That's too bad, because you're mine."

Virgin or Whore

Rose

Tristan sends a litter to carry my things. I don't have many, and it's almost embarrassing to see the half empty cart moving towards his domus. When we're practically there, a commotion near the forum stops us. The crowds are shouting something and I strain to hear it.

"What is it?" I ask one of the servants.

He shakes his head, craning his neck to see. I follow his line of sight until I see it, too.

It's a large iron box, big enough for a woman, a couch, and some food. My stomach flips, and I hear them then, the virgins weeping.

"The vow-breaker," the servant says, although I've already guessed. The women following the box are in white stolas and head-dresses, their cheeks streaked in tears as they follow the disgraced priestess. The box itself is silent and I wonder if she's already run out of air and food. The Vestals are given more than any of us, sacred in and of themselves, but it means they have the most to lose.

By breaking their vow of chastity, willingly or not, they forfeit everything. Not just their status, their relationship with Vesta, or their ability to be free from men's claims on their bodies or their time. No, they lose their lives, too.

"Where do they bury it?" I ask. I can't bear to think of the her inside, shrouded in darkness when she's spent her entire life tending and worshiping the flame. Every day she's seen the red and gold of the hearth and in the end they plunge her into absolute dark.

"Edge of the city," he says. "Can't spill the blood here, and if she were to cut herself in there, it would curse us all." I doubt he's worried about the city. Just himself.

I swallow and tell them to find a way around, so that I don't have to see.

It's always better if you don't have to see.

I haven't forgotten the priestess, but when my litter arrives at the domus I feel safer, less exposed. As if the Vestal would curse me for even seeing her torture, for seeing and doing nothing. What I see now is the opposite. The domus is all extravagant rooms, beautiful art, and a plethora of flowers. Instead of weeping, it's silent in its majesty. Almost nothing could make it seem more magical except, perhaps, Tristan. He's a golden god, welcoming me on the steps.

It's a whirlwind of being shown my rooms, the grounds, and then hours later I sit on Tristan's right.

"I'm happy you're here." He leans over to kiss my hand. While I hated leaving Daisy, I know that the sooner I fit in here, the sooner I can bring her. Tristan's right; I don't understand his familia. I don't understand the patricians at all. As a plebeian I've worried over food, money, and marriage. With two of those removed, I can't fathom what occupies his class.

Once I study them and understand, I can figure out how to carve a space for my sister, or hope Augustus finds her a suitor to whom Tristan won't take offense.

"I can't believe it." I smile. My freedom is weighted. Each breath away from my pater takes me further from Daisy, and I hate that they're linked. But for tonight, I decide to enjoy it. To bask in Tristan's golden glow.

"You look beautiful," Tristan says, eyeing the hair piled on top of my head, the golden ringlets stacked so high I have the urge to duck when stepping beneath archways.

My smile widens. "I'm glad you like it." I wish he preferred a less time intensive style, but it's worth it for the way he looks at me now.

Tristan shifts in his chair. Sips his wine. "I will have to send a seamstress tomorrow, though." I look down at my tunic.

"A seamstress?"

"You'll need more tunics, and gowns and stolas for once we're married." It strikes me then, how much everything is about to change. My domus, my name, my pater, and even my clothes. It's all going to be different.

The nervous energy coils in my gut, so I just smile.

Tristan stands, coming in front of me. "I love you, Rosebud. I love you so much it makes my chest ache. All I think about is you." He reaches out to cradle my face in his hands, and for some reason I think back to the garden, to the way he gripped my arms so painfully, the shattering glasses. A flash of fear, like Jupiter's lightening, strikes through me, gone as quickly as it came.

He plants a tender kiss on my forehead, so warm and sweet that I feel myself lean forward, despite my wariness. "I love you, too, Tristan," I say, and I mean it. Tristan is complicated, but that's how love is.

"I'm sorry," Tristan murmurs against my skin. I think he means for his jealousy over Augustus, but I can't be sure.

"It's okay. We're learning," I remind him.

"Yes," he says, his hands coming to my waist. He lifts me onto the table, shoving back my plate. "I'll learn to control my temper."

He kisses my neck, and I can't help the small whimper that breaks free. "And I'll learn what I need to do, what it means to be a part of your familia," I gasp beneath him.

"And you'll need to learn how to thank me," he says, voice gruff as he breathes into my neck. His hands are roaming across my back, my hips. Desire fights with uncertainty, I know this isn't ladylike. I know we should wait.

"The servants," I say, helpless against his passion. He kisses me hard, teeth crashing into mine. He wants me so badly he can hardly control himself. Perhaps I shouldn't have worn my hair this way, my tunic so loose.

"They know better than to come in," he says, dropping to kiss above my breasts. "Say you're mine."

"Tristan, we should stop." I'm not sure if I want to. I'm on fire, my skin burning and smoldering beneath his touch, his lips.

"Say it," he groans, hands wrapping around my ankles as he presses himself between my legs, our clothing the only thing separating us from breaking propriety.

"I'm yours," I whisper. "But, Tristan. We can't." White dresses. White sheets. If I don't bleed on our wedding night, there will be questions.

"I won't ruin you for the wedding, but I need to show you how to thank me," he says, pausing.

"What do you mean?" I'm panting, confusion and want and uncertainty making my heart gallop in my chest.

He takes my hand and puts it between us, so it's resting on his hardness. I try to remove my hand, but he grips my wrist tighter. "I could have anyone, but I love you." He kisses my forehead again. "I want *you*. So, give me what I want. Thank me. And Daisy can move in the day after the wedding."

A strange sort of numbness moves through me. I expected this on our wedding night. I thought I'd have more time to be ready, to understand.

I've heard whispers of the transactional nature of intimacy, of course. Women gathering water telling each other how they shared the bed a few extra nights for this or for that.

I didn't know love worked that way, too.

Tristan slides me off the table, and I obey, standing before him, chest heaving. His hands come up my waist, resting on top of my shoulders. Then he pushes me down onto my knees, leaving my tunic in place. He brushes a curl off my cheek and says, "So beautiful, Rosebud." His thumb rests on my lips, tugging tenderly at the bottom one. "Let me show you how to say thank you. Let me show you how to be my wife."

Tristan keeps his word, and I know I'll still bleed on our marriage sheets. Afterwards he kisses me everywhere but my mouth.

My swollen lips feel numb, tingling after so much friction. He says he loves me, wants me, that I'm perfect. There is an odd sense of pride that I undid him. That he wants *me*.

I just wish it hadn't been *for* something. I wish it hadn't felt like a trade.

I wish my pride wasn't warring with shame.

There is much to learn about marriage, I suppose. Will Daisy have to learn all of this, too? Will her marriage be different?

I'd assumed her dichotomy had been a metaphor for those who marry and those who don't, but now I wonder if she meant exactly what she said.

You can be a virgin or a whore.

Too

Luella

Cassius looks horrified. "Stones! How many times have you almost killed me?" he asks. I'm explaining how I typically profile and attract my praeda, although I leave Mia's involvement out of it.

"We're not married," I say, smiling.

He grunts at my joke and moves another pawn forward. We've taken to playing Latrones each morning since we visited the temple of Venus a full clipse ago. It's a cautious trust we've built, but Cassius has been true to his word. Each day we spend the morning together. The afternoon *sapa* we take 'privately' with a flora. To the rest of the Domus Aurea it likely looks like Cassius is either training or bedding me, either of which is his right. Instead, each of the floras is telling us everything they can about the Emperor. What he likes, what sparks his temper, how he takes his *sapa* and his meals.

Any and every detail that we can use so that I can do what needs to be done, hoping for something to illuminate a path forward.

The worry for us all is that the Emperor has no need to take a wife, and unlike Ledo who preferred his women to play a specific role that a wife could embody, he is more complicated. My usual plan might not work.

"I can't pose as a flora," I say throwing up my hands. Imperial floras are chosen at a young age, as Flavia explained. And then they are raised in the Vestal temple where they are kept chaste until the Emperor chooses them. If I had wanted to infiltrate them I would have to be there for years, proving how devout I was. We didn't have the time. And since the Emperor hand picked them, I don't think I can just infiltrate the floras already in the Domus Aurea.

"Can you impersonate someone?" Cassius suddenly asks.

I shake my head. "It's nearly impossible to replicate someone that already exists. I can make things new, but trying to imitate others enough that someone wouldn't notice? I don't trust it." I take a breath and admit what we're both thinking. "And if I fail..."

"It would be a death sentence for whomever you impersonated." He bites his lip, the movement drawing my eyes.

I shake my head, moving forward to take one of his pawns. "I won't risk them."

"That probably wouldn't work anyways..." Cassius muses out loud. "Not with the way he binds the floras. You'd never be able to slip something in his drink or his food posed as a flora." The women he chooses feel random, but what he does afterwards is starting to fit a pattern.

I run my finger over the edges of the board. "Cassius?" He looks up from the board and frowns at what he sees on my face. "When your brother broke my wrist, it seemed like he was jealous."

His eyes darken, but he nods. "I've had very little in life that my brother hasn't taken from me. It's why I don't want you out with that face alone."

"But if we can't nail down a profile, if we can't find a way for me to get close without raising suspicion... Could we use that?"

He's shaking his head before I've finished speaking. "Luella, he's too dangerous. He's not a kid who's lost his temper or even a man who likes to flaunt his control. He's a monster."

"Cassius, you brought me here to help you. Now you don't want me to get close to him?" I try to keep the frustration from showing. Calm and in control. "This is what I do."

He looks away, having the decency to look shamed. Tightness grips my chest and even though I'm not sure I want the answer, I ask anyways. "What's changed?"

Cassius runs his hand through his copper strands before letting loose a sigh. He turns to look at me.

"Has anyone ever told you that you have beautiful eyes?" His are searching, searing, and I hear more than feel myself swallow.

"Not as often as you'd think, considering how hard they are to change." I smile and am the first to look away.

He nods, as if I've confirmed something. "You're right. Nothing's changed." He takes one of my pawns. "That doesn't mean we should be reckless. And we are not using his jealousy."

"Give me a good reason why."

"Because," he lowers his voice, like saying it out loud will manifest it right here, "he doesn't just rut women Luella. The stuff he does to the floras? The stuff Ledo did? That's the usual. If we play with that jealousy too much, if we push him the wrong way? He'll snap."

"I know," I say.

"He won't just use you. He'll kill you. Or use you in his twisted rituals, then kill you. I'm not going to let him do it again."

I lean forward, fighting for control. He said *again*. The problem with secrets is that they stay sticky, like the strands of a web. Sometimes I am surprised by which ones cling to me and which ones fall away. And now, I'm loosing track of which are mine and which are Cassius'.

"If we don't come up with a better plan, we won't have a choice," I grind out.

"We'll find one," Cassius growls. "One that doesn't leave you at the mercy of a monster, Luella."

I move a pawn forward and take his dux. A win, but hard earned. "I'm very hard to kill, Dominus."

He's lost in thought and doesn't answer me.

He forgets that I'm a monster, too.

Kiss & Kill

Luella

The Senate dinner is a once per clipse affair for Praetors and Senators to dine with the Emperor and the Dominus. Of course, the *Concilium Plebis* is technically allowed to attend, but somehow the date always seems to change and they are not notified. Cassius didn't want to bring me, but I reminded him that I need to see the Emperor and interact with him if I am to eventually fulfill our plan.

Which is how I end up three seats down from him, smiling politely as he tells Cassius that without a familia there is no way to ensure I'm not a 'common meretrix.'

"Her status doesn't matter, does it brother? I want her, so I will have her," Cassius says. I remember his measured words that first night we danced and I can see now that he's played this role for years. He likely did the same to protect his siblings.

"So protective, brother." The Emperor smirks, the sharp planes of his face falling into the expression naturally. Then he shifts his eyes to me and I see what I picked up on before. Jealousy. Envy. Possession. He doesn't care for me, of course, but he doesn't like that Cassius has something that he doesn't.

The conversation moves to matters of state. The other women look down at their plates, eating quietly as I am expected to do. So, I do. But I listen as well.

The senator next to me is speaking to the man at his side. "The date can't be set until he chooses his sacrifice."

"Well he needs to hurry," the man next to him says. "Everyone else is ready."

"Bacchus prefers a specific style of sacrifice, and you know he won't take one who doesn't fit his type for that."

"If it has tits, it should be enough."

I don't look up, but they must decide they shouldn't be discussing the matter here because they quickly change the subject to more appropriate dinner conversation, like the price of prostitutes and grain, and eventually healers.

"They are filling up, not saving any beds," one of the Senators says, "it's not right."

"You'd have them turn people away?" Cassius says.

"What if a Senator or Praetor needed care, and there were no beds?" a different man says. Praetor Caul I think.

"And your life is worth more than theirs?" I hear myself say, from a stupid, far away place.

Caul's face reddens. "Excuse me?"

"I just mean that you are less likely to need care than the common people, Praetor," I say, looking down. I've made a mistake.

"Control your whore, Cassius. Or I will." Caul's voice cuts through the low din of conversation.

Cassius stands so quickly his chair falls back. Before I can blink, he's holding Caul's throat. "Perhaps you've forgotten that I am the Dominus, Caul. And you are a Praetor." He tips his head to the side, considering. "Are Praetors divined by the gods to rule?"

Caul doesn't answer, because of course they are not. The Evandia line rules until the gods help another line to topple it, as the Evandians did to the Gaius line and the Gaius line did to Nepos before them. The Dominus might not be Emperor, but he's the second most powerful man in the republic.

"You," Cassius hisses, "were chosen by *my* line. And you can be replaced." He shoves Caul back in his chair and holds his arm out to me wordlessly.

I stand, tilting my chin and placing a hand on his arm. When he walks me by the Emperor he says, "I apologize Imperator, but I'll be retiring with my betrothed."

The Emperor nods, but he's looking at me again. So I look back, channeling something shy and hopeful and naive. Something that might remind him of his youth, and I drain one of my stones just a little so that for a moment my eyes shift colors into the dead ones of my past.

His eyes widen ever so slightly, and I smile.

Cassius leads me through the corridor, and some might think he is taking me away to punish me as Caul suggested, as is his supposed right. Only I know his hand is featherlight, the warmth of his fingers a caress instead of demand. Pulling me into his rooms, he releases me. "Jupiter's stones, what an idiota."

"Dominus, you can't lose your temper like that," I reprimand. Perhaps with my little trick of the eyes it could still work. I have to lead the Emperor on the perfect amount, and if he thought Cassius was so affected by me, his need to push his brother might overtake his desire to have me. I needed the latter to take over, not the former. I let out a breath through my teeth. "I shouldn't have spoken, though. I'm sorry."

"Shouldn't have spoken? He was being absurd!"

"Yes, but women have no place to speak over a Praetor."

"I know you don't believe that," Cassius says.

"Usually men don't care if we believe it." I smile, the bitterness coating my lips.

"I do." He steps closer, his eyes searching mine.

I reach my hand out to touch his jaw, dragging my nail along the stubble the way I've longed to for days. "You're delightfully naive sometimes, Dominus."

His hand presses against mine, holding it to his face and he leans into the touch. "Maybe I'm just an idealist. Maybe I see a different future for the republic."

Heat floods me at the look in his eyes, the warmth in his hand, and hope in his words. It's reckless to touch him. I'm the naive one, pretending that Cassius is doing any of this for any reason besides his own revenge, his own ambitions. I know exactly what will happen when I kill the Emperor.

The republic will need a new one.

I reach into my pocket and wrap my fingers around a cool stone. I don't need to see it to know the color is leaching from it, the yellow, orange, or red paling and then bleeding to black.

He knows I can do this, but I've never shown him. That was a mistake. I need us both to remember who and what I am.

The black widow.

Tisiphone.

Venefica.

I mold myself into a younger woman with dark hair and suns-kissed skin, dark eyes and thick full lips. I transform into temptation, but not just for him. "I'm restless. I'm going into the city."

"What are you going to do?" Cassius asks, still holding my hand.

"I'm going to play a game."

"I want to come," he says, just as I knew he would. Just as I hoped.

"You can decide." I shrug as if it's no matter to me, as if I thought he'd be content to let me leave all alone after the dinner we'd had. "It's called Kiss and Kill."

Meet Me at the Maero

Luella

I lean towards Nero, and even though I can't smell him, I can feel the alcohol seeping off of him by the ruddiness in his cheeks, the sweat on his brow and his chest, and the swaying of his large frame.

Cassius is cloaked and drinking in the corner of the tavern. His knuckles are white around his glass as I brush my lips against Nero's ear. "You're very handsome."

A grin splits his very average, and very married, face. I wouldn't kill him if he was just a cheater, but his wife is in Mia's back room right now after the brute broke four of her ribs. That does earn a spot on my list, especially when Mia says the woman would be dead if Nero hadn't been interrupted, that the woman has multiple fractures of different ages all throughout her body. Perhaps she'd hate me for ending his pathetic life, or perhaps she might like to know what it is to have a body that is her own.

I know I would.

His hand wraps around to grope my ass and I squeal, falling forward into his arms. In the crowded tavern it was easy to spike his cerevisia, but now I have to lure him out before he drops. He chuckles and I press myself closer, knowing I'll have to scrub the scent of him off me. He grabs my hair and kisses me roughly, drunkenly. I moan into his mouth and feel the evidence of his desire between us. I fight the gag working its way through me, biting his lip instead.

"I do like 'em feisty," he says.

I smile, because what woman doesn't enjoy being diminished to one fuckable trait while simultaneously being compared to the collective 'them' who've already endured his pathetic rutting.

He pauses to take another swig of his drink and then begins to tug me towards the back of the tavern. I follow him through the exit and into the back alley.

"Let's walk to the Maero," I say, peeling down the shoulder of my loose tunic, showing that I have nothing underneath.

"I'm happy right here," he says, pressing me up against the wall to kiss me again.

I run my tongue up his neck, the salt making me shudder. Then I suck his earlobe into my mouth until he bucks his hips forward. Now I have him. "I want to be loud when you fuck me," I say.

He grips my hips, grinding against me as he recaptures my mouth. "You're a little *meretrix*, aren't you?"

"Take me to the Maero and I'll show you exactly what I am," I say. Timing is everything, and this alley isn't the best place to do what I do.

He grabs my hand and starts to drag me down the alley, and I turn back to see Cassius coming out the back, eyes wide. I press a finger to my lips, motioning him to be quiet as I follow Nero. Thankfully he's too intoxicated to notice Cassius trailing behind us in the dark.

One street over are the stairs to the walkway along the Maero, and I let him lead me down. His steps start to sway as we move. As usual, my timing is spot on.

The path is dark, but as we land on the walkway and round the corner the sound of the water drowns out any revelry on the street. It's just us, and likely up on the stairs is Cassius, but I don't worry about him. Good citizens don't wander this far from the city at night.

Nero pushes me against this new wall, wasting no time ripping my skirts down. I let him, and even tug down my top so my breasts break free, my nipples puckering in the chill.

He reaches for his own pants while trying to tear my underclothes free, but now he's slowing.

"Problems, sus?"

"What did you call me?" he asks, and I hope I see what I think I do. His eyes widen and I smile. Yes, it's there. The fear.

"Sus. Swine. Porcus," I say, yanking his shirt towards me so our bodies collide. "What else could you expect from a whore?"

Nero blinks, confused. Over his shoulder I see Cassius at the foot of the steps, watching, tension radiating from his shoulders and one hand on the blade at his hip. I smile my most wicked smile at him. I've never had an audience before, but I know he needs to see what I do. His strange protectiveness is going to interfere with our plans. And if he keeps being... him, perhaps my own feelings will as well.

This will fix it, though. This will remind him that I'm not a beautiful thing.

I'm jagged. Sharp.

A tiny little spider in the center of a giant web, just waiting to strike.

Nero blinks again at my smile. "See you in a few," I say as he sways and finally topples to the ground.

I don't adjust my clothes. I use my nakedness as a weapon all its own on Cassius. I don't need his honor or protection or anything else he's trying to give me. Shivering, I lean down and hog tie Nero. Cassius moves to help me and I wave him away. "I always work alone."

I use one hand to squeeze his jaw down and open, tipping the contents of the next vial into his waiting mouth.

I don't look at Cassius as I wait for Nero to wake, and after a moment he stirs, his eyes fluttering.

I slap him, hard.

"You stupid bitch," he seethes, spitting at me.

"That's not very nice," I pout.

He sees Cassius then. "Help me goodman, she's crazy! Help!" Cassius doesn't move and Nero struggles in earnest now, the knots growing tighter with each move.

"Nero," I tsk. "Your wife sent me." Cassius didn't know I visited Mia. I'd left him at the Domus Aurea and returned after I spoke to her. "Four broken ribs?"

Cassius and Nero flinch, although I suspect for very different reasons. "Whatever she says is a lie," Nero says.

"And the neighbors who dragged you off of her?"

"She's probably fucking them."

"Is that any way to talk about your wife? And what about your first wife? Was she fucking everyone, too?" This is his third wife in as many years. The problem with men like Nero is that they believe that there are no consequences, and without shame or fear, they grow predictable.

Easy praeda.

He spits and I shrug, taking out another vial, this one the smallest. I tip just a few drops into Nero's mouth and smile as he sputters, trying to spit out the bitter liquid.

I sit back on my heels, still fighting to keep my eyes off Cassius. I don't care what he thinks.

Nero's throat starts working, a loud gurgling sound as he realizes what I've done. "What did you— w-w-what did you give me?" He groans.

"Some incentive," I say. "How many times have you hit your wife, Nero?"

"M-m-make it stop," he moans, the venom is the most painful that exists, although the effects are short lived. Mia's developed it into a poison that helps me keep my hands mostly clean, when needed.

"Answer the question, sus."

"I did it, okay. P-p-please make it stop."

"How many times, Nero?" The words are slow and patient, almost kind. "Be a good boy," I say.

"I don't k-k-k-know," he wails.

"Too many too count?" I say, pouting.

He nods, tears streaming down his face and I nod as if I understand. Those wives, always misbehaving. But I only see one disobedient party here, and unfortunately for him, I need to make a point.

Usually I just dump the poison in now, but instead I take the asp venom and pour the remaining contents into his greedy gullet. He screams, the sound so loud it pierces my eardrums.

I look to Cassius, giving into my urge, and see his face is shuttered, stony.

When the screams start to irritate me, I reach in for the last vial and pour the red poison into the abyss of sound.

"Throw him in the river," I tell Cassius as I adjust my clothes. I don't wait for a response as I turn to leave him, because I don't care what he thinks.

And after tonight, I've ensured he won't care about me, either.

DROWN

ROSE

IT DOES GROW ON you, the *sapa*. Over the last clipse I've grown fond of the drink, and fond of the ritual of it in general. Every day at the same time, in the same place, I drink the sweet dark liquid and it takes the edge off. Each sip dilutes the plebian parts of me.

This is what the patricians do.

Best of all, Tristan is there. His hands are never on me. He's not whispering sweet words or setting me on fire with his hands and his lips. He just... talks.

He lets me know him. Learn him.

And I'm greedy for it.

"It's a pathetic excuse for reform." Tristan sips his *sapa*, letting the glass dangle from his fingertips with an ease that would make even the gods jealous.

"Isn't that the one about the Sabines?" I ask, leaning forward. Tristan is not fond of the changes that Augustus has been advocating for.

"Yes, the one my idiot brother brought to Senator Marcus." He's also not fond of Senator Marcus.

"It's not a good bill?" I don't know if I'm allowed to ask about politics, but I usually do. I certainly can't give advice, but a good wife would listen to her husband and empathize with him, no matter the topic. Besides, Tristan talks longer when I do.

"It places all the responsibility on the Imperator instead of on the people. If people want to buy sabines, sabines will be for sale. That's the way of the world."

"Oh," I say. Without The Sabines, would the same women just be sold somewhere else? Maybe they'd be even more mistreated without the oversight of a building?

Tristan waves a hand. "Enough unpleasantness. How are you enjoying the domus?"

His hand reaches across the table and I smile at him, grasping his cool palm. "It's beautiful here." It is. It's beautiful and grand; and so, so lonely.

I've spent my life with Daisy sleeping next to me; sharing space, sharing air, sharing life. Now, I sleep alone. I spend most of my days alone. And besides appearing at *sapa*, I'm expected to do... nothing. At least as far as I can tell. I think after marriage I'm meant to take a role with Camilla, running the domus domestically. And of course, trying to give Tristan a son.

My stomach twists and I'm not sure which makes me more nervous. Tristan hasn't asked to be thanked again, and I'm grateful. Not that I don't want to learn to please him, I do.

We're just supposed to wait. I've always known this.

I want to wait until after our wedding. I want to do things the way I'm supposed to. I also want to make Tristan happy.

"Rosebud?" Tristan asks. I must have missed what he said.

"Yes, Tristan?" I smile, drowning my doubts with another sip of *sapa*. Taking the edge off the uncertainty.

"I said, do you need anything?" He's beginning to stand and I realize this is his way of ending *sapa*. He doesn't stay long with all of his important work waiting for him.

"No." I shake my head. "No, thank you. I'm quite content."

Tristan leans down, capturing my lips. I wait for the heat from before, but it doesn't come. Perhaps my senses are dulled by the drink. Perhaps I've had too much. "Of course you are." His hand dips behind my head and he kisses me more forcefully, as if he can tell my heart isn't in it.

I kiss him back, arching into his hand. He likes when I do that.

"Rosebud," he groans into my mouth. "I won't see you until the wedding."

It's in two days. I bite my lip. "I won't see you tomorrow?"

He looks down at me, shaking his head softly. "I have meetings and I'm attending a new temple." I tilt my head to the side and he continues, "If it ends up being something I enjoy, I'll bring you sometime. For now, it's just an experiment."

I nod, trying to hide my disappointment. A day without *sapa* means a full day alone, watching the twins dance around each other or pretending to read.

But I needn't hide anything, because Tristan is already turning away.

A Curse

Luella

There's no more time. Cassius understands what I am now, and I think I know what to do.

I'm ready.

I'm rushing towards our rooms, moving swiftly down each corridor in the late afternoon. The suns cast double shadows, although tomorrow will be the shadowing, the coldest day of the clipse. A day of rest, although not for me.

Instead, I'll push Cassius to initiate my plan and by next clipse, this will all be over.

I turn the last corner to our rooms and collide with none other than Caul and another Praetor I don't recognize.

An undignified grunt escapes me and I move around them. "I'm so sorry, Praetors." I dip my head, but Caul is holding my wrist and when I try to move away he yanks me back.

"Just who we were looking for. The Emperor requests an audience." He sneers and I realize too late that they were waiting for me.

Fear rises, and I don't wait to see if it's warranted. When intuition speaks, I listen, especially in situations I haven't orchestrated. I scream for Cassius, my voice shrill, "Dominus! Cassius, help me!" I don't know if he's near, but perhaps Flavia or another flora will still hear me.

Caul yanks me against him and wraps his forearm around my neck, squeezing until I can hardly breathe, much less scream. The other Praetor checks the hallway and they begin leading me away. I struggle, knowing I can't acquiesce.

In one moment the circumstances can change. I know this. I slow my struggle, taking slow breaths through my nose. I feel for the vials in my pocket, for the stones, but my cooperation warns them and the other Praetor sees my hand in my pocket and rips it out.

"Witch," he hisses when one of the vials comes out in my hand, shattering against the marble and spilling the violet liquid onto the floor.

Caul's arm tightens around my neck, and despite my urge to keep my wits, I struggle anyways. My head pounds, my face is hot, and I realize I can't breathe at all. He's going to kill me.

Then he loosens his grip, just a little. They must want me alive, and awake. Caul spins me around and slams me up against the wall, hoisting my hands above my head with one hand and punching me in the face with the other. I cough as blood pools in my mouth and I would likely crumple if he wasn't holding me up. "Don't you ever disrespect me again," Caul says throwing me to the ground. He kicks me and then I feel the weight of him on top of me, his hands working on his trousers.

Something wild in me breaks free and I scream, scrambling forward only for the other Praetor to kick me in the chest when I try to rise. My chest crunches beneath his boot and I make a noise between a gasp and scream, collapsing onto my stomach. Caul grabs my legs, dragging me back towards him. Then he's on me again, knees digging into my thighs as he tries to hold me and undo his trousers at the same time.

The other Praetor drops onto my upper arms, his shins crushing me into the marble floor. He leans forward, body draping over me, as he begins to rip at my dress. I remember something then, the pearl between my back teeth. Mia told me not to use it, but I don't care. I won't let them take this.

I try to work the pearl free but the panic makes my movements choppy and I bite my tongue when the nameless man rips my undergarments free. Air rushes over the exposed skin and then over my entire back, my head. The man isn't over me anymore.

"She's mine," Cassius growls, throwing the man off me. His boots are in front of me and I could lick them for how pleased I am to see him. He draws the sword from his hip and steps to the side of me, swinging it with a whistle.

Caul doesn't have a chance to say anything before the blade slices across his jugular. He collapses onto me, the weight shifting from my thighs to my back and I scream as I'm coated in his blood. Cassius shifts me from beneath the weight of the corpse, and lifts me into his arms. I see the other man crumpled against the far wall. Cassius threw him just right for his skull to crack, and blood pools around him, too.

The hall is bathed in blood, as am I.

Cassius carries me away and I take one last look over his shoulder at the crimson scene. I can't help but wonder how much more blood will have to spill before this is all over?

"Get out," Cassius snaps to the servants in the imperial Baths. It has as many pools as the public ones, but each is smaller, and more elegant. Frescoes and gemstones adorn the walls above and below water, each pool a vibrant vat of color. The best ones are cast in a hazy fog as steam rises off the surface.

Cassius starts to take off my bloody and torn dress and I flinch. "Luella." He touches my face, his hand warm but firm. "It's me. I need to remove this so we can clean the blood. Okay?"

I nod, letting him peel down the wet fabric from my shoulders. Nothing hurts and a distant part of me says that this is shock. You remember shock, Luella.

She just screams so pretty.

"I was just about to—," I gasp as I move to pull down a sleeve, spikes of pain from my shattered ribs breaking through the fog. "—to escape. You didn't need to interfere."

We both know it's a lie but Cassius has the decency to say, "Sorry, I didn't think."

"Now he'll know I'm a weak spot for you," I say, clenching my teeth as I step out of the gown. I'm in my underthings, but the strap to one side of my tunic is broken and my undergarments are ripped down the back. I can feel myself shaking, my body still unsure if I should be running or fighting.

"These are rubbish," I say, dragging them off. I rip the seam on the side of my tunic and salvage the small yellow stone, the one I'd sown in when I moved to the Domus Aurea. Then I toss the remnants of the garments towards the center of the room.

Cassius is looking down in a very respectful attempt to maintain my privacy and I'm keen to let him until I lean down to pick up the warm water ewer. A hiss escapes me as my ribs shift and Cassius looks up. "Stones, let me do it."

"I thought you'd never ask," I manage, trying and failing to keep my tone light. I straighten, breathing slow. "I need the healer after this."

"I should have let you flay them," he says.

"Haven't seen me be cruel enough?" I say, remembering how he had withdrawn at my methods last night.

"There is no such thing as cruel enough for that," he says. I can't decipher exactly what he means and I'm too tired to try.

In attempt to avert his eyes, Cassius smacks my cheek with the ewer. "Ow," I snap.

"Sorry," he says, dumping the next ewer of water over empty air.

I sigh. "*Matulo,* will you please just open your eyes? I'm not shy and I can't do it myself."

I'm not shy. After all, I make these bodies for eyes to see. They are unblemished save calculated things. A mole above the left side of a lip. A smatter of freckles across the bridge of a nose. A sliver of a scar across a hand or shoulder. All to appear more real. And so I am used to gazes that undress, that demean, that imagine all manner of things that nearly actually occurred just now, and I know that's not how Cassius will look at me. He will be collected, methodical. Courteous.

Except he's not. His eyes roam across my face, moving between my eyes and down to my lips and then lower to my collarbone. Cheeks darkening he dips the shaking ewer into the water and pours it over my shoulders, the warmth streaming in rivulets down my bloody skin in the steamy air between us.

I'm more naked than I've ever been, beneath that gaze.

Once the blood is mostly gone, Cassius holds out an arm, letting me lean on him as he leads me to the hot bath. I tenderly lower myself into the steaming water, glad for his arm to steady me. I sink all the way in until the water reaches my chin and take a deep breath before submersing myself. The water rushes across my face, fills my ears, nose, and the spaces between each strand of hair and my whole body loosens.

When I come up for air, Cassius is sitting at the edge of the pool with his trousers rolled up past his knees and his feet soaking. "Are you all right?"

I don't answer right away but when I do my voice is softer than usual. "It's different, when you're not prepared." I lean my head back against the edge of the tub right next to Cassius, looking up at him. "Thank you, Cassius."

His hand drops to my hair, smoothing it back. "I think I'd know those eyes in any form," he says. A smile plays across my lips and he brushes his thumb across them, like he's making sure it's really there. "I think I might know you, in any form, Luella." He says it like it's a curse, like it'll break him, and I stop smiling then. Because I know he's right.

Whatever this is, it'll doom us both.

The Act

Luella

The square neckline of my wedding dress is low, the fabric taut with my labored breaths. The gauzy fabric pools at my feet, and the tight bodice hugs my newly healed ribs. We've been at the temple of the Furies for hours while Cassius' own Praetorians announced our wedding in the streets.

The temple is beautiful in a hard, unforgiving way. Instead of arches, the lines connecting the columns are straight and severe. The marble columns and altars aren't adorned with jewels or flowers, but instead with metal. Gold, silver, and bronze inlays show each of the Furies meting out judgment. The columns around the courtyard at the center are woven tight with ivy, the only touches of color in the space. The dark leaves are almost menacing, their sharp tips creating small fangs of shadow on the white pillars beneath.

Ceremony only requires us to sign paperwork to be wed, but Cassius has other plans.

"We will be a beacon to the people, to the plebeians. To the women," he had told me last night after the attack. "And with a public wedding, it will be harder for the Emperor to move against you. And..."

"And once he thinks you've had me, he won't be as interested?" I finished for him, seeing his discomfort.

It was likely true. The jealousy might ease enough for us, for me, to stay safer while we worked towards our goal. As for being a beacon, I hadn't understood before.

I do now.

Cassius is in his white and gold imperial jacket and trousers, while I am in solid white with gold nerium flowers stitched along the hem of the dress. We look like gods. Add that to the fact that we're exchanging vows, a practice that is highly unorthodox, and we're doing it in the temple of revenge and punishment?

Cassius doesn't just mean to kill his brother. He wants to destroy the fabric of his reign.

The furies have three symbolic priestesses: Tisiphone, Alecto, and Megaera. Each is adorned with metallic paint. Megaera is bronze, Alecto is silver, and Tisiphone is gold.

"We are here to unite two souls as one," the priestess representing Tisiphone says. She had tied a golden rope around my waist, which Cassius is meant to untie during the ceremony.

"Dominus Cassius Evander, do you take Luella to be your wife?" Tisiphone continues. My last name doesn't matter, as I'm expected to be Luella Evander or even just Evandia now. Belonging to the Evanders.

But bold, brilliant Cassius has other ideas. He drops to his knees in front of me, clasping my hands in his. "Luella Amulius, I would marry you in any temple, in front of any gods. I would know your soul through any eyes. I will honor you and your wishes. And, I will not let you become anything, except that of your own choosing. Will you do me the honor of becoming the Domina Luella Evander?

He asked permission. He prostrated himself before me.

He knelt.

Cassius Evander had just won the hearts of every woman and every good plebeian man in Divus. But not mine. Still, I smile, soft and sweet beneath my gold veil. Another calculated break in tradition, to abandon the red.

"Rise, Dominus. You do me a great honor." But I don't kneel, or even bow. I meet his gaze. "You are nothing like I expected, yet I find myself in awe of your bravery and integrity. I would love to become the Domina Evander." My words are rehearsed, but I mean them nonetheless.

Cassius unties the knot at my waist, the golden thread hanging loose, and gathers me into his arms as Tisiphone says, "The Furies bless the Dominus and Domina Evander!" His lips find mine, more tender than I expected, and my breath leaves me in a rush. He pulls away, a small smile on his lips.

The temple comes into focus around us as the crowds' cheers grow louder, chanting our names and our titles, I can't help but be affected by the spectacle, by the hope.

And that terrifies me.

This is the most dangerous time, for me. Cassius and I must return to his room without drawing the Emperor's attention. While the people are not surprised that he didn't attend the wedding—he's a busy man after all—he will be, since he was not informed it would be taking place today.

Cassius thinks that until the marriage is consummated, the Emperor will be interested in me.

So we rush back to a separate suite he had prepared for us, near the servants' exit of the Domus Aurea. Hidden.

When we enter the rooms I notice the pristine white linens first. Marriage beds and their white linens. My shoulders tense, but Mia gave me just the vial to remedy that situation and the first thing I do is fold down the top sheet and lie in bed.

Cassius gapes at me as I roll around in the sheets, thrashing through the pillows and tangling the sheets about my legs. I move to the side and eye the area that aligns with my waist, then dump the bright red contents of a vial onto the sheets. A small smear of blood forms and I lay back, returning the empty vial to my pocket.

"There, consummated."

Cassius rolls his eyes as if this was very juvenile and says, "It doesn't happen *that* quickly."

"Have I wounded your pride, Dominus?" I laugh.

"Not at all, Domina. I just want to make sure you have the facts," he says, challenge in his eyes.

"And what are those?" I swing my legs over the side of the bed, coming into a sitting position and resting my head in my hands and my elbows on my knees.

Cassius comes to kneel in front of me, our faces lining up. "I would never expect my Domina to do so much work, nor bleed so early." He captures a hand, kissing each knuckle slowly. The warmth I felt at the ceremony returns and I bite the inside of my lip.

"Not all women bleed, especially if it's done right," I challenge. "Besides, I'm hardly chaste." I shake my hand out of his hold.

"Even more reason to take my time," he says. "Remind you why you married me."

"We both know why I married you," I say, quirking a brow. Perhaps this is the trap I had been anticipating clipses ago, waiting for me to admit my treason.

"Yes, but do you know why I married you?" He recaptures my hand, kissing my palm and laying it against his cheek. "Do you know that I can hardly breathe when you leave my sight? That our plans mean nothing to me if they risk you?"

"You don't need that act here, Dominus. You've already won the people."

"I don't care about the people." His eyes search mine, the blue and gold like a midday sky with not just two but many suns, many rays of light. "Luella, I care about you." I'm not breathing, not daring to move and Cassius must sense the tensing muscles in my legs and the roaring in my head to run, because he rushes to continue. "I always wanted to eliminate him, to stop him from hurting our siblings. And then I wanted revenge, yes. The republic, though? I don't care about the republic. Then I thought about what you've done, what you've been trying to do all by yourself. To fix things, to save people. That's why I wanted the spectacle at the temple."

"I don't understand." My words come out softer than I intend, curious instead of insistent. It frightens me, that I don't see his motives as clearly as I see my praedas'.

"I bowed to you, Luella. I named you my equal, the Domina. I don't need any of that to take down the republic."

"Then why did you do it?" My heart thunders in my ears, the treacherous, dangerous thing that it is.

"So that once we destroy him, I can take the city." I nod because that's become obvious, but he goes on, bringing my hand back to his lips. "So I can take this city, and give it to you."

Time stands still and I think perhaps I am fevered. Had Cassius poisoned me and now the hallucinations have taken hold?

"I don't want the city." Do I?

"You deserve it. You won't have just the city, either; you'll have everything," Cassius says, fervently. I shake my head again. "If you don't want it you can change your face, leave me, and never look back. You can play your game with me, kiss and kill. But perhaps... you will want to stay."

"I thought that night at the tavern, you were... shocked," I say.

Cassius laughs, the sound deep and throaty. His lips move up my arm, to the inner side of my wrist where he nips at the skin. "I was aroused, Luella. Mesmerized. It didn't seem like the best time to beg you to let me taste you."

I shake my head, confused. "Cassius are *you* ill? Feverish?" Perhaps we have both been drugged.

"Perhaps it's the block shape of my head, scrambling my wits." He smiles and puts his hand on my cheek, the mirror to how he placed mine on his a moment ago.

"You are a *matulo*," I whisper. Then he kisses me, soft lips and pressure and yearning and passion all pressed into me so perfectly that for a moment I lose myself in it. Cassius leans forward and I fall back to the bed and then he's over me, deepening the kiss and I feel breathless, heady.

"Wait," Cassius says, scrambling off me.

"Cassius what—" I start to ask, but Cassius tugs me after him, so we're both standing. Then he's walking me backward so that my back is against one of the posters of the bed.

"I'm not your mark, Luella. I'm not trying to take from you," he says, kissing me again. His hands are gentle at the back of my neck, then at my waist. "I want you to see what I mean."

I can't think as his hands squeeze my waist and caress my hair and my cheek. As my blood rushes and my core heats and all I can actually think is that I want. I want Cassius, on me and near me and with me. He kisses my jaw next, then a spot on my neck that sends a shiver through me and

Cassius must feel my skin pebble because he kisses it again, biting me softly.

I give in to the desire heating my skin. The fire engulfing my nerves and my senses. My hands wander across the plane of his chest, his shoulders, into his red hair.

Cassius brings his lips to my ear, brushing against the shell as he whispers, "Tell me what you want, Lue." But I don't know exactly what it is and a whimper escapes me. More. I just want more.

I must say it out loud because Cassius kisses below my ear, and then he's behind me, kissing my neck and the column of my spine where it meets my hairline as he undoes the multitude of buttons holding me together. My dress falls to the floor and Cassius' hands aren't on me anymore but his mouth is. He's biting my shoulder, grazing my neck, and I realize he's taking his clothes off, too. He comes in front of me again, gaze heavy as he takes me in.

"Any form, any face, I would desire you." I doubt that very much, but I care even less at this moment. He's beautiful in a way I wasn't sure a man could be. The muscles of his shoulders spread down into a strong chest that then tapers to the v-shape above his manhood. A cock is just a cock, and I stand by that, but Cassius' doesn't make me want to gag.

Everything about him makes me feel desire.

"Don't be so dramatic, *matulo*," I say.

He huffs a laugh, kissing me once more. Then slowly working down, kissing the tops of my breasts, the plane between. He slips my nipple into his mouth, sucking hard until my back arches and then he repeats the exquisite motion on the other, twisting the first between his fingers.

I'm burning, growing impatient with his teasing, his tenderness. "Cassius," I growl.

"Yes, Domina," he says, dropping all the way to his knees. Then he lifts one of my legs, my weight shifting to the other, and places it on his shoulder. He traces my inner thigh with kisses as one hand holds my leg in place and the other steadies my waist, pinning my hips back against the bedpost.

It's only a moment, but it's torturous. His copper hair gleams in the fire light and his golden skin tangles with mine. Then his mouth is where I crave him and he's featherlight, kissing and testing and tasting.

I moan, trying to tilt my hips forward against his grasp and I realize he was waiting for permission, because now he's frenzied. His tongue thrusts into me, warm and insistent, and I reach down to tangle my fingers in his hair. He devours me, drinking in each thrust until I feel the tension coiling low. My hips move faster, my grip on his hair tighter.

Cassius growls something into me but I can't hear it over my own whimpers, and then he's sucking that sensitive bundle of nerves into his mouth. I unravel, feeling the tension break as wave after wave of pleasure rolls through me.

Still Cassius doesn't stop, his mouth gentler but not slowed. My legs are shaking as his tongue moves through me, and my knees become weak. I tighten my thighs until I'm squeezing his head in place but he makes a low sound and presses in, hungry.

"Cassius," I gasp, "I'm going to collapse."

He pauses, reluctantly, and kisses my inner thigh. I twitch, my skin too sensitive, and push him away. He laughs. "Sorry, I didn't mean to get carried away." Then he swoops his arms beneath my shoulders and knees, lifting me like he did that day in the hallway, when I was covered in blood.

Even with that thought, or perhaps because of it, I melt into him. Satisfied. Safe.

He lowers me to the bed, and I have the urge to stretch like a cat in the suns, savoring this moment of languid pleasure. Cassius has other plans, though, and his mouth starts at my neck and travels down my body until I'm panting again with desire.

"Must you tease me?" I say.

"I'm not teasing, Domina," he says. I don't need to see his smile to hear it, and then he reaches the apex of my thighs. "I'm worshiping." Once again the warmth of his mouth, the scrape of his beard on my thighs, and the alternation between sucking and licking has me bucking my hips and holding his hair. I feel the pressure building again and I just want Cassius.

"More," I pant.

Cassius shifts and suddenly I feel his fingers easily slide through my wet center, and he sucks harder on the sensitive flesh. I cry out in pleasure and surprise and Cassius moans, too. His fingers thrust and curl while I grip his copper strands, not caring if he can breath or move. I'm too consumed by my pleasure and I think I'm saying his name or praying to the gods but soon I fracture all over again, shattering under his touch.

He gentles further this time, wringing each drop of pleasure from me until his touch sends shivers through me. I sigh and Cassius moves up, wrapping me in his arms. I reach for him, but it only takes a moment to realize he found his pleasure as well, without me even touching him.

He laughs, without an ounce of embarrassment. "I told you. I would desire you in any form. I don't need to take anything from you except the sounds of your own pleasure." He kisses the side of my forehead, his breath warm across my brow and his own forehead hot. "But I will try to contain myself so I can pleasure you any way you wish, next time."

Next time. I freeze, not daring to speak. Not wanting to ruin this moment with my sharp words. Not wanting to ruin Cassius with my jagged edges.

His chest moves slowly, relaxed, and I finally take my own deep breath, feeling sleep begin to tug at me and realize I can smell Cassius for the first time. He smells like forest trails and sunshine, like his room. That combined with his warmth and the satisfaction coursing through my body draws my own breath out slow, calm.

Just before sleep claims me a whisper of sound reaches me. "Goodnight, *cor meum.*"

Goodnight, *my heart.*

CHOICE

ROSE

THE HALLS STRETCH OUT before me, dual shadows caging me in on the way back to my room. The wedding looms ahead of us, but I don't have to plan anything. Camilla will take care of it all. My choices would probably be too plebeian, anyways.

Once I reach my rooms I'll be there for the night, so instead of heading straight back, I begin looking for a detour. Certainly there is more to see here.

To my right is another long, mostly dark corridor with a number of doors off the main hall; perhaps one of them—

"Ouch!"

My body collides with something warm and impossibly large.

"Gods," I rub my face and look up into Augustus' sheepish face. "Didn't you see me?"

"Didn't you see me?" he retorts.

"What's down there?" I point down the hall I'd been staring at, refusing to look at him.

"Guest rooms, but the wing is closed right now." Augustus shrugs. "Not enough guests, I suppose." He's staring at me, and I refuse to meet his eyes. "You have a habit of running into me."

"Perhaps you have a habit of being in my way." The words have left me before I've calibrated them and my hand flies to my mouth.

Augustus just laughs. "Ah yes, no idea where Daisy gets her spirit, huh?"

"*She's* rubbing off on *me*," I defend.

Augustus grabs my elbow, leading me to the side of the hall where we won't be noticed immediately if someone were to come this way. He's not laughing now. "I wanted to talk to you about Daisy."

My stomach sinks to my toes. "What?"

I can't look away from him now. His eyes are searching and for a moment I'm frozen in their depths. Our chests are a breath away, and his warmth seeps through the air and into me. My eyelids flutter and I take a shaky breath in. "Augustus?"

He clears his throat. "I think I found Daisy a match. My friend is a good man, his familia is at the lower end of patricians but they do well enough to waive a dowry. He's in the legions, though, and won't be back for two quads."

Two quads.

Daisy can hold out that long. Besides, Tristan had said she could move in here after the wedding. He would keep his word.

"I know it's not ideal, but he's a good man. I wanted to make sure it was someone I could trust."

Something swells in my throat. "Thank you." It's everything and not enough all at once.

"But Rose?" Augustus reaches down, taking my hand.

I stare at it a moment, his callouses and warmth searing my flesh. I want to lean in and I want to step away. "Tristan wouldn't like this."

"Rose, I could find you a match... too."

The warmth evaporates and I try to move away in earnest, but Augustus tightens his grip.

I'm shaking my head, but he goes on. "You don't have to marry him."

"What are you talking about?"

"He's not like you think he is," Augustus whispers, his words urgent.

"He *saved* me," I hiss. He might be right. Tristan isn't how I thought. But did I think things would be easy and perfect? My life has never been either of those things. Tristan's saving me in more ways than one. Soon he will save Daisy, too.

"Why was he there?"

"What?"

"Why was Tristan right by The Sabines when you needed him?" Augustus asks.

I shake my head, refusing to question the circumstances of my rescue. "I got lucky. Would you rather I be sold right now? Chained up in that... that place? With the type of monsters who patronize that place?"

"Don't you understand? It's a prettier place, but the monsters here are the same."

I rear back as if I've been slapped, the words striking through me with white hot fear.

"He loves me."

"He loves nothing," Augustus growls.

"What other choice did I have?" I snap back. The words are low, angry. How dare he bring this to me now? Tristan *saved* me. He loves me.

"Me," Augustus says and I'm shaking my head before the word has left his mouth.

"I can't do this. I love Tristan. I won't betray him." For a bitter, hopeless, disgusting moment, I remember being on my knees in front of Tristan and consider that Augustus wouldn't want me anyway, if he knew. That there's no choice, now that I've been dishonored. Ironic, considering what Tristan once said about his brother. I shove that thought aside, pretending it never existed to begin with. "You should go."

Augustus doesn't say anything for a moment, studying my face. "I'm going, Rose. Pater's sending me away this clipse. I don't know that I'll be here to protect you."

From my husband? "I don't need you to worry about me." I hold my chin high, daring him to argue.

Augustus cups my face, running a thumb along my cheek. Shuddering, I draw back. This isn't me. I love Tristan. I was made for him.

Augustus' hand lingers in the air, over the ghost of where I stood. His expression nearly breaks my heart. It's yearning and fear and desperation. It's all the things I know all too well.

"I'm happy, Augustus." My words are heavy, suffocating, but I don't know why. I mean them.

I am happy.

So why does it hurt so much when Augustus leaves without a word?

Sold

Luella

I awake in a nightmare. Dark. Damp. The sounds of screaming. Rats crawling across my limbs. I try to move but my arms are too heavy, and I quickly realize they're chained to the floor.

I shake them harder, panic crawling up my throat and something inside me cracks. Where is Cassius? The heat from last night. The way I wondered if I'd been drugged...

A broken hollow sound leaves me in the form of a chuckle, which grows until I'm laughing so hard I might vomit. The laughs stick in my throat, sounding more crazed with each one, until I realize I'm not laughing. I'm sobbing.

I cry until I feel myself again. Until the woman from last night is washed away by the salt on my cheeks.

I was drugged. On my wedding night.

Cassius played my very own game on me, and I was so naive that I didn't notice. I fool men by blending in, Cassius fooled me by standing out. Whatever was in the wine was sneaky, too slow to be noticed right away, and not the same as what I usually use and dose myself with daily to build tolerance.

If last night was the kiss, I know what comes today. But I am not praeda. I'm the black widow. I'm Tisiphone.

I'm revenge.

Perhaps it is minutes, or perhaps it is hours, but slowly the screaming dies out. A key scrapes in the lock to this small room and before I can move back the light from the hall blinds me. I flinch back, trying to cover my face but the chains don't reach. I close my eyes instead, waiting.

"Grab the witch," a male voice says. A bag is placed over my head and the chains are unlocked from the ground, leaving my hands heavy as someone drags me forward. I fight the panic and listen to each noise muffled through the bag. How many men? Where are we going? What can I use to escape?

I'm yanked forward and I stumble, biting my lip. I can't reach my pocket if I even still have vials in there. I'm helpless without my potions and poisons.

No, that's not true.

There are my wits.

There's a man to each side, and one in front, from the sounds of their steps, the grasp of their arms. I don't struggle because every ounce of strength will be needed before the end. I know that.

The only light comes from torches, the flames hissing in the damp air as the men lead me away from the small cell in which I awoke. I keep my breathing steady, counting my steps and my breaths.

I refuse to let panic take me, as I have every day of my life for the last ten years. I will not crumble, no matter what happens. I will survive. It's just a body.

This is my mantra.

I will not crumble. I will survive. It's just a body.

I remind myself of the time Silas didn't take to the sleeping drought and I smashed a vase over his head. I reminisce on the time Brutis tried to rape me before the wedding ceremony and I slit his throat. I remember the feel of Maximus' hands wrapped around my throat when he refused the wine I had poisoned and I stabbed my thumb into his eye, blinding him.

I have never crumbled. Janus has saved me, yes, but I also have saved myself. And I will continue to do so.

Slivers of pain shoot through my palms and I fight to unclench my fists. The stone floor is cold and dirt sticks to the soles of my feet as they shove me into a new room. I stumble but don't fall and the man to my left decides that was a mistake. He kicks the back of my knee and I collapse, chains rattling and bones jarring as my hands join my feet in the damp dirt.

I stay there, on my hands and knees, waiting. The hush of the room tells me someone else is here, and they are in charge.

"Remove her hood," he says.

They do. We are underground. There is no light, no windows. Yet, the archways, the columns, and the altar before me tell me where I am. A temple. The room is worn limestone, but the altar draws my eyes. It's brown with rust and death, coated in the remnants of the types of sacrifice that no good Divusian would use. The men here wear masks of the god Bacchus, identical to the cursed fountain that mocked me for clipses. All except the man who sits before me.

The Emperor.

I expected Cassius, or Flavia. Perhaps they are here, and masked. Either way, I expected a face, a name. I expected someone to be here to gloat, but since they are not, I play the game. I wait to see who will speak first.

"Evandia," The Emperor says.

"Imperator," I greet, as if this is a pleasant passing in the hall.

"Cassius has decided to make good on his promise." He smiles, teeth bared in a feral grin that sends a shudder through me. It hurts. The betrayal that I had convinced myself wouldn't come.

"You'd like me straight from my marriage bed?" I risk to say, hoping it will dissuade him that I was so recently with another.

"Your marriage consummation isn't complete. You are Evandia and I am Evander."

He searches my face and I remember the little shift of the eyes I had shown him that day in the dining room. It was a mistake, a miscalculation. I worry once again that I do not understand this man. Perhaps this will not be so bad as it seems if the only issue at play is the jealousy that I had planned for.

I bow my head, itching to reach towards my skirts, to the lifelines that I pray to Janus are still there. I don't dare, though, not with all eyes on me, and they are on me. The hair raised on the back of my neck, the hush of the room, the collective bated breath; they all tell me this.

The way his closeness, the fervor in his eyes, and his grip on my skirts tells me what he will do, just before he does it. Soon, I am naked, my vials shattered in the pockets of my nightgown across the room.

My face is pressed against the floor, and now my cheek matches my palms, which matches the stomach and the breasts and the body that I inhabit as I watch for what could be minutes, or could be hours, as the violet and white liquid of my shattered salvation seep into the nightgown and onto the dirt floor.

As the day or night continues, the me that stepped into this room seeps away as well, and all I hear are the words from my nightmares.

She just screams so pretty.

I wait for him to be done with the body that isn't mine.

It's controlled and not all at once, and... it's just him. It's a lesson, so there is no frenzy, no excessive cruelty. Of course there is no intimacy either, even the forced kind. I never thought I'd be disappointed that a praeda hadn't kissed me, but I've loosened the pearl hidden between my teeth and am unable to use it. I hold it between my tongue and the roof of my mouth, just in case, afraid the clench of my jaw will release it needlessly.

It takes me a moment to realize it's over, the numbness and pain mingling to a crescendo of untethered despondence.

Part of me screams to pay attention, that these are the moments where they will think me bent to their will, but my vials are gone. My pearl will only work if he gets close. For a moment, I will allow myself to be exactly as I appear; broken. I accept the familiar swell of injustice and rage and pain and shattering self.

The bag is placed over my head, but before I leave the Emperor calls to me. "See you in a few days, Evandia."

If I am to live to return, it means I will not be killed. Which means that the Emperor is not afraid of me.

He thinks me just a woman, available for him to use.

A *venefica* in what I've done to Cassius, maybe, but not her.

Not Tisiphone.

Not Vidua.

I feel the jagged edges of me falling into place, into a semblance of a person as I piece each moment together. Cassius sold my body, but not my secret.

WHO?

LUELLA

My rooms are empty when I return. It's a gracious word for the way they shove me into the chamber, the bag still in place, the only clue to my whereabouts the warmth spreading across my skin from the afternoon suns as I lie on the plush rugs. I remove the hood, but I don't rise. The dirt on my skin and the salt on my cheeks just feed the rage inside of me. I debate going to Cassius and slitting his throat. I debate castrating the Emperor and shoving his pathetic member down his own throat.

I still might do that one.

I change into a clean shift, filling the pockets with Janus' blessing stones and replacement vials. I don't remove the shift in the bathing chambers of the Baths where Cassius took me before. I scrub around the material until my skin is pink beneath the white garment. I keep scouring my skin, the shift wet and sticking to the ground pumice coating me. Protecting me. I don't stop until the pink turns to red and my skin screams in protest.

I will need to see Mia today to heal my injuries and check for infection, although shame urges me to stay away.

My chambers are still empty when I return, as are Cassius'. I change into a dress suitable for traveling, transfer my vials and my stones, and discard my wet shift.

Perhaps Mia will tell me 'I told you so,' and I can pretend this is another poor choice. I can pretend this is a learning opportunity, a plan

I was attempting, a way to set the Emperor at ease around me so I could kill him next time.

Perhaps I can pretend I'm still in control.

The streets are busy, and the noise grates my nerves like fine cheese. I wrinkle my nose and take a deep breath, entering Mia's clinic.

While I wait I pick my cuticles bloody and wonder if I will cry. Perhaps she will hold me, the way I know she does.

"Stones, Lue." Mia enters and does just that. She doesn't ask me anything, just folds me in a warm embrace. Her healing power spreads across my body, and I refuse to apologize for the great gulping breaths I take in her arms. Her power tells her enough that when I finally catch my breath she just asks, "Who was it?"

I don't want to answer, don't know if I can.

But Mia's silence is gentle, and I finally set it free. The name that lives in me as a whisper, a secret, and a curse.

"Tristan."

THE DOVE

ROSE

THE TEMPLE OF VENUS is intoxicating, the myrtle blossoms filling the air as a light breeze separates petals from stems. I'm already in my white wedding dress, modest and trimmed in gold to match Tristan's white and gold robes. Everything has a red haze as I look through my wedding veil. White for purity and red for luck and fertility.

Tristan doesn't come in. "Venus is for women," he says. Perhaps she is, but Venus blessed our match with her festival and with her favor. I know it. My hands are sweaty, wrapped around a struggling dove. Its small talons and little beak grasp for purchase against my slick skin so it can fling itself away.

I've never brought a live sacrifice before. My stomach turns. I could set it free and Tristan would never know, but the priestesses would.

My steps are steady and sure as I move towards the altar and my heart thunders in time to the dove's, beating against my palm until I don't know which belongs to me.

The temple is empty, cleared by the Praetorians, as I drop to my knees in front of Venus. The columns cast gilded shadows across the courtyard, as if the myrtle trees and I are caged here. The dove has finally exhausted itself, lying still in my hand.

"Venus." I take a sharp, shaky breath. "Bestow your favor upon my marriage. Open my heart to love and grant me the wisdom to serve my husband." I lower my hands, still caging the dove. It stays there, frozen in fear. Can I kill it?

I'm supposed to break its neck, quick and painless, but my hands are immobile. I'm supposed to do so many things, but what do I want? I want to build a life, one that's nothing like the one I've had before. I want sweetness and hope. I want what I was made for.

I want a life filled with love.

I've followed tradition my whole life, adhered to expectations set forth by my mater and pater, and doing so gained me so little. When I was vulnerable, when I told Tristan the truth: that's when Venus changed my life.

If we want to break the cycles that have broken us, shouldn't I break this tradition, too?

I make a decision, the first of my new life, and uncurl my fingers.

The dove flies away, unharmed.

My wedding isn't a grand ceremony; only me, Tristan, and a Jupiter priest. Too much of his life was pomp and circumstance, Tristan said. This would be better than that. Intimate.

"I promise to provide for you, lead you, and fulfill my duties as your husband," Tristan repeats after the priest. It's hard to see his face beneath the red haze of my wedding veil, but he doesn't smile, doesn't look happy. The shadows of the temple shroud his features and I feel a chill at the back of my neck.

My familia isn't here. After the temple of Venus, we'd stopped at my old domus where Pater had signed the paperwork that released his right to his eldest daughter, entrusting me to Tristan and his familia. Daisy had bowed and smiled at us, sending us off with happy wishes. Tristan's pater was too busy to attend the signing, but no one minded. Tristan wasn't old enough for this to be a spectacle yet. Besides, I don't need Pater's reminders about my role tonight.

"I vow to obey my husband in all things," I repeat after the priest. Tristan nods across from me, his silent approval easing something tight in my chest.

Minutes later, we're on our way back to the Domus Aurea to dine and retire to our marriage bed. The excitement and nervous energy course through my tangled thoughts, until I realize Tristan's led me to the garden.

Except it's different. Instead of orange trees and grapes, the entire central walk has been replaced with...

"Roses," I whisper. The smell hits me now, almost overwhelming in the still evening air. I can almost taste the petals, loamy and sweet .

Tristan steps closer. "A wedding gift, Rosebud. I wanted to give it to you before dinner." He tugs me into his arms, and they aren't as warm as I want them to be. I lean in closer.

"I love you, Tristan." He captures my mouth the way he always does, but he's more insistent tonight. Our teeth clash and I flinch away, trying to find a more comfortable rhythm. Tristan growls, gripping my hips to stop me.

"Don't call me that," he says. He releases my mouth, moving his lips and teeth to my jaw. His hand tangles into my hair and he drags my head back so he can access my neck.

"What should I call you?" I'm breathless, dizzy with it.

"You call him Augustus." He punctuates the sentence by biting me along the side of my neck, the fragile skin trapped between his teeth, and

I can't help the whimper that escapes. Panic shoots through me. He can't know about Augustus and me in the hallway. "But that's not his name." He bites again and my hands come up of their own accord, gripping into his shoulders in protest, but the traitorous things refuse to push him away. I can't. "And she calls him *princeps*." He moves to the top of my shoulder now, teeth grazing, and my head angles to protect it, trying to stop his access. Desire and fear wrap around me, the way they often do with Tristan.

"He told me that was his name," I whisper. "It just became a habit to continue." I think my explanation will remind him that I didn't choose it, but I'm not good at reading people, at reading him. His grip tightens in my hair and he yanks even harder.

The scent of roses threatens to turn my stomach as the fear overpowers everything else. My muscles slacken and my eyes drop. I know better than to fight this.

"Because you spend so much time with him," Tristan says, his tone condescending. "My sabine wife, trying to fuck any patrician cock she can find?"

A tear slips down my cheek, because nothing has changed. The cycle we vowed to break is already repeating, and I remember that Augustus said the monsters are here, too. I think past the hurt, past the fear I've known my whole life. My mind wants to survive. "No, my love. I just want you."

Tristan's hands are rough and cold. The contrast against my skin feels like shattered dreams and a broken future.

I should have snapped that dove's neck when I had the chance.

Nothing

Luella

I lock the door between our rooms when I return, although I'm tempted to enter Cassius' chambers to take the keys to mine. I doubt it matters. If Cassius or the Emperor want to enter, they will.

I ignore the knock that sounds through the room just as I begin to drift into sleep. His knock is louder the second time, rattling the door.

"Yes?" I say when I rip it open, trying not to slur the words with a pearl under my tongue. A vial of paralytic is in my fist, my thumb on the stopper.

He leans down to kiss me and I flinch back. His eyes widen. *"Cor meum,* what's wrong?"

I had planned to play this out. On my way back from Mia's I had considered the retorts I could use, the venom I could inject into Cassius and Tristan to poison their brotherhood, to distract them. Now each one shrivels on my tongue as I see his concern. It enrages me.

"What's wrong?" I step forward, taking pleasure in the way he steps back. "What's wrong is you coming in here. You'll have to borrow his chains if you want to touch me again."

"Chains? Luella what are you—" He doesn't finish the thought because frantic knocking begins in the back of his room. Flavia flings herself through the servants' door before he has a chance to answer.

"Dominus," she gasps, her chest heaving as she takes greedy breaths. She sees me and pales. "Domina," she rasps, nearly shoving Cassius out of the way as she falls to the floor in front of me. She grabs my free hand, the one not in my pocket, with both of hers. "*Vidua*. We didn't know."

"Didn't know?" I say at the same time that Cassius says, "know what?"

She looks between us, as if realizing what she's interrupted, that Cassius still doesn't know. She can see my rage, although I wonder if she thinks it's for her because for a moment she just stares at me.

"I just heard," she finally whispers.

I nod, not sure if I'm relieved or angry. Is Cassius so useless he can't protect his wife on her wedding night? Or is this all a ruse?

I yank my hand out of Flavia's grip. "You tell him," I say, shutting and locking the door between us.

Cassius rages. Furniture shatters and glass breaks. He screams at Flavia. He pleads with me to let him in. He begs for my voice, for my anger. He tells me that I was gone when he woke and he thought I was in the Baths. He vows to kill them all. He apologizes for letting me down and he asks for forgiveness.

I lie on the bed, under all of the blankets. I'm motionless, held in place by more pillows than I need. Hearing him hurt shouldn't please me, but it does. Because even though I can see it now, the lie Tristan tried to place between us, I still blame Cassius. Perhaps because he didn't keep me safe. Perhaps, more unforgivably, because he made me feel safe in the first place. I blame him for the lie and the distraction. But most of all, I blame him so that I don't blame myself.

I know that I will not survive that.

"*Cor meum*," he says quietly, his voice muffled against the door. "Domina, please. Let me in."

I let him cry and scream and beg, and I don't offer my pain to ease his. I'll share nothing with him again.

THREADS

LUELLA

CASSIUS BRINGS ME THEIR heads. Not all of them, of course, but the three men who wore masks and watched. I am his wife, after all, and he is allowed to do with the men as he wishes.

He could kill me, too. A good Divusian woman cannot be raped, because if I was where I should have been, if I behaved appropriately, what man would take me? If anyone finds out, I had it coming. Cassius could divorce me and shame me. He can kill me, just like he can kill the men who saw me.

He just can't kill the Emperor.

The Emperor's will is divine, so Cassius can do anything but retaliate. Any challenge to the Emperor's position would doom his own future.

Tristan really is quite clever.

"What am I supposed to do with them?" I ask, not masking my irritation. The heads don't bother me, but the valiant gesture does. They were mine to seek vengeance on. Tisiphone doesn't need a lover to exact revenge and a black *vidua* doesn't need a husband to help her hold the knife.

"Whatever you wish, Domina." Cassius eyes me warily. It's been two days since I've agreed to see him, and I've only allowed it now because I fear the Emperor will take me again soon. I have questions for Cassius.

"I would have wished to do it myself," I snap.

Cassius looks down. "*Cor meum*, I did mean to bring them alive..." His voice fades into the tapestries and I understand his meaning. He lost his temper.

"Are you even sure it's them? They wore masks."

"I'm sure." His jaw clenches and he withdraws the masks from a bag at his waist. I look away, hiding my flinch with movement. Bacchus is such a bastard.

I study the tapestries a moment before speaking, gathering courage for a conversation I am not sure I'm ready to have. "Cassius, what is your history with your brother?"

"What do you mean?"

"This is more than rivalry. More than jealousy. You hate him."

"What's not to hate?" A line appears between his eyes and he takes a step closer, his fist clenching at his side as if he is fighting the urge to reach for me.

I turn to him and I drop my own mask to reveal not my actual face, but my true emotion. I let him see the rage and the hurt, the fear and fury. "There. Is. More." I know it, but I need to hear it from him.

Cassius gestures to the bench at the end of the bed and sits. I don't join him, instead crossing my arms over my chest. He sighs in resignation but begins.

"When we were boys, I met a young woman. She was..." his voice cracks. "She was beautiful. Kind. Brave... but she was from a lower familia. I asked my pater if I could court her, officially."

It's not what I expected and I sit next to him on the bench, silent.

"My brother knew my intentions. He argued with Pater that she wasn't right for me. That if anyone should marry a plebeian, it should be him to show he was an Emperor of the people. My pater... he agreed. He said I should marry politically. Unite the republic with Nocia or another country someday."

"I don't see—" I start to say, but Cassius interrupts me.

"Our mater was ill, but she didn't agree. She told Tristan that he wasn't ready to marry. I said we should just wait. Everyone should wait, because I knew I could change Pater's mind with some time. We were young. It didn't have to happen then."

Something inside my heart cracks wide, blood rushing into the spaces, pressuring the entire thing to fracture. Oblivious, Cassius continues. "Tristan hated me. He hated me so much..."

"What do you mean?" I ask, even though a part of me knows. I've already heard this story, just not like this.

"He married her. *Her*." His voice is cold, like he can't think about what he's saying. "He wanted to upset our mater. He wanted to take from me. And part of him must have known what he would do... because he married her quietly. They signed the paperwork. No fanfare. The next day she was gone. I didn't find out until later what happened... He..."

He takes a deep breath and tries again. "He... killed her." He says it so simply. Like dead girls aren't fractured bones and sinew and salt, salt, salt.

"Then..." his voice breaks. "Then he went to her Pater and ..." He can't continue, his tears silently trailing down his cheeks, like the streams in his paintings around the room. It feels cruel to make him continue when I know the rest. I know it like I know the men of this republic. The way I know their depravities and the way they hurt and the way they take their dying breaths.

I know it, but I wish I didn't.

"Oh." It's all I can think to say, all I can gather as the pieces of me grate against one another.

"He said he didn't know I actually cared about her. Like that made it better that he ... I almost killed him then. We fought and when they finally separated us I swore I'd destroy him, but he moved the twins into his care the next day."

"What did your parents think?"

"Mater was furious. She was always hard on him. Cruel, even. She didn't see how she fueled his hate for me by being... her." He looks down at his hands. "My mater died a few clipses later, and then Pater not long after."

"How?"

"Poisoned. I think he'd been poisoning Mater for years, but he didn't move slow with Pater. Not that I could ever prove it was him."

"Oh," I say again. Eloquent as always.

"Luella, I'm so sorry. I'm the reason... I thought we were safe."

It tempers me to hear the guilt in his voice. I almost tell him it's not his fault, but that wouldn't be fair to either of us. It's Tristan's fault, but that feels too easy and too hard at the same time because I can't hold him accountable yet. I'm here with Cassius, though, and he could be that. Accountable. He could be many things, I think, if I let him.

"Does he ever talk about his dead betrothed?" I ask, tugging a thread I'd toyed with dangerously before.

"Flavia says he calls some of the floras her name at times..." He shakes his head in disgust. "And I do think he regretted it to some extent. He wanted what I think he's always wanted."

"What's that?"

"Love," he says simply. My breath whooshes out of me at that, but he goes on. "Or I guess, for her to love him, and not me."

"Did she love you?" I don't know why I ask.

He shakes his head. "No, but maybe she could have. If I had the chance to... to love her. And that was enough to doom her."

My breath sticks to my ribs, heart trying to drown out anything more Cassius might tell me. The dual suns mock us, giving shape to the twin shadows that we are in that moment: rage and grief, loss and sorrow. So much darkness and pain in our pasts and our sticky, tangled threads keeping us from our future.

Black and Blue Bride

Rose

I know nothing but pain.

Agony.

Betrayal.

Each breath fractures inside my chest as bones and blood seize my lungs. Don't you dare take a breath, they say. You should obey your pain, they reprimand.

But I can't obey, my mind too stunned and my heart more broken than my body. My eyes are swollen, making it nearly impossible to see past the blood and the flowing tears. A haze of red fills my vision, as if my wedding veil is sutured over my eyes, taunting me.

My throat is raw from screaming, but the rest is worse.

Lash marks. Bruises. Brands.

The memory is already fading, distant against the agony of the present.

Tristan had asked for things that I couldn't comprehend, couldn't stomach. After the garden, he'd brought me to his rooms.

And he'd made me scream.

There's a goat lying next to me, it's throat slit and dried blood coating its fur.

"We match," I tell him sagely. We're at the bottom of the trash chute, to be dumped outside of Divus when it's full. Tristan would have his wife die in a trash heap, without even the courtesy to dump me here himself. I can't remember who did. His friend?

I have always been destined for this, I remember. For the life of a goat: To be sold to The Sabines, or Tristan, or anyone else. I'd always have ended up here.

But I don't care. I can't die. I have to find Daisy and run. She'll come looking for me, she'll ask questions in a few days when I don't visit her.

I don't want her anywhere near the Evanders.

Blood smears as I try to push a lock of hair out of my face. It's matted and stiff with blood and semen, patchy from where he ripped pieces out at the root. Distantly, I wonder if the sobs are coming from me or the goat.

If crying doesn't hurt, I won't feel it.

All I am is pain.

"Thank me," Tristan had screamed when he'd first snapped, slapping me for my stunned silence in the face of his brutality. I drag myself out of the trash bin, a small cry echoing against the cobblestones when my body hits. A wave of dizziness threatens to overwhelm me, but I take a deep breath through my mouth, spitting the blood away when it pools in my throat.

"Call me *princeps*," Tristan had said as he whipped me with the flagrum, flogged me like a criminal. I shake my head. I can't think of this now. I have to escape.

I have to get away.

Away.

I stick to the alley, empty at this late hour, but between the darkness, my blurred vision, and the dizziness threatening to topple me, it's not long before I'm well and truly lost. I step down a new street and hear a man and his friend urinating behind a row of shops. I jerk back, the male voices and the smell of urine in my hair sending fear coursing through me.

I stumble away, down a different path, until the sound of the city becomes muffled. I'm too far out. I'm lost. Alone.

Black and blue on my wedding night, like Pater always knew I would be.

A sob tears through me as I fall onto a step that goes not up, but down. Ah, a tomb. Exactly the place for me.

It's not a tomb that greets me, though; it's a temple. A temple with arched doorways and a small pond in the center of the room. At the back of the temple is a statue of a two-headed form morphing between feminine and masculine features, neither man nor woman. Many faces, many lives, many beginnings. A promise that means nothing to me.

I fall onto the altar, thoughts sluggish.

"I should have brought an offering," I whisper, naked and shivering on the stone floor. Then I laugh, remembering that I'm a goat anyways.

"Do you like goats?" I ask the shifting statue, my voice like gravel beneath a Praetorian's boots. I close my eyes.

"She just screams so pretty," Tristan says, but to whom I'm not sure.

I bolt upright, gasping in pain. Is he here? He sounds so close. So real. The edges of my vision swim in black and the puddle around me is all wrong. Why did I sit in the pond?

It's not water. It's blood.

"I'm sorry Daisy," I whisper, sacrificing myself on the altar of a god I've never prayed to. Perhaps he'll take pity on me when I die, and bless Daisy in this life or the next.

Maybe he'll protect her.

"I'm sorry Daisy," I say again. I know it's no longer if I die.

It's when. Because Daisy forgot one of the options before. One I'd seen firsthand when the Vestal priestess suffocated in a box before my eyes.

We can be virgins or whores.

Or corpses.

Hearts' Sisters

Luella

Taln answers the door to the closed infirmaria, his usually brown face a sickly two shades lighter. A bead of sweat marks his brow even though the suns have almost set and a cool breeze whispers down the cobbled streets.

"Taln, are you alright?"

Taln nods too many times, the motion hurried. I look behind me and to the side but can't put my finger on what could be wrong besides his awkwardness. Perhaps Mia told him something about me?

Is he afraid?

"Where's Mia?" I ask, keeping my tone gentle.

"This way," Taln says, turning to lead me into the dark hallways. Not a single light shines, each room instead yawning with darkness as we pass on our way to the back room. I grip the vials in my pocket and the stones in the other.

It's too dark. Too quiet.

One of the stones at my fingertips seems to whisper to me. It's small and smooth, shaped like a single grain of wheat in the bread that's always sustained me. I follow Taln down the hall, hesitating for just a moment. I pop the small charged stone into my mouth and swallow hard. After doing it once, it feels right to do it again. I trace each stone, until I find another that reminds me of grain. It follows the first, and I decide this is either the wisest or stupidest decision I've made in awhile.

I manage to stuff three more of the grain-like stones into my mouth and swallow them dry. They settle cool and heavy at the base of my belly as Taln stumbles ahead of me.

"Taln, is Mia alright?" I prod as we enter the private area.

He hesitates. "Y-yes." Taln steps aside to let me in the very back room. Perhaps Mia had a bad patient again, or one who had died. That might set off the boy.

Moving into the backroom I see that Mia does have a patient, but they are very much alive. Three men stand in the room, Bacchus masks on their faces. One holds a knife at Mia's throat, and the other two rush to flank me. I side-step, elbowing the closer one in the throat. Regret rings through me like a bell as Mia makes a strangled noise. The brute holding her squeezes the knife ever closer, drawing a small trickle of blood. "Don't make me kill the healer, *venefica*."

I freeze. How did they find Mia? Why? Surely not because of the Emperor's games. They must know more. I lock eyes with my friend, my friend for ten years, and try to see what she knows. She tries to move her eyes to the side, like she wants to shake her head but can't against the knife on her throat.

She hasn't told them anything.

"Why have you accosted my healer?" I say, mustering my most unaffected and Domina-like voice. I channel Cassius in all his righteousness, Ledo in his arrogance, and the Emperor in his dismissiveness.

"Cause she's friends with you, *venefica*," the man holding Mia says. He seems to be in charge, and while the other two men haven't grabbed me, they do block the door behind me. Not that I would run while my friend was in danger. Taln huddles off to the side. "Or should I say, *Vidua*." He grins at that, as if it's funny to him that I have this name.

Then he shifts to the side, intentionally, cruelly. There's someone behind him, crumpled against the wall. Someone who was very much alive yesterday, but no longer witnesses the horrors of the republic.

The last of seven favors her pater traded for, finally joining her sisters.

But she wasn't a favor to me, or to Cassius. She was just Flavia. The man must see my eyes, wavering on her still form, her bruised face, her bloody back. He doesn't have to tell me what my eyes have already pieced together, but he does. "She told us all about your secret. Working with the Dominus to eventually kill the Emperor. She didn't know how you changed your face or what magic you possess." He laughs. "But she knew enough." And once she was used up for her information, she was discarded, like so many others.

I meet Mia's eyes again. I can't risk her, too. "I'll come with you," I say.

"No!" Mia moves forward as if on instinct and the man holding her slices the blade straight across her throat. A choked, gurgled sound comes from Mia as her vocal cords tear beneath his blade and I scream. I scream and scream and scream as I watch the woman who braids my hair, who first called me Lue, who is the sister of my heart, crumple to the ground.

Not Broken

Rose

I dream. I dream of Tristan's first kisses, soft and hungry, sur-rounded by blooms and bustle and hope. I dream of his brother, his nickname beaten from me so now his real name is bruised on my insides. I dream of thorns wrapped in my fist, blood trickling down my forearm. The scent of roses and blood permeates, the sharp metallic scent so mingled with pain that I don't know if I'm feeling it fill my mouth or breathing it in.

I dream of my face, morphing like the statue I'd collapsed in front of, my features moving through a kaleidoscope of physicality. I dream of the golden haired man who turned into a vengeful god, and I dream of how he ordered me to say thank you. I dream of his rage and fire and blood, and soon I don't know which is mine and which is his.

Finally there's a resonant voice, calling my name.

"Are you ready for a new beginning?"

I open my eyes, urgency gripping the back of my neck as I take in the unfamiliar sanctuary. The temple.

I remember.

The suns are mid sky, casting dual shadows throughout the temple, the columns slicing their darkness across the pond.

I might think it all a nightmare if I wasn't still in a pool of my own blood, the liquid dark and sticky now. Cooled and tempered. My back screams but my lungs no longer protest, no longer swim in their own fluid. I take in a greedy breath. My stomach still burns where Tristan branded me. "You're mine now, Mater," he'd said. Mater.

Images flash, his voice an echo in my mind. "My mater favored him…" My memory is a deluge of horrible words spilling from Tristan's wrathful lips. "Did he punish you?" He'd asked about my pater.

I shake my head. The thought takes hold, though, and I turn and vomit off the side of the altar, choking when the movement brings pain so intense that I cough on it as I scream.

I should be dead. I knew it last night, but now my lungs are functioning and somehow… I'm alive. I look to the statue of Janus and decide I'll bring them as many goats as they want, but first I need to find Daisy.

I look down at the blood and dirt crusted onto my skin. Then I look to the small pond. I can't travel through town with the suns up this way. Less blood, more clothes.

Stepping into the cool water, I slowly and painstakingly wipe the blood off my skin. The water clouds but I don't worry about that. A little blood and dirt won't hurt the plants; rather, they'll probably relish it, blooming anew with the nutrients that were scoured from my flesh.

Naked and shivering, I search the temple for something to use as clothing. I find a sack that likely held an offering or grain at one time, and rip it into something resembling a shift to cover my breasts, stomach, and hips. And then, I stumble from the temple.

I am black and blue and bruised, but I am no longer broken.

Husband

Luella

I don't struggle anymore. I don't know how I am still breathing, how my heart could still be so traitorous as to beat. A bag falls over my head and I'm loaded into a litter like a large parcel. Distantly, I wonder why they didn't wait for me to return to the castle and think they either wanted Mia to confirm my story, or they weren't ready to take Cassius.

I suppose it doesn't matter.

I'm nowhere I have been before. Underground again, but in a different place. The damp, stale, earthy scent fills my nostrils, reminding me of that night. I curse my nose for allowing me this return of my senses. I don't want it, the memory.

They chain my arms above my head and remove the bag so I can see I'm hanging in the center of a circular chamber. The altar is not at the front of the room, but instead right below me. My feet barely reach a circular dais, raised a few footlengths from the floor, but it's enough to steady myself. My shoulders scream as I twist, taking in the room. Closest to me, the Emperor wears no mask, but beyond him a circle of masked men and women fill the room. I'm surprised by the women, but their shape is obvious beneath some of the robes. Perhaps that is a shortcoming of mine—to judge men more harshly. After all, did Flavia truly betray me or did another flora betray Flavia? Or has it been Cassius all along?

I suppose it doesn't matter, either.

The domed roof allows water to trickle down along a few of the columns, which calls to mind the fountain. The sound of water seems to follow my suffering as a shadow.

The Bacchus masks are all black except one, which is white and must be the priest. His tall, thin frame steps forward. "Who claims this sacrifice?"

Many step forward at that, but the Emperor speaks before anyone else. "She's mine."

The menace in his voice, the need in his eyes, the word sacrifice—all are hints about how this night will go. I should be piecing it together. I should be making a plan.

I should be following my intuition but I don't, because my soul, my intuition, my heart? It's lying on the floor in the very back room of Mia's infirmaria, begging my heart's sister not to leave me the way my first sister did.

The priest in the white mask claps his hands as protests fill the air. "The Emperor has claimed her; you may make your own sacrifices."

At that, more people enter the large chamber. A mixture of women and men, some appear to be willing while others are drug by their hair or their clothing. All are in white shifts like the ones I had seen the floras wear before.

I was so conceited to assume I was the only person the Bacchantes might hurt tonight. I've been so naive. How many people have died because of me at this point? The women Ledo beat when I angered him or for training. The two sisters the Emperor slaughtered the night I tricked him with my eyes.

Mia.

It was too much. The tide of this broken world with men like Tristan in charge crashes through me, punctuated by the beginning festivities around me. The Bacchanalia is something I wouldn't wish on anyone. It starts innocently enough, with *sapa,* but drinks begin to spill, the pleasuring and punishment of the sacrifices commences, and soon the room is a mass of writhing bodies.

It's chaos. My eyes snag on a young man as a male and female Bacchante degrade him, the way I was just days ago. Tears stream down his face when I meet his eyes across the room, but then the hips of the monster thrusting inside his mouth block us. A flora next to them is enjoying herself, grinding on the masked face of a Bacchante, laughing as his hands roam across her hips and breasts. It's whiplash. Pain and pleasure, consent and rape, moans and screams and flesh. It breathes its contradictions along my neck and I look up to see the Emperor hasn't moved. He's staring at me, one of the few still fully clothed.

My arms are numb, my shoulder pain fading as the weight of my body further stretches the nerves. The revelry blurs around me. Time does not exist. I do not exist.

Until the Emperor comes to stand before me.

Tristan.

No one notices us, too absorbed in their drink or their deviances. His clean skin and hair mock me, dusted in gold powders and perfumed water while I hang in dirty chains. He reaches out a hand and I can't help but flinch, remembering the last time he touched me, and he smiles. His hand falls before it reaches me, he's not quite close enough to touch. To spit at.

"I heard you and Cassius had some plans for me? How were you going to get close to me, *vidua*?" he says.

"I've already been close to you," I say, infusing as much bolster into my words as I can.

He's not a stupid man. He is cruel and depraved, but not reckless. As I have been regarding him, he has been doing the same to me. He moves behind me, as if he knows my mouth is only capable of poison. Pulling my hair back he whispers into my ear. "So eager for more, Evandia?"

I swallow hard and for the first time consider what would happen if I simply bit the pearl and drank the poison myself. It might kill me to use it anyways, but to break it open only for that? I've never believed that I would welcome death, but with Tristan's hands on me, Cassius surely locked away or otherwise occupied, and Mia's blood soaking the hem of my gown...

I don't bite the pearl.

But I do die.

That's what it feels like as I draw power from the pebbles I swallowed, as I shift into the form I promised myself I'd never take again.

My old body.

My dead body.

The idea had begun to form since I was last underground with Tristan, since he'd drugged me on my own wedding night. He haunted me, and I think I'd like to haunt him, too.

I shift my hair to a darker, wheat blonde. My eyes to the grayish blue that used to watch my sister in the mirror as we braided each others' hair. My hips widen, my breasts shrink, and my cheeks sweep upward, sharper than they are sweet.

"I'm not a *vidua* yet, Evander." My voice is higher and lighter than it's been in over ten years. Maybe not exactly the same as my youth after the damage, but close.

"The Dominus is of no concern to me," Tristan scoffs, disdain dripping from each word as if offended by the very idea that anyone would dare to question him.

"I don't mean the Dominus, Tristan," I say. Very few know his name and even fewer would use it, now. He freezes and finally notices the subtle changes I have made. The death I just underwent in front of him. The resurrection.

He moves in front of me and his eyes widen in recognition and shock. And, most deliciously of all, in fear.

"Husband," I say, letting my lips turn up in the corners. It's the shy smile of a 20 year old girl, not the smirk of a woman who has spent the last 10 years murdering men. Men who had no right to marry her, because she was already married. Men just like her husband.

My husband, Emperor Tristan Evander.

Used to Be

Rose

My pater is in his cups already and coins leftover from my *coemptio* cover the table. I realize now what a fortune Tristan gave him. How much was for me and how much was for silence?

He needn't have bothered. Bottles of full strength *sapa* litter the floor, their thin metallic coating making it look like our domus is full of fallen stars. Maybe it is. Pater's dreams, my mater's life, my future.

"Where's Daisy?" I demand, not able to muster the usual respect. What could he do to me, now that it's all been done?

"Ha," Pater scoffs. "She's filling in for you, you ungrateful *meretrix*!"

I shove past him, knowing if my nose wasn't shattered he'd smell like sour wine and sweat. Perhaps the scent of wood would temper it, showing he'd actually worked this clipse. When I reach the room where my sister and I grew in each other's hearts, it's empty. Something shifts in me, my bones grinding, ribs rearranging.

"Where's Daisy?" I demand, shaking him. His head lolls on his broad shoulders and he glares at me.

"That husband of yours came for the meat he paid for," he scoffs. "We owed him a wife and he didn't have a wife."

The shifting turns to quakes, and the world tilts beneath me. The suns shatter into a million shards, like the glasses Tristan shattered at my feet. Neptune's tides rise from the Maero to drown and deafen every nerve inside of me.

"Tristan came for her?" I whisper.

"That disrespectful chit didn't even come himself," Pater says, as if he even remembers.

I'm already running, my feet splitting and bleeding on the cobblestones as I race back to the Domus Aurea, back to the garbage chute I'd barely survived.

Praying. Crying. Pleading.

"He came for the meat he paid for," Pater said. Meat.

Goats.

Virgins, whores, or corpses.

That's all we are to Tristan, after everything.

My side aches, my feet bleed, but now that I'm here I can't look. I pace blindly, flies swarming me.

Finally, I gather the courage to see what I already know is there.

And I scream.

I don't know how no one hears me. I scream with every fiber of my soul as I heave my beautiful, kind, dead sister from the trash chute.

I scream as I drag her to the Maero to wipe the trash and the fluid and the blood from her golden hair and skin.

I scream for the hours it takes to drag her body to the edge of town, where I find an abandoned domus with a lake, and dig with my bare hands until my nails shatter and my fingertips bleed.

I scream over her grave until my throat is so ragged that nothing comes out.

And in the end, all that's left are the jagged pieces of who I used to be.

So Pretty

Luella

Tristan steps back. Forward. The room around us means nothing, is nothing. Instead I see the man who raped me and murdered me in every way that matters. I died more than once the night of our wedding, because he took the only thing that I loved, then.

Daisy.

And he's done it all over again, taking the only thing I had dared to love, now.

Mia.

"Please, Tristan." I bite my lip. "I'll do whatever you want, be whatever you want. Just take me out of here." I look around, widening my eyes, scrunching my nose. I'm afraid, I tell him with my body. I'm sorry, I beg with my eyes. "Please."

I see his confusion in his furrowed brow, but something else is there, too. Eagerness. It's in the way he leans in when I speak, the way he bites the inside of his cheek as he considers.

Moments of indecision, when life and death balance on the edge of a blade, seem to slow. The world around us has frozen and the air leaves my lungs in infinitesimal amounts, a single heartbeat lasts minutes, and the blood rushing in my ears slows to a static roar.

No one else sees this, the moment that will define my future. Tristan smiles, wicked. "All I ever wanted was to hear you say please, Rosebud."

He comes behind me, releasing my chains from overhead, but not from my wrists. The numbness in my arms means the weight of the chains is unbearable, and I collapse. Tristan gathers the chains and begins to drag me from the room. The few who notice us make no move to stop him from taking 'the sacrifice,' too lost in their own pursuits. No one notices a woman running, or leaving, or being dragged. Not around here.

He pulls me out of the chamber and down a long hall. Fire races down my arms with each step as blood fights to return feeling to my limbs. It's agony and it's bliss. It's one step closer to why I am here.

At the end of the long hall is a staircase that we ascend in a clamor of chains and curses, me stumbling constantly and Tristan cursing me for it. Finally we are in halls I recognize, the Domus Aurea. He hauls me further until we come not to the dungeon he raped me in just a few days ago, but the room he raped me in over ten years ago.

His room.

The red and gold and white of it churn my stomach. So little has changed since my first wedding night. A large circular bed sits not against any wall, but in the center of the room. Its linens are white, of course, and the rug beneath it a deep burgundy. One to display his depravity, and the other to hide it. Replacing rugs is trickier than replacing linens, after all. There's a small seating area off to the side, not a true study since that is through the connecting door, and a small table to take breakfast on the other. There is nothing inherently disturbing about the room, but I know the small table next to his bed holds much more than it ever did before. The floras tallied his chains, whips, and knives for me, and in his closet are more. Metal brands and acids to burn, and bars and clips to pinch and pry and open.

Anything he can use to make sure he hears the sounds he wants.

Each poster surrounding the bed has hooks at varying heights, which work in concert with his chains and bars and clips. He could hang my chains from the top as they displayed me in the dungeon, or down near the floor so I had to bend over, or any place in the middle.

He tethers my chains so my hands are at waist height. No need to stoop or to strain; a kindness really. Just as the thought forms, Tristan strikes me across the face. I whimper and he does it again, harder.

"Who are you?" he demands.

"Your wife." It comes out a snarl, the way I wish I had spoken to him back then.

"My wife is dead." He draws himself up, part indignation, part concern. Questioning himself that night.

"I was close to dead." I nod. "As you can see, though, I live."

"It's not possible. You're a witch. You've taken this form to haunt me."

"Haunt you? I'm returning to you, husband. Didn't you miss me?" I know that I was his first. He had been hesitant. Ecstatic but unorganized, not sure what he was seeking. By the end of the night he'd known.

She just screams so pretty.

It's like he hears where my thoughts have traveled because he unhooks one of my chains, stretching it out to one of the other posters on the bed. My arms are stretched wide but I'm facing the bed instead of Tristan. I won't be able to see him, which means I won't be able to read him, or draw him close enough.

"Can I see you?" I ask. I let it come out low, let my desperation leak into my words.

I hear the air whistle before the crack. The sound before the pain. The whip bites into my flesh with such excruciating accuracy that I know these years haven't done anything to temper his appetites. They've honed them.

My scream pierces my own eardrums. "Tristan," I moan, the pain overwhelming.

"Don't." He snaps the whip down again, and I cry out. "Call." Crack. "Me." Crack. "That." His voice rises to match my screams.

Tears stream down my face. I missed my chance. I missed my chance and this time he really will kill me; I can feel it in his precision. He knows exactly how far he can take someone before death, which means I won't die soon.

I'll die after he's given me a thousand little deaths.

I'll die after I stop screaming so pretty.

Before

Rose

I am seven, which means Daisy is four. That's always how it is for me, my life measured by the existence of the only light left. It wasn't always that way, of course.

There had been another light, once.

It had been snuffed two years before, consumed by the shadows of this place. It was bitter, to know our mater was gone.

That Daisy and I had not been enough to make her stay, and simultaneously understanding the call of the light spilling onto the streets outside the threshold of this dark domus.

Daisy is digging in the cupboards, trying to help me find just one more bag of flour.

There has to be more flour.

The sting of tears wells in the corners of my eyes as I contemplate asking Pater for the coins stamped with the man of two faces on one side and a ship on the other. I'd need two for a loaf, but for the flour the baker charged ten. The bag could make them twenty loaves, but getting ten discs at once?

There has to be more flour.

A small squeal and then shattering glass. My heart stops. "Daisy!"

Scrambling over to where Daisy had disappeared a few moments earlier, I drop to my knees to see her sitting in dark amber liquid, shards of the bottle scattered around her but the base still intact.

Daisy begins to cry when she sees the look on my face. The terror.

"It's okay, Daize," I say, extricating her from the shards of glass. "It'll be okay."

It probably won't, but I'll try to make it so.

"Papa will be so mad," Daisy sobs into my chest.

"Pater," I correct softly. Only when Mama had been here had he been Papa. This makes Daisy wail harder, a sharp and swift reminder of what?

The Mater she probably can't remember. Or perhaps, of the sister who was less afraid, less cautious.

Maero take me, I hate the helplessness of holding my baby sister as she cries. I pet her hair and take my own deep breaths, showing Daisy how to calm herself.

Children are to be seen and not heard. At four, she understands the rules, and the consequences of breaking them. Slowly, shaky breaths replace her stifled sobs.

"I did this," I say sternly, meeting her watery eyes. "If Pater asks, I did this looking for flour."

"But Pap- Pater will be so mad," she whispers. We both know what she doesn't say, what it means.

"I'll be okay. This is what big sisters are for."

Daisy clings to me, our blonde hair tangling together as our small hearts beat rapidly against one another.

"It'll always be me and you, Daize."

"Promise?" She hiccups.

"Promise," I say, already knowing it's a lie.

REWARD

LUELLA

TIME ISN'T REAL, IT'S a construct to mark the mundane. Let dough rest for one hour before stretching and folding. Allow twenty minutes for a sleeping drought to take hold. Schedule fifteen minutes to braid your sister's hair.

Pain like this isn't mundane, not to me, and so time no longer exists. Perhaps I am whipped for only another minute, or perhaps it is days, but finally he stops. My legs have long since given out. My arms are numb again and I'm covered in sweat and tears and blood.

Salt.

He comes up behind me and rips my head back, making me cry out, and whispers into my ear, "Did you miss me, Rose?"

I whimper again and the sound makes me want to grind my teeth. I worked so hard never to be here again. Never to mean that sound. His hand comes around my neck, like a lover's caress. This is the way someone like Cassius might touch me, and it's so at odds with what's happening around me that I almost lean into it. Then, because the hand belongs to Tristan, the touch turns cruel. He squeezes tighter and I can't speak, can't breathe.

"I said, did you miss me, Rosebud?" Another tear streams down my face as I remember our wedding night. The mind games. The assault. Of course he'd gravitated towards the followers of Bacchus in the years after as he tried to find a place where his sadistic pleasure belonged.

He's still holding my throat but I try to rasp the words out. "I'll only scream for you, *princeps*."

His grip loosens. "Say it again."

"I'll only scream for you, *princeps*." The words feel hollow and broken in my mouth, like dried eggshells, empty and cracking beneath my teeth.

"Rosebud," he says, coming around to kneel on the bed in front of me. "Say it again." He puts a hand between my legs, rough and punishing.

I scream. I infuse every ounce of feeling into it as I can and when he withdraws his hand I say, "Thank you, *princeps*."

That does it. He releases both of my chains and throws me onto the bed. On my back he comes to lie on top of me, pushing apart my legs. He slaps me and I let out a cry. "Thank you, *princeps*," I say through the tears. He's frenzied now, getting exactly what he wanted those years ago: a submissive and obedient wife who loved whatever he did to her. Perhaps I would have eventually, if he had groomed me and tempered himself in the meantime. Instead, I had tried to flee.

I don't try that, now. Tristan wraps a hand around my throat and pushes himself between my legs. I try to say something, but he's squeezing too hard and a rasp comes out. He presses his hips forward and I squeeze my thighs tighter, trying to keep him away. "Say it," he commands, pressing into me once more, his golden face eager.

It's almost sad, how desperate he is for the name his mater would never call him.

I move my lips, but don't allow any sound to come out. He leans in closer and widens my legs with his, frustrated that I'm not giving him what he wants, until our breaths mingle. He loosens his hold on my throat and says, "Say it, *meretrix*."

"Thank you," I say, biting down hard on the pearl. As the warm poison explodes in my mouth I spit directly into his, the tasteless and odorless concoction landing right where I aim. "Tristan."

His head rears back and his face reddens. Before I can say anything he punches me in the face, hard. I feel a tooth shatter beneath his fist and blood pools in my mouth. I spit again, but it doesn't hit him, landing weakly on my chest, spattering on the white sheets streaked with the blood from my back. My arm, heavy with chains, swings around and I catch him on the side of the head. He falls to the side, freeing me from his weight. I don't know how long the poison will take to work on either of us.

"Thank you, Tristan," I repeat. "For showing me what a pathetic, disgusting creature you are on our first night, so that I didn't have to spend my life enduring you." I scramble to my feet across the bed from him.

"I was enduring you, you beggar whore, but it was worth it to taste your sweet, sweet sister." His grin falters as I lunge towards him screaming, swinging my chained hands as weapons, unfaltering as he tries to shove me away.

One of the chains whips his ear and eye, and he reaches a hand up to the fresh blood. I try to hit him again and he blocks me, throwing my arm to the side and punching my ribs. I cry out as I double over, but I'm not done and I swing at the same place again. He brings his other hand up to block his face and I bring my chained fist in again, finally making contact on the side of his head.

"You." I swing the other hand quickly, catching him on the opposite side of the face. "Should." I swing from the other side again and he just holds his hands in front of his face, protecting his nose and eyes. "Scream." The other hand. "Prettier." I can feel myself growing weak, but I can't die like this. I won't die unless he does. I won't let anyone else lose a Daisy or a Mia. I won't let anyone else endure this man who holds so much power he doesn't even know what to do with it except hurt, hurt, hurt.

I must slow enough for him to gather himself because suddenly I'm crashing into the opposite wall and crumpling onto the floor. It's my body this time. Not someone else's. Not a mask.

Mine.

It's bruised and whipped and bloody. And it hurts.

"I'll fuck you to death, you stupid sabine," he screams, grabbing his metal scepter that he uses when presiding over the Senate.

"Because you can't get it up, can you Tristan," I taunt. I wrap the long end of the chain around my fist. "Not even man enough to fuck me with your own cock."

When he springs for me, I'm ready. I swing one hand and when he moves to block it, I swing the other, catching him yet again on the side of the face with the force of all my body weight. The momentum brings us both to the ground and instead of scrambling away from him, I fling my naked, bloody body onto his. Screaming, I roll him onto his back and raise both hands over my head, bringing them down with a satisfying crunch.

My mind feels muddy, churning like the eddies of the Maero.

Tristan's not moving. He's not fighting me. But I keep raising my hands together, letting the momentum carry the weight of the chains into him once.

Crack.

Twice.

Crunch.

The poison is towing me under and my movements are becoming sluggish, but I need him to die first. It's the principle of the thing, really. I've already died so many times.

Isn't it his turn yet?

I raise my hands again for what I know is the final time, and swing everything on top of Tristan, folding over his mutilated face as my chains grind gold into red, flesh into bone, and revenge into reward.

We're woven together, like the two faces of Janus. Past and future. Forward and back. Perhaps neither of us can exist without the other, two sides of a monstrous coin. Darkness drags me down, and I can only hope neither of us wakes.

LUELLA
ROSE

AN OLDER MAN FINDS me curled over Daisy's half buried body. He sees me, turns on his heel, and leaves. I hope he comes back to kill me.

That thought comforts me as I drift to sleep, but when I wake up, I'm not dead. Obviously. I'm in the man's dark arms and he's telling me everything will be okay. His voice is soothing, kind.

I don't trust it one bit, but my traitorous body succumbs to sleep once more.

When I wake this time, I'm in a dark room with two doors, one solid and the other with a small portal to open and see who's outside. Another woman is here, and she looks a bit older than me with brown hair. I can't see the color of her eyes since both are swollen closed. The bruising looks fresh if I know anything about black eyes, which I do.

I'm cleaner than I've been since I don't know when, and I'm in a new tunic.

I try to speak, but it comes out as a rasp, my throat still so raw from screaming. I try again and manage, "Where?"

The woman looks up. "You're in the infirmaria. Been out since I arrived."

"I can't be here," I say. I sit up, not knowing how to tell her that I can't be seen by the Emperor, by my pater.

"Only the women know about this place," she says, gesturing to the back door with the slit. This must be the back of the infirmaria I see everyday near the Baths. The alley behind likely serves to ferry women to the safety that must be kept a secret, else the men would take that, too. "And I'm guessing a woman didn't do that to you." It's not a question, so I don't answer.

"Healer ran out of stones fixing you, so she had to leave. She'll be back."

I'd heard she was blessed by Apollo or Aesculapius, but never was sure. Blessings are rare. The Senate said it was because we were already divine as Divusians, which means it's probably the opposite. I lie back and it's as if I'm floating over my own body, watching myself exist in a place I know I don't belong. My eyes close against a fresh wave of regret, the what ifs and should haves strangling me.

After a few moments I ask the woman, "Who did that to you?"

She smiles, baring her teeth, maybe not realizing or not caring that the front two are chipped. "You first."

"My husband."

She nods. "*Idem*." *Same*.

"Before that, my pater," I say.

"*Idem*," she says again. Silence settles between us again, heavy as the burden of feminity in an empire ruled by men. It makes me angry. No, not just angry, incandescent.

"We won't have peace will we? Virgins, whores, or corpses." The words are sharp, enhanced by the gravely quality of my worn vocal chords.

"I pray to Tisiphone," she admits. "To make me a widow. To give me freedom."

"A widow?" I ask, but I realize what she means. It's... freedom. "A widow..." I say again.

The woman closes her eyes. "He'd never see it coming. Tisiphone would be beautiful even as she slipped a dagger into his chest." A contented sigh looses from the woman, as if the image of her husband's blood pouring from him would be like the sounds of a bubbling stream or a string melody.

There must be so many like us, those who want nothing more than to escape our own matrimony, leave behind the pain of obedience. To be free from the lie we're fed from the moment of our birth, whispered to us in our maters' protective embraces and lectured from beneath our paters' fists. Released from following generations of women who say, 'see, like this,' and the men who say, 'or else.'

Someone should stop the cycle. Someone should say, 'not anymore.'

"What's your name?" I ask.

"Skylar," she says. "But it doesn't matter. I'm 'ia' in every way that counts." The way I was Octavia to my pater's Octavius. The way I'm now Evandia to Tristan Evander, even if he doesn't know it.

"Do you ever want to run? To start over with a new name?"

"Mmm." She hums her assent, content to keep what it would be to herself.

I think about who I might want to be now. I can't be Rose anymore. I could be like many men and use my middle name. It was unusual for women to have middle names, but my mater had insisted, giving me and Daisy the same one.

"It was my mater's name," she had told me, "and she didn't have any sons. So her gens is already lost to the world. Luella Amulius will never exist again, but Daisy Luella and Rose Luella will. She can live in you girls, she can keep you together."

"My name's Luella," I tell Skylar.

She nods, as if she knows I've just decided this, and her approval feels good. "I like it," she says.

"*Idem*," I say, closing my eyes against the memories of Mater, of Daisy.

The pain drags me back into sleep and restless dreams where my face transforms. First I become my mater, slipping a dagger into my pater and staying to raise Daisy and me. We're laughing at the festival, and she's teaching me to bake bread instead of leaving me to learn it on my own at age five. Then I'm Skylar, slitting her husband's throat, smiling when the blood sprays across her chipped teeth, eyes flashing green with hate and triumph.

My face begins changing faster, shifting and morphing between my own, Daisy's, and the likeness of the goddess Tisiphone. Our features start merging, like the statue in the temple of Janus where the god's whispered words and magic must have healed me enough to give me a second chance.

'What do I do?' I want to scream, but the words won't come. Instead I see myself, Daisy, and Tisiphone, morphed into one beautiful face with blonde hair and the bluest eyes with twin specks in the right one. One red as a rose, the other daisy yellow. I see this person who is me and isn't.

She kills man, after man, after man. She slits throats, and poisons, and finally she kills Tristan with her own two hands wrapped in the chains of marriage. She shatters his face with centuries of pain and obedience and betrayal. The sound of shattering bones as his skull collapses in on itself startles me awake, reality crashing over me.

Drenched in sweat and shaking, I look around the room once more, rage rising like the Maero in summer.

Someone *should* stop them.

And it's going to be me.

The Widow

The pain that wakes me is two-fold. My back and wrists and face scream in agony at my shift in movement. Worse, though, is the pain of remembering that Mia is not here, will never again chastise me.

I'm done, Mia. I promise if you just come back, I'll be safe. I'll bake bread and help you in the infirmaria and swim in the frigidarium, and stop making you worry.

I don't want to open my eyes. I'm afraid to see what the world looks like now, but then he speaks.

"How are you feeling, *cor meum?*"

"Why must you call me that?" I say, the jagged little pieces of me feel sharper than ever. As if the whip was a whetstone last night, each touch from Tristan another new fracture.

"It's how I feel. Why does it irk you so? And what would you rather be called?"

I finally drag my eyes open and gasp. "Jupiter's stones, what happened to you?" Cassius' usually golden face is black and blue, one of his eyes is bloodshot, and red seeps from a gash across his cheek. His lip is split and swollen and blood stains splash across his chest as if he was whipped, too. We're in the nerium room, the traitorous frescoes and tapestries welcoming this new, yet old, version of me.

"When you didn't return I knew something was wrong... but Tristan dragged me into a trial. I was flogged for my failure at Bai-Zu last night."

A legion conquest over six years old. Tristan had restrained Cassius the least incriminating way he could, through politics. Cassius would have been brought before the Senate to be lashed.

"How many?" I ask.

"One hundred. With the five-pronged flagrum," he says, shaking his head. A death sentence. "The Senate protested and they all left the room after ten. Tristan was already gone so it was just me and the flogger."

"He stopped?"

"Tristan may have friends among the Praetors and Senators, but I have friends where it matters." He doesn't say any more, but I understand what he means. His friends are the people that Tristan manipulates. Manipulated?

"Cassius, is he...?" I close my eyes again, afraid to hear the answer. Afraid that I did it, and more afraid that I didn't.

"He's dead, *cor meum*. You did it." He reaches out and grabs my hand, gentle with the skin I broke by wrapping my chains around them. "I'm only sorry you had to do it alone. And I'm sorry you had to pay such a high price..."

He reaches his free hand out to brush a finger across my temple, where I'm sure I'm bruised. I turn away. "Flavia, Mia...they're gone." I tell him.

"Flavia, yes, but Mia isn't." He smiles in a sad sort of way. "She will have lasting damage, and she can't speak or use her powers right now, but she's alive."

I move to sit up. "I have to see her," I gasp against the pain, my back tearing anew.

Cassius moves to lower me back to the bed. "Soon, *cor meum*, soon."

I let him lie me back and I close my eyes.

Crack. I hear the whip. I feel Tristan on top of me, forcing into me and each time blends together. My first wedding night. The night I was punished as Luella. The night I became a real widow.

Crunch.

The sound of broken bones and flesh as I smashed Tristan's face in with feral rage. Black and blue and blood.

I open my eyes. Cassius looks back at me with something like longing. Adoration. The same thing I saw on our wedding night. Love. *Cor meum*, he says.

But his face is golden. Even his hair is tinged with it, the red and gold copper strands mussed in the low light of late day. He got what he wanted. He's the Emperor now.

"I can't do this, Cassius," I say softly, gently.

He shakes his head. "Don't say that Luella."

"You got what you wanted; let me go."

"Of course you can go," Cassius growls, rising to stand over my bed. "I'm not a monster! But I love you." He falls to his knees, grabbing my hand again. "I love you, Luella. Whatever you can do, I want that."

"What if I can't stand it? To see you in his robes, in his rooms. To hear you addressed as Imperator? To see your face…" I choke on it, the idea of loving the brother of my worst nightmare. Of being married to an Emperor again.

"You can change it. Make me into whatever face you want to see. I don't care."

"It doesn't work like that. Besides, you need this face to be Emperor." A small laugh escapes me. "Would you give that up?"

"I think you'd hate me if I did, if I changed nothing after everything you sacrificed, but I still would, if you asked me to."

I hate that he understands me. "I wouldn't ask for that, even if I could change you." With a dark chuckle, I add, "Besides, I'd hate for you to be made into anything other than that of your own choosing."

He looks down at our hands. "Please," he whispers and I blink back the tears mounting on my lower lashes.

"How did you recognize me?" I finally say, remembering that he's never seen this version of me, the version that's mine.

"I told you, Rose." I take a sharp, careless inhale before my ribs and back protest at the sudden movement. "I would recognize you in any life. I'd know you in any form."

"You knew?" The words beg to be answered as much I want them to be ignored.

Cassius nods. "Not at first, but then those eyes…" His gaze lingers on my right eye, on the two specks that are so hard for me to alter. He runs his fingertips up my arm, the barely brushing touch sending goose-pebbles up the back of my neck. It's soft. It's right. "And I didn't know how that could be. Then the longer we spent together, the more I saw you, the more I started to hope. And then I stopped caring, because it didn't matter who you were or had been, because you were simply… you."

I don't know if I'm breathing, existing. I don't know what he's saying and I do. "Don't, Augustus," I beg. It's different than before. It's different if he knows everything. If he knows I didn't choose correctly all those years ago. If he knows the depths of my suffering, the past that shaped me. It means he's not seeing the mask, the persona, the body I've created.

He's seeing *me*.

He smiles softly at the old nickname. "All that matters is that I love you, *cor meum*. And I'll keep loving you as long as you let me."

A soft sound escapes me, a strangled cry or perhaps a plea. I close my eyes.

But then I hear it again. The crack of the whip, the crunch of bone.

She just screams so pretty.

I yank my arm away, instinctively fast at first and then more slowly, reluctantly. "Please," Cassius says again. *Begs.*

I don't want to have the power, but I don't want him to have it either. I want to trust, but how can I? Rose can't do that anymore, and I don't know if Luella can either.

I don't know which version of me I am anymore.

I don't know if I know me, without my list of praeda.

Who am I, if I'm not revenge?

"I need time." I don't know what I need, but I want Mia and space and to be far away from the gods-forsaken Domus Aurea where I finally became what I always wanted to be.

A widow.

THE SOROR

Cassius, the stupid, beautiful *matulo*, gives me what I said I needed.

Time.

But he took what he needed to do it, which is space.

It's only been two days but part of me already yearns to see his face, to hear more than his muffled meetings in the fleeting moments he's been in his room. Securing power is never a simple task, and I imagine rallying his supporters and ensuring Tristan's fall in line is happening quickly and quietly, long before the public will even know Tristan is dead. The Evander line can't be seen as weak, or a new power will try to move in.

I've seen the Domus Aurea healer a few times, but no one else has come to my rooms.

Until today.

The knock sounds again, accompanied by a vaguely familiar voice.

"Imperata?" She calls and I feel myself flinch. I'm sitting on a floor cushion, staring off as I have found myself doing more than I'd care to admit. It's a flora, but I can't place which.

"Enter," I call out, not rising.

A young woman with black hair and wide green eyes enters. She's one of the floras who had shared information about Tristan with Cassius and me.

"Hello, Rine."

"Imperata." She bows much lower than I'm comfortable with. "The Imperator would like to know if this room is still acceptable or if you'd like your things moved?"

When I don't answer Rine, she takes a deep breath. "He also wanted to say the healer said you are cleared for travel as of today, and that you may do with that information as you wish."

"Did he give you a letter to give to me, too?" I ask, remembering the way he'd sent me the list before.

Rine shakes her head. "No, Imperata." I don't know why I'm disappointed. Perhaps I've asked for something I don't actually want. Then I think of her wording. 'You may do with that information as you wish.'

Cassius doesn't know what to do, doesn't know what I want.

That makes two of us.

Rine leaves, and I slip out of the Domus Aurea easily, wearing brown hair and freckles. A small bag hangs over my shoulder with my leftover potions and stones. I left Cassius a note, but he won't like it.

"Thank you, *matulo*. For everything."

I don't know if I'll return, or who I would be if I did.

Besides, there's somewhere more important for me to be right now.

The domus is small, with most of the land dedicated to the garden in the back where Agrippa tilled the ground to make his and Mia's dream come true. Where I'd stumbled ten years ago, bloody and broken, into the arms of my new sister.

I knock before entering, but don't wait for an answer. Taln is there in a moment and when his eyes widen, I realize he still doesn't know.

Reaching into my pocket, I drain a stone, until I look like the Luella he knew. He steps back.

"It's okay, Taln. Everything's okay now."

I wrap my hand around another stone, this time transforming into the first face he ever saw of mine. Julia, wife of Silas. "It's always been me."

"Julia?" He asks.

I smile, crouching down to his level. "I like Luella best, but you can use whatever you want."

"You want to see her?" He seems less shocked than I expected.

I nod. "Did Mia tell you?" Standing, I make my way to her bedroom.

"She told me a little bit. Not your name, but what you were doing." Ah. He just didn't know the face I had worn today.

When I open Mia's bedroom, I realize how much tension I'd been carrying. I hadn't believed she was alive, not really. Hadn't been able to until I saw her lying on the bed, her hair wrapped in silk, eyes closed. Her chest rises and falls, as if she's sleeping deeply.

Taln lets out a cry of relief and I turn to shush him before realizing he's still in the entryroom. The noise came from me. I cover my mouth and check if I've woken her, and see Mia's beautiful brown eyes looking right at me.

"Am I dreaming?" she asks, her voice like gravel and glass.

"You know I only appear in nightmares." I smile, falling onto the bed and wrapping my arms around her as gently as I can manage through my half-laugh, half-sob. "I thought I lost you." I'm crying in earnest now, my relief so sharp and strong in the aftermath of the last few clipses, maybe in the aftermath of the last ten years.

Her arms are around me in a breath, and then I can feel her crying, too. "Me too, soror. Me too."

I kiss the top of her head, then sit up and kiss the backs of her hands, holding them to me like she'll float away if I let go.

My own voice mirrors hers, cracked and broken with emotion instead of injury. "He's gone. It's finally done."

A clipse later, Mia motions for Taln to pour us water, tapping her empty glass against the pitcher gently. Taln quickly fills both of our cups before bowing out of the sitting room. I've moved in, for now, to make sure Mia's not alone, only to discover she wasn't anyways.

"When did he move in, miss 'I don't take in strays?'" I smirk.

"Well, someone mentioned that it went okay the last time I did." She smiles, and while we're both mostly healed, her scarred throat is a constant reminder of what I've put her through.

"Maybe they spoke too soon."

She follows my line of sight and sighs. "We're alive. We're together. That's more than I ever hoped would come of this."

It hurts to hear her say it, how much my revenge almost cost us both.

"I still can't believe it, Mi." I shake my head. "How did we both know to try ingesting the stones?"

"I think the gods guided us. Although, Janus could have done a little better job. I still can't believe you just swallowed whole stones." Mia had the idea to start grinding the stones into a powder and ingesting it the very day she'd been attacked. She said she'd swallowed her first dose just that morning, to see if she could heal her morning patients before telling me about the technique.

I laugh. "Yeah, I already told them how I felt about those stones coming out the other end."

"Stones, indeed." Mia says, face serious. She meets my eyes and we can't hold it in any longer, both of us laughing too hard to speak, hers a croaking rasp and mine louder and more unbridled than ever.

"What will you do now?" Mia says, catching her breath.

"I don't know what I'm going to do," I say. We both know what I *should* do.

"You want to help this city? This is how you do it. You can't keep going after individual praeda. There are always more." She coughs, taking another small sip of water. "Change the system, Luella."

"He'd do it without me." I know it's true. I know that with or without me, Cassius will try to change things. "And what if I don't love him? What if I can't? If I use him that way am I any better than Ledo or Tristan or any other man who tried to use another?" I shake my head. "I won't do that."

Mia shakes her head like she's disappointed. Her black braids fan her ebony face. "Tell him the truth. Besides, how do you know you don't love him?"

"I don't know that I can love anyone," I confess. I don't know that I'm capable. I've seen too much, and if Cassius is decent then I know even less about what to do with him, how to behave.

Mia, as always, knows the tenor of my thoughts. "You could try being yourself, Luella. No games. No goals. No roles to play, no faces to wear. Just you."

I'd never considered it, not really. I'd never thought I could just be... me. Cassius had, though. He'd seen me when I hadn't even seen myself. And he'd loved me in all my forms. Could I do that, too?

"Perhaps," I tell us both.

THE WOMAN

TIME IS FOR THE mundane, I once thought. Real time, though, is a creature. It's moody and irritable, prone to fits of ecstatic speed and depressive slowness. I feel it now, living in Mia's domus, how the upcoming mortua season cools the air and the creature that calls itself time tries to curl into itself, ready to slumber.

The forum feels it, too. It's emptier than usual and I'm able to move easily through the stalls. I buy ingredients for bread, items that had once felt like gold, now so commonplace. I find a new mortar and pestle for Mia, as her current one looks worse for the wear we've put on it since consistently grinding our stones.

The Senate will remain out of session for the next two quads during mortua, but I still linger on the steps, wondering what he's up to.

I turn to leave and notice something out of place. At the top of the steps, instead of a bust of Cassius, or even Tristan or their father, there's a new bust adorning the entrance.

Tisiphone.

My heart stutters. It's not just that it's a message for me, because of that I'm sure.

It's because there's a woman in the Senate, the very first.

And even though she's made of stone, I know she's just the beginning.

The next day I can't help but travel to the Furies' temple. It's as beautiful as the day Cassius and I wed, all gold, silver, and bronze. It's mostly deserted, except for a priestess speaking in low tones in the front of the room.

I don't know why I'm here. I'm hunting praeda I have no intention of catching. I should return to Mia's. I should forget about the Evanders, the republic. I could even leave Divus.

At the very least, I should leave the temple.

But I don't.

My heart begins to race before I know why, and my feet carry me forward, towards the altar. One of the priestesses, in gray robes, stands over a man as he kneels. His broad shoulders are bent forward as he prays, and his copper gold strands catch more shadows than sunslight.

Breathing shouldn't be this hard.

Air stutters in and out of my lungs. I don't decide what happens next; my feet pursue their own self-preservation, darting behind a pillar in case he should turn.

The Imperator.

Cassius Augustus Evander.

My husband.

The pillar is close, close enough that his prayers carry. "I've already asked so much, but I still can't see it all. Show me who else needs your judgment, Tisiphone. Alecto, give me your righteous anger and help thwart the jealousy of the Senate, Megaera."

Cassius makes the traditional offering in return, grain and goats.

"Leave me, please, priestess," Cassius says.

"I'm sorry, Imperator. I wish I could give you a different answer." I desperately want to know what she means, but I know I need to leave, lest he see me crouching behind a pillar like a common thief. It's not my way to spy. Kill? Yes. Poison? Absolutely.

Spy and sneak and hide? Only in plain sight.

I turn to leave but Cassius' voice freezes me, his words lower than before. I strain to hear him, leaning closer.

"And if you see fit, please send her back to me. Show me what she needs me to be. For this request, I give you what she's given; my blood."

A small gasp escapes Cassius and I know he's sliced his palm. Offering human blood to the gods isn't a ceremony performed often. Some believe it will only open the gates to human sacrifice, while others just dislike the discomfort of it.

The only gods who ask for blood are Bacchus and Mars, but even Mars would only ask for it from the battlefield. And Bacchus, well. He's a bastard.

When Cassius stands to leave, his clothes rustle and his sword scrapes the ground. It startles me out of the rage induced paralysis that my thoughts of Bacchus conjured, and I maneuver around the pillar to keep out of sight.

I peek out at the exact moment Cassius disappears from view, leaving the temple.

My sigh cuts short, startling into a scream when a hand brushes my shoulder.

"Hello, *pullus,*" the priestess says.

"Stones, you scared me."

"Did you think I was your husband?" she asks, cocking her head. Her dark brown curls spill off her shoulders with the movement and I know my mouth has opened in a most undignified way. Not that I'm too concerned with how ladylike I appear these days.

"I don't know what you mean," I say, my voice betraying the lie beneath.

"Then I suppose you don't care that he comes every day?" She hums, considering. "Or that he makes the same offering each day."

"The Imperator has plenty of goats and more than enough grain," I mutter.

"Not that one." She shakes her head as though I'm as hopeless as I feel. "He asked me to leave because I told him to stop offering blood to the Furies. They will grow fat on it, gluttonous. I told him they wouldn't force you to do anything and his blood was worthless."

The words pass my lips before they've formed in my mind. "Then why does he keep doing it?"

"She bled for us, I'll bleed for her," she mimics in a deep voice. "I think he threw some curses in there, but I won't repeat them while in a place of worship."

I take a step back. "Every day?" It's been clipses. Quads. Multiple quads.

"And he leaves an offering on the dais, with a note." I step forward. "Since you're not his wife, though, perhaps you don't care what they said?"

"You've read them?" I ask.

"Of course not." She looks as offended as if I'd recommended she defecate on the Furies' altar. "I did save them. In case."

"He's the Imperator," I admonish. "You can't share his personal communications with a random woman." I feel defensive of the letters, not him. Definitely not him.

"A random woman wouldn't have been swooning behind a pillar." She meets my stare and I know I'm scowling.

"Fine." I loose an irritated breath. "May I see them?"

The offering makes me cry. It's not a goat, or blood, or food. It's none of the customary or even non-customary items.

It's for me.

The small basket at first appears to be full of roses, except each and every one had been beheaded, leaving just the long thorny stems. Not a petal in sight.

My hand is over my mouth, trying to hold back what I'm not sure. A curse? A sob? A laugh, maybe.

"I didn't save all the stems. This is just from today, but here are the notes."

Each is a small piece of parchment, rolled and sealed with imperial purple wax. I count them. Then I count them again.

The priestess didn't lie. There is one for every day since I left the Domus Aurea.

Sixty-four in total.

My legs don't crumple so much as they fold, as if they give in to my heart which has grown so heavy that it can no longer defy gravity by remaining so high in my chest.

The priestess places her hand on my shoulder and murmurs, "I'll give you privacy, Imperata."

I don't flinch, at least not perceptibly; my mind is too curious, too greedy for what's in these letters.

If I expected poems, or ballads, or stories, I would not have known Cassius very well. That is why, when I crack the seal on the first, I am not at all surprised to find none of those things.

Cassius writes like he speaks, with purpose.

I miss you, cor meum.

-Matulo

That's it. I smile at the simplicity, the honesty, and then open another.

I love you, cor meum.

-Matulo.

And another. *Thank you, cor meum. I hope you're safe, cor meum. You're brave, cor meum. I'll write to you forever, if you like my letters, cor meum. You're the best latrones partner, cor meum.*

And on and on. Sixty-three simple, sincere sentiments, all signed the same way. Not one is addressed to me. Not Rose, not Luella, not Skylar.

He doesn't call me Tisiphone, or Vidua, or even Domina or Imperata. I'm not a title, not a name.

Just the woman that he loves.

I pick up the last one and open it.

It's always been you, cor meum.

-Matulo

THE BAKER

I PLACE THE ROUND ball of dough in a rattan basket, clap the flour off my hands, then move to another mound that's ready to be folded. The heat from the ovens dampens my brow and my dark hair clings to my forehead where tendrils have escaped the crown braid I wear.

I've been working in this kitchen for a full clipse now, hired as the new baker.

I'm just curious, I tell myself when I apply.

I enjoy the dough crusted along my cuticles and the smell of wheat. Plus, there is a cook here who knows his way around the soup kettle, and his wife Bernice makes sweet pastries to rival any I've attempted.

I just want to stay busy, I say when I tell Mia about the job.

"Can you make that mushroom stew again, Claude?" I ask, moving the dough aside to rest before it's final folding.

"Cassandra, you've asked for that thrice in one clipse!" Claude chides.

I once thought I had never met a decent man, but I'm starting to wonder if I never looked.

I was searching for praeda, eyes glossing over anyone who wasn't. I saw men like my pater, like Tristan, and they went on my list. Or, I saw boys and men like Taln, who were abused the way we were. There was no in-between. Abusers and the abused. Predator and prey. Even *vidua* and praeda, because every time I close my eyes I still hear the crunch of

Tristan's face and know that I broke something inside myself that day, too.

There are monsters in the world and perhaps I will always find them, because like calls to like.

"Don't you give that girl a hard time," Bernice scolds. "If she wants that soup, stones help you, you better make it!"

"Don't put me out, Bernie. I'll make the gods-forsaken soup." I might expect irritation to line the admission, but not from Claude. He laughs, looking at me like he wouldn't have denied me even if Bernice hadn't threatened him.

"I can help," I offer.

Claude waves me off. "You make the bread, I'll make the soup. Bernice can just look beautiful." He winks and Bernice and I match eye rolls, but Bernice also lets out a small groan. She tosses a crisp white dishtowel at him. He catches it swiftly and offers her a little bow.

I'm just having fun, I tell myself today.

I was worried, during the interview. I didn't think he'd be there, of course, but perhaps he would be keeping an eye out on newly hired servants. Or he would have issued a warning to alert him of women who looked too familiar.

Were these fears logical? No. They didn't rule me, because I would never allow that. But they did visit. Whisper.

And it was all for naught. I am having fun, though. Mia is healed and I've moved back to my domus. Her back room certainly isn't empty, but it's different. No violent rituals, no nightly floggings. No floras at all.

Domestic disputes. Praeda I can easily and quickly manage, although some women know by now, and they beg Mia not to tell Tisiphone. They wish to return to their normal lives. They aren't ready for safety or for freedom, because the fear is still too thick.

That's their right, but I certainly don't have to like it.

A young man appears in the doorway, probably around Taln's age. He nods to Claude, the respect due to the head of the kitchens.

"He's ready," the young man says, and I realize Remus must have already set.

"I'll have it sent right up," Claude nods in return.

My lips move against my better judgment. "I'll take it, Claude."

He just stares at me, as does Bernice. They don't know much about me besides that I'm a young woman, and I'm a baker. I'm average height, with brown hair and blue eyes. I'm old enough that I'm assumed a widow or a spinster. And, I've avoided leaving the kitchen the entire time I've been here.

I only offer because I like to be helpful. Right?

Finally, Claude slides the completed tray over.

I only take it because I'm curious.

What's the harm in that?

The halls confirm my suspicions, only Romulus casting his shadows across the marble pillars. The tapestries are different than before, no more excess. No more condescension.

There's one of a woman knitting beside a pond, a soft smile on her face. A temple of Vesta filled with small candles, making it glow, the hearth flame almost emanating warmth. An archway with large yellow blossoms clinging to the underside, bursting with light.

The tray is heavy, because of course it is. Claude doesn't even take the trays up, letting the 'young saplings' do it. That's what I get, for letting my curiosity get the better of me.

When I arrive to the chamber I assume is his, I find no Praetorians outside. I set the tray on a table but when I knock, there's no answer.

Suspicion and necessity war within me. Can I even open this door? Should I?

I probably shouldn't, but I do.

And it's nothing like I expected. The room is completely empty. No bed. No posts.

Nothing.

Footsteps echo down the hall and I turn to see one of the Praetorians. My gut clenches. I do have vials in my pocket, and a knife. Will I need them? That's what I've really been wondering since I started working here.

If it's as real as it seems.

"Good lady, are you lost?" he asks, the term of respect making me squint.

I tell him what my mission is and he smiles, shaking his head. He tells me where to deliver the tray and I hurry away. I should have asked Claude where to deliver this monstrosity before I walked out, but I was too busy convincing myself this was a good idea.

I find him exactly where the Praetorian said I would.

And now I know this was a terrible idea.

He looks good.

He's in the atrium where we took our *sapa*, the hideous fountain nowhere to be seen. Instead, there's a new statue. It's two faced, like Janus. Yet statues outside their temple always depict Janus as male, and this statue is decidedly female. The faces are similar, with only the noses and ages a bit different. One slightly younger, perhaps late teens, and the other a grown woman. The younger is smiling a shy type of smile, while the other smirks, knowing.

I look away from the statue to him. He's writing on a large parchment and I can see it's some matter of the republic, numbers on the top showing which article of the Senate it would fall under. His copper hair is more mussed than usual and he's not clean shaven the way he usually is, instead sporting a dark smattering of hair that looks the exact right amount of rough.

"Thank you," he says without looking up. "You can leave it anywhere, I'm just finishing up."

I should say something, but I'm not sure my voice will cooperate. I'm not sure what I'll say.

I can't wear the mask around him anymore.

Setting the tray on the table, I turn to leave when I hear, "Wait."

I turn, keeping my eyes downcast, not sure if I should trust my voice. "Yes, Imperator?" It works and it obeys me. Thank Janus.

"I haven't seen you before," he says, letting it hang in the air between us, heavy and full of promise.

"No, Imperator."

He makes a humming sound, and I feel it in my bones, vibrating through my soul. I finally raise my eyes to meet his.

Sharp. Piercing.

Knowing.

His blue orbs widen ever so slightly. "Would you like to stay?"

"Stay, Imperator?"

"To eat?" He doesn't wait for my answer before moving over on the bench, making room for me.

"I shouldn't, I'm working."

The corners of his mouth, which were beginning an upward trajectory, freeze. "As you wish, of course."

He knows. Just like I know this is my choice. He won't push me here.

"I brought your tray to the old Imperator's quarters," I say.

"Did you think I'd ever be able to sleep there?" he asks.

I look away, then back to him. He hasn't looked anywhere except me. "I'm not sure what I expected."

"I'll be turning that wing into a temple," he says.

"For whom?"

"Whomever she tells me to. Tisiphone, Venus, Janus. Whomever makes her feel the most powerful in erasing him."

I don't bother pretending I don't know what he means. I don't play the game we once played.

"What about how you'd like to cover him up?"

He waves the scroll at me. "I'm already working on that with the Senate."

My steps are slow, halting, until I stand before him. Our fingers brush as I take the scroll and the warmth shocks me, but not as much as what I read.

I knew Cassius would make changes without me. I knew he wasn't his brother. Still, I didn't expect this.

It's a law that would create a new type of marriage, one where a woman no longer belonged to her husband. She could continue to belong to her closest male relative or... to no one. He would grant all women the freedom that only widows like Mia had enjoyed before. To own land, to sell more than their bodies.

"Cassius..." I manage.

"It's just a start, but I need to do more politicking before I can push more through and eliminate the old ways. You could help... even if..."

He clears his throat. "Even if you want to work in the kitchens and you want nothing to do with me. You could still tell me what to do."

"You'd let me dictate laws?" I scoff.

"Let you?" He shakes his head. *"Cor meum,* you're always in control here. And we both know you've been denied your right for over ten years."

"What right?" I ask, tilting my face towards him.

"To rule, Imperata. You've been Empress for ten years."

I have, I suppose, been married to an Emperor for that long. A version of me, at least. "That means our marriage didn't count. I'm finally a true widow."

Cassius reaches forward, removes the scroll from my hands, and places it on the table. Then he reaches forward again, clasping my hands in his larger ones. "I said it then, and I say it again. I'd marry you in any temple, in front of any gods, and as many times as you'd let me. Even if you won't have me, I'll still answer to you."

I can't help the way I sway towards him, like a flower reaching towards the light. "What if I will?"

"Will what?"

"Will have you?"

He grins, his face brightening enough to make up for the missing sun. "Then I just have one question."

"And what is that?"

"What's your name?" His eyes are teasing, but I see the relief there, too. The joy. I don't realize I'm smiling until his finger reaches out to trace my lips. He draws me closer, so I'm standing between his legs.

I lean down, wrapping my arms around his shoulders. It feels right, it feels like the reason I'm alive. My forehead meets his and for a moment I just breathe in his air, sharing life with this man who saved me as much as I saved myself.

Finally, I have my answer.

"Luella," I say once.

Kissing him softly, I whisper it again, "You can call me Luella."

THE EMPRESS

"Divusians don't do this," I tell Cassius for what must be the hundredth time.

"Divusians didn't *used* to do this," he corrects, as usual.

"It feels ridiculous," I argue.

"It's important for the people to see you as ruling in your own right." This isn't the first time I have heard this argument, and I agreed to it. Now that we're here in the forum and I can hear the crowds, though, my nerves have started to fray. I'm not used to being so visible. I'm used to blending in, playing my role.

I suppose this is a role, too.

Wife to the Imperator, Cassius Augustus Evander.

Imperata.

Empress Luella Rose Amulius Evander.

Luella gave me the strength to take revenge for my sister, but Rose was the me who lost everything. Amulius was my mater's familia name, before she married my pater, and Cassius is the only man I'd allow to call me his equal. I broke tradition by keeping my old name and taking his. Four names? The Senate had a fit.

But it was right. I'm all of those things and more.

And I'm done hiding.

I look to Cassius and nod, and we move from behind the curtain, hand in hand.

"People of Divus," Cassius says, voice booming to resonate across the marble pillars. The seats are full of Senators and on the floor and through the doorway is a sea of plebeians. "I'm pleased to present to you, our Empress, Luella Rose Amulius Evander." A cheer from the plebeians, many of whom will remember me from our wedding in the Furies temple. If they notice my hair a bit darker, my nose a bit different, or my eyes less bright, they don't say anything. I wear my real face now, the one I'd shied away from for so long. The Senators are more subdued, unsure of what this new power dynamic means for them, for their politics. I'm sure many supported Tristan, and others are likely Bacchantes themselves.

It feels right to claim this as myself, in my own body.

Cassius looks to me, waiting for the crowd to cool, for the cheers to die down, before he speaks again. His eyes never leave mine. "Your Empress has worked tirelessly to keep the women and men of this republic safe for years." He's playing up the rumors that have been circulating since we were married by Tisiphone's priestess. Whether he admits it or not, he has a way with the people. "Now she can do it from where she belongs, at the head and the heart of Divus."

The crowd cheers, and I hear it whispered loudly by some, chanted by others.

"*Vidua*," they whisper.

"Tisiphone," they chant.

"Justice," more intone.

Cassius places a small golden diadem on my wheat waves, the circlet offset by thorns and small leaves, the twin to his. He doesn't kiss me, or raise our hands, as I expected. Instead, he kneels.

"One cannot inherit Divus. One must take it." The crowd cheers louder for this, the Divusian motto of might. "You have taken it from the corrupt Tristan Evander, a traitor to our Divusian women and men." My cheeks threaten to flame. Can he blame me for the death of the Emperor? What will the people think?

They scream, they cry. New chants rise up as Cassius continues. "You are chosen by the gods, by me as Emperor, and now..." he gestures to the crowd, still kneeling. "People of Divus, do you accept your Empress?"

He's a genius. I see it when the Senators realize what he's done. They pale as the crowd screams its assent.

"We choose!"

"Empress! Empress!"

"Tisiphone! *Vidua!*"

I turn to them then, and bow. The hush is immediate. "Thank you, Imperator. Thank you, people of Divus." Pulling Cassius to standing, I raise our joined hands.

"To the future."

The screams are deafening, my ears near to popping, but I look to Cassius and we both smile.

"To the future," he mouths back to me.

Cassius moved rooms. His tapestries and frescoes came with, the once traitorous nature scenes feeling more true than ever, as we just admitted to trying to topple the old ways. It feels good, freeing.

We do not have separate chambers here, just one large bed. It's not swathed in white, but deep green to match the walls. The suns have set, and I can feel the events of the day buzzing through us both, our bodies nearly vibrating.

He steps closer to me once the servants depart. "How are you?" He takes my hand and tugs me into his chest. His lips find mine, warm and tender.

"Better now," I murmur against his lips. I told him I liked the scruff and now he refuses to shave, the coarse hair tickling my cheek.

"Luella," he whispers into my neck. "*Cor meum*." He's kissing my neck, my jaw, trailing his lips along each space in between. "You were incredible."

"As were you," I say, tilting my head to allow him better access to my neck. A shiver runs through me as his teeth graze the sensitive spot just above my shoulder.

We haven't done more than kiss in the clipses since I left the kitchens. Claude still lets me come down to bake, but they've hired a true baker now. One who isn't consumed with running an empire.

Cassius must remember this at the same time I do, because he stops, his breath ragged. "Sorry, *cor meum*." He kisses my forehead, lips gentle at first. Then he leans in and lets out a breath on my forehead. "Forgive me?"

I tip my head up and kiss him, harder. "There's nothing to forgive," I say. My hands begin to seek him, his heat. I push back his shirt, tangling my hands in his hair, greedy for him.

He's frozen for a moment, as if he can't decide what he should do, but then he's kissing me back, breathing life into me with his lips. "We can stop, *cor meum*."

"I don't want to, do you?" I say, biting his neck. The guttural noise that escapes him curls my toes, brings fire to my core.

"Gods, no. I dream of this every night." I know he's not lying. He talks in his sleep sometimes, whispering my name, and I always wake clutched in his arms. "But if you're not ready…" He draws back to look at me, eyes searching.

"Cassius," I say it slowly. "I want you, now." He snaps then, his hands finally matching my own, roving across my back, brushing my hips.

I wrestle his shirt off, reveling in the strength of his arms, the taper of his muscles below his breeches. He's hard, his generous length clearly visible. He doesn't show that he's eager, though. Instead, he takes his time, kissing every inch of exposed skin until I'm the one removing my clothes.

"Cassius," I whimper, tugging down my dress. He chases the fabric with his tongue, his teeth, kissing each inch of skin as it emerges from the dress, until his mouth is on my breasts and I gasp. He slips my nipple into his mouth and sucks gently. My back arches and I whimper again. He growls, moving to the other while his hand finds the one he abandoned, twisting it enough to make me tremble.

"Tell me to stop," he says, his tongue flicking out over the beaded skin.

I moan. "Don't stop." He slides my dress down to the floor, following it until he's on his knees, kissing my stomach, my hips, my thighs. I need him, my thighs clenching as my core heats.

He walks on his knees, pushing me back towards the bed, kissing my waist all the while. The backs of my legs meet the bed and he molds his hands on my waist, settling me on plush green linen. He kisses my knees, then the inside of each, then he nuzzles them open, so my legs fall to the sides enough for his head to start moving towards my core, kissing my legs as he goes, until finally he's there.

Nipping the inside of my thigh, he inhales sharply. "Tell me to stop," he says again. I reach down, stroking his cheek, tangling my hands in his hair. Then I push his head forward.

When his tongue meets my core I tip my head back in relief that he's finally, finally where I want him. "Yes," I pant. "More."

Cassius obliges, his tongue circling that sensitive bundle of nerves and his skilled finger coming to my entrance. I tip my hips forward. "More," I tell him. He slides one finger inside of me, his own moan vibrating through me.

"More," I tell him and he doubles his fingers but I'm already shaking my head. "No, more of you." I tug on his hair.

"Luella, let me worship you," he says, almost pleading. He's scared. I know he is, because as much as he wants me he doesn't want to lose me, either. He thinks I will see Tristan in him, the way I told him once that I couldn't stand to be married to the Emperor.

"Let me choose how I'm worshiped." I capture his mouth in mine, tasting myself on his tongue. It stokes the fire in me higher, passion and purpose mingling into one.

Reaching between us, I grip his hard length, and his head falls forward into my neck. "Gods, Luella. You'll undo me in seconds." I loosen my grip, guiding him towards my entrance.

"I don't mind." Smiling, I kiss him deep, wrapping my legs around his waist until he slides into me. The breath leaves me and Cassius freezes. I bite his lip, tipping my hips forward, eliciting a tiny bit of friction. "Cassius, more," I demand. He does as I ask, slowly sliding his length into me. I feel myself clenching already, release so close I can almost touch it.

Not yet, though. Cassius breathes me in as he moves, slow at first, and then faster. Our cries mingle together until I don't know where I begin and he ends.

Then one of his hands tangles in my hair and something about it feels disturbingly familiar, painfully reminiscent of another time. "Stop," I manage to say. It's a cracked whisper, and I know as I say it that it will be swallowed by his passion.

Except it isn't. He stops before I've finished the words, his breath ragged. "What is it?" He presses up, still leaning over me, his weight shifting back, ready to do whatever I ask. Cerulean pools meet mine, and the concern, the love, is overwhelming. I feel my own eyes welling with tears, but I shake them away.

"You," I swallow hard, "caught my hair. I don't..." I don't need to finish, his hands instantly moving away, widening his stance so that his body drops lower.

"Tell me what you want," he whispers. "I'm not him...not any of them. Please, *cor meum*."

My legs are still around his waist and I twist them, tugging him to the side. He complies, easily rolling onto his side and then his back. I follow, straddling him. I reposition us so he meets my entrance again, heat and warmth urging me forward. When I slide back onto his length, Cassius puts his hands above his head, keeping them away from me. "Tell me what you want," he says again.

I don't answer, finding the small forward movements that hit the spot I want. My hands grip his chest and soon I feel that pressure building again.

Cassius has his hands together, like he's praying. I can see how hard he's working to keep his hands off of me, to keep from thrusting into me. To make sure it's all completely in my control.

When the pressure threatens to blind me I finally lean forward, kissing him. He meets me with all of his restrained desire, the heat between us building.

"Touch me," I ask. "Make me forget, Cassius."

Once my words register, Cassius' hands are on me in a moment. He runs them along my hips, my sides. "I love you," he says, kissing me. "I love you," he mutters, gripping my hips with the perfect amount of pressure. "I love you," he whispers, tilting his hips up to meet mine.

His hand comes behind my neck, not pushing me onto his length but instead making sure I can't escape his lips, his words.

"I love you, *cor meum*," he promises, shattering my past into pieces as I come undone.

EPILOGUE

CASSIUS KISSES THE TENDER flesh of my neck, his breath warm against the morning chill. The suns have not yet risen high enough to cast their dual shadows into our chamber, but the stars have fled as the darkness begins to melt away. It's too early.

"I want to go to the gymnasia today," I say, nestling further into Cassius' warm chest. His heart feels steady against my ear. It's the only sound that helps me sleep, that drowns out the sounds of cracking whips and crunching bones.

"Mmm can we not exercise here, *cor meum*?" he teases, nibbling my ear. I swat at him.

"We have new Senators to appoint today. I will need more than a romp." My blood boils at the prospect. We've been rooting out supporters of Tristan's, because even with him gone, they fight against what we are trying to do. They fight against the female Senators who have joined their ranks. Mostly, they fight against me. I have new names now, although *vidua* is still one. Now I'm also the *Venefica*. The Empress Whore. The *Meretrix* Mater.

The plebeians have taken to my new edicts, and support from the *Concilium Plebis* is high. The Praetors and Senators, on the other hand, will not relinquish their order, their way of doing things.

"The Bacchantes are hiding themselves well, so we may need to make Mia more accessible to victims. Will you ask her what she thinks?" Cassius kisses my collarbone, moving to hold himself over me. "What about a romp *and* the gymnasia?"

I capture his mouth, feeling the way he molds to me, adjusts to my needs. As though he truly would know me anywhere, in any body. I hope that one day I will adjust to his as well, that I can give more than this jagged version of me. I nip at his lower lip and his tongue finds mine, searching and needy.

I can't help the moan that escapes into his mouth, the sound I only make for him.

"Stones, *cor meum*."

"I'll ask Mia," I say, the words breathier than I intend when Cassius dips his head down to the top of my breast. "We have executions today, too."

His tongue flicks across my nipple and I arch into him. "Luella, I'm not sure if you know what hearing you run this empire does to me, but your talk of executions is not helping," he says between my breasts, moving to the other nipple.

"Cassius, you're ridiculous."

"I love you," he laughs, skimming his teeth along my ribcage as his hand grips my hip. "Now tell me if I have time for my favorite breakfast or if you'd actually like to get up?"

"We can celebrate tonight," I say, gripping his messy red locks and guiding him up to my lips again. I kiss him once, twice.

He kisses my forehead. "Deal, but if you visit Bernie I want my own sourdough this time. Claude only sends up a piece of bread. *One* piece, Lue. I'm wasting away."

"I left your dough to rise overnight, actually. You'll have your own loaf by dinner."

Cassius freezes, as if he doesn't believe what I've said. "You made me one?"

I smile. "Yes, *amor*." I leave the rest unsaid, because he understands what it means for me to offer him something I made. Something I didn't break. Something I love.

It's the principle of it, of taking the first step to smooth at least one jagged edge. It's refusing to wear my mask or play a role. It's over ten years in the making, this thing that Janus promised me and the people of Divus. I remember what the god asked me that day in the temple, when I bled onto their altar.

"Are you ready for a new beginning?"

Finally, I am.

GLOSSARY

While some terms are adapted from latin, many are entirely fictional. Please consult academic sources for accurate translations and mythology

Asp—A venomous snake known for its painful bite

Belua—Monster

Cerevisia—A fermented malt beverage

Clipse—Measurement of time that spans five days, there are four clipses in each quad

Coemptio—A reverse dowry, where the groom's familia pays the bride's

Divus—A city on a hill founded by Romulus and Remus, together. After forming their divine city, Remus determined that Romulus did not have the best interests of the city in mind and kills his twin in the night. Because of this, he's cursed to be the smaller and darker sun in the sky

Eclipse—Also called the shadowing, when the smaller, less bright sun (the Traitor/Remus) blocks out the center of the King/Romulus. Because the less bright sun is so much smaller and dimmer, it creates a shadowing effect. This happens once a clipse (aka the end of the week)

Flora—Imperial harem worker

Idem—Same

Infirmaria—Clinic or sick house, place for the infirm

Lace herbs—Herbs used for contraceptive purposes

Latrones—A two-person board game where all pieces are shaped the same except one, a king piece called a dux

Mater—Mother

Matulo—Insult meaning blockhead

Meretrix—Often used to mean high-end prostitute, but also used as derogatory term for a woman deemed 'improper'

Pater—Father

Posca—Drink made by mixing vinegar and water

Praeda—Victim or prey

Pullus—Young bird, used as a term of endearment for children

Quad—A time period of four clipses (20 days)

Remus—The smaller of the two suns, only 10% as bright as Romulus. Also called 'The Traitor' after the myth around the founding of Divus

Romulus—The larger of the two suns, responsible for the majority of heat and light. Also called 'The King'

Sabines—The name of a brothel known for its cruelty. The women in it are also referred to as 'sabines' and are typically from conquered nations. The women are slaves, owned and sold by the brothel

Sapa—Wine sweetened with honey, still named after a previous sweet wine that was aged in lead barrels. The old version was toxic, leading to lead poisoning and death. Sapa is also an occasion, similar to an afternoon tea

Soror—Sister

Venefica—Sorceress, witch. Also, woman who poisons

Vidua—Widow

Vir vult es deus vult—A husband's will is god's will

ACKNOWLEDGEMENTS

Thank YOU for reading this book and going on this journey with Luella and Rose. This project was such a wild ride, and I hope you enjoyed it even half as much as I enjoyed writing it.

To Jessica P, thank you for being the first person to read my very first book. Without your sunshine, I would never have made it to my first 'the end.'

Beth, this book is a testament to your encouragement and insight. I'm so thankful for your unicorn dust and am so honored to have you work on these stories with me.

Jessica F and Alessandra, thank you for being the first eyes on this story and loving all the rage I poured into it.

Patty, my publishing guru, thank you for lending me some of your spirit to get it done.

Kaitie, your love for this story helped more than you know. Thank you!

Thank you to my amazing alpha and beta readers. Melissa, Jo, T.J., Ben Logsdon, Isla, Tay, Tracey, Lindsey, Stephanie, K.J., L.B., J.L.O ., Holly, Leila, and Hannah, your time and feedback was invaluable. This story would be a mess without you.

Emmaline, my amazing editor, thank you for answering my endless questions and sharing my excitement for this story.

To my husband, thank you for coming up with the worst character names for me. Maybe someday one of them will make it into the book. I couldn't do any of this without your love and the way you support all of my dreams.

To my parents, thank you for reading everything I write, even when I tell you not to. Mom, you're the best cheerleader, and Dad, I'm so thankful that you shared your love of fantasy with me.

Lori, thank you for supporting me in everything from our love of office supplies to reading fantasy even when you weren't sure if you'd like it. I'm so lucky to have a MIL like you and am forever grateful for you (and your eagle eye proofreading)!

Seeing this list is incredible, because I know it's not every person who has encouraged me, let me vent, or helped me navigate my author journey. I can't thank you enough for making my dreams come true.

ABOUT THE AUTHOR

Rhiannon Rollness is a fantasy author, nurse, wife, and mother. When not balancing all of these on the trapeze of life, you can find her reading, obsessively listening to the same song on repeat, baking muffins, lounging by her pool, and daydreaming.

In her stories, you'll find a mix of fantasy, myth, and science. If you like books that remind us that the human experience is sometimes best explored in magical places, you've come to the right place.

Follow @rhirhi_readsnwrites on Instagram for updates on her work, bookish musings, and more. Join Rhiannon's mailing list at rhiannonr ollness.com for exclusive updates and content.

www.ingramcontent.com/pod-product-compliance
Lightning Source LLC
Chambersburg PA
CBHW031841310726
48972CB00005B/1366